"Do you trust me?"

Did she trust him? "Do I have a choice?"

"No. You're in my hands now, Miz Summerville. You don't eat, you don't sleep, you don't even blink without me there watching. From this moment on, you don't leave my sight until I'm satisfied you're safe."

Oh God. She squeezed her eyes shut.

"Any questions?"

Yeah. A really big one. In his hands Muse might very well be safe from James Davies. But…

Who on earth would protect her from Remi Beaulieux?

Dear Reader,

Once again, we invite you to experience the romantic excitement that is the hallmark of Silhouette Intimate Moments. And what better way to begin than with *Downright Dangerous,* the newest of THE PROTECTORS, the must-read miniseries by Beverly Barton? Bad-boy-turned-bodyguard Rafe Devlin is a hero guaranteed to win heroine Elsa Leone's heart—and yours.

We have more miniseries excitement for you with Marie Ferrarella's newest CAVANAUGH JUSTICE title, *Dangerous Games,* about a detective heroine joining forces with the hero to prove his younger brother's innocence, and *The Cradle Will Fall,* Maggie Price's newest LINE OF DUTY title, featuring ex-lovers brought back together to find a missing child. And that's not all, of course. Reader favorite Jenna Mills returns with *Crossfire*, about a case of personal protection that's very personal indeed. Nina Bruhns is back with a taste of *Sweet Suspicion*. This FBI agent hero doesn't want to fall for the one witness who can make or break his case, but his heart just isn't listening to his head. Finally, meet the *Undercover Virgin* who's the heroine of Becky Barker's newest novel. When a mission goes wrong and she's on the run with the hero, she may stay under cover, but as for the rest…!

Enjoy them all, and be sure to come back next month for six more of the best and most exciting romance novels around, right here in Silhouette Intimate Moments.

Yours,

Leslie J. Wainger
Executive Editor

Please address questions and book requests to:
Silhouette Reader Service
U.S.: 3010 Walden Ave., P.O. Box 1325, Buffalo, NY 14269
Canadian: P.O. Box 609, Fort Erie, Ont. L2A 5X3

Sweet Suspicion

NINA BRUHNS

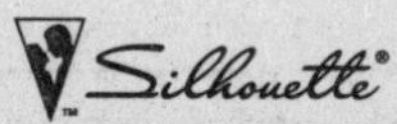

INTIMATE MOMENTS™

Published by Silhouette Books

America's Publisher of Contemporary Romance

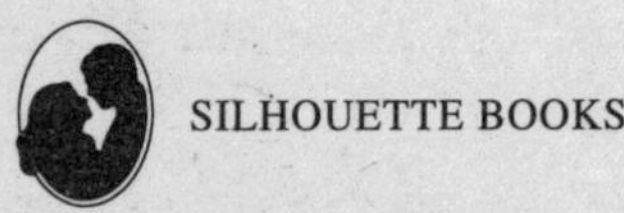

ISBN 0-373-27347-9

SWEET SUSPICION

This edition published by arrangement with Harlequin Books S.A.

Visit Silhouette at www.eHarlequin.com

Printed in U.S.A.

Books by Nina Bruhns

Silhouette Intimate Moments

Catch Me If You Can #990
Warrior's Bride #1080
Sweet Revenge #1163
Sins of the Father #1209
Sweet Suspicion #1277

NINA BRUHNS

credits her Gypsy great-grandfather for her great love of adventure. She has lived and traveled all over the world, including a six-year stint in Sweden. She has been on scientific expeditions from California to Spain to Egypt and the Sudan, and has two graduate degrees in archaeology (with a specialty in Egyptology). She speaks four languages and writes a mean hieroglyphics!

But Nina's first love has always been writing. For her, writing for Silhouette Books is the ultimate adventure. Drawing on her many experiences gives her stories a colorful dimension, and allows her to create settings and characters out of the ordinary. Two of her books, including this one, won the prestigious Romance Writers of America Golden Heart Award for writing excellence.

A native of Canada, Nina grew up in California and currently resides in Charleston, South Carolina, with her husband and three children.

She loves to hear from her readers, and can be reached at P.O. Box 746, Ladson, SC 29456-0746 or by e-mail via the Harlequin Web site at www.eHarlequin.com.

This book is dedicated to the wonderful, fabulous, amazing critique partners who have helped me through the highs of writing and publishing the stories I love, as well as the times I've wanted to quit or wanted to put all my unruly characters on a southbound plane, crash it and type The End. Cynthia, Michele, Pat, Jeanette, Adrienne, Priscilla, Stan, Enola and Kieran, here's to you!

Chapter 1

She was prettier than her mug shot.

FBI Special Agent Remi Beaulieux leaned his elbows back on the crowded bar, popped a stick of Juicy Fruit into his mouth and contemplated the woman working the crowd.

Prettier and more cheerful. The FBI photographer must have caught her on a really bad day. He lifted his shot glass and took a sip of tequila. Not that it mattered. He'd just wanted to get a look at her in person.

Remi's specialty was undercover work, posing as a bad guy, convincing the other bad guys to trust him long enough to hang themselves. After weeks of meticulous planning and putting his cover in place, tomorrow he'd be slipping into the James Davies crime organization, playing the part of a drug smuggler drumming up business.

He wanted to know all the important players by sight. Muse Summerville had been the FBI's inside man—or woman—with Davies, right up until two weeks ago when she'd ended her relationship with Gary Fox, one of Davies's main gofers.

He watched as she lifted the hair off her neck and made eyes at about the tenth guy in as many minutes, a big dude in a Harley T-shirt and combat boots.

Obviously she was real broken up about it. Not that Remi was interested in the details of Muse Summerville's love life.

Still, he couldn't help but admire the view. A lithe, tall blonde with miles of shapely leg and a cute, flirty sundress short enough to make a man pray for a stiff wind. No wonder they were swarming around her two deep.

He took another sip of tequila, wiped a bead of sweat from his temple and watched as she gave a woman a big hug and started talking with her animatedly, all the while smiling and waving to passersby who greeted her.

Popular lady. No surprise. Her background file said she had lots of friends. But what did surprise Remi was that there were just as many women as men. Now, that was interesting.

The big old wooden paddle fan twirling above the dance floor must have been doing its job, for she tipped her face up and let the breeze caress her face. It was a gesture so sensual a low hum of appreciation rumbled from his throat.

She was surely not what he'd expected.

The Eyes Only FBI file on Muse he'd skimmed earlier was thick and revealing to say the least. It had been filled with page after page of information she'd gathered on James Davies over the past six months, as well as a sketchy profile of Muse and her flamboyant lifestyle. In person, Remi had been expecting a jaded, streetwise woman with no hint of vulnerability, flashing sex appeal like a neon sign.

Bien, she was sexy, all right. And obviously used to taking care of herself.

But that's where the similarities ended. Despite the short dress, spike heels and bright lipstick, there seemed to be a genuineness and intelligence about this woman that defied her reputation as a wild-living party girl. She was intriguing as hell.

Not that she was his type.

He suddenly realized she'd caught him watching her. Her gaze faltered as it collided with his, moved on, then returned.

Wrong.

She was just his type. In fact, she was so much his type it was almost scary. Scary enough to make him take a giant mental step back.

Garde, mon fils. Careful, boy.

It would be foolish to make contact. He wasn't authorized, and he had no reason to speak to her. Muse Summerville was the FBI's ace in the hole against James Davies, the only informant still alive whose testimony could put Davies away for good. In two days Remi'd be deep undercover, trying his damnedest to locate the bastard so they could arrest him and get him on trial.

So far Davies didn't suspect her. By making any contact at all, Remi could put both her and himself in unnecessary danger. Especially since a few days ago she'd reported she was being followed.

No problem. He'd only watch her for a little while, then slip away before she really noticed him.

Except her gaze was still on him.

Against all caution, he stared right back. He could see her swallow, then whisper to the woman next to her, who gave him the once-over and shook her head, but shot him a flirtatious smile.

He lifted his glass in an answering salute, but held Muse's gaze the whole time. Damn, he'd like to meet her.

Dieu. Jamais. Reality check.

What would he do if she actually walked over and introduced herself? Tell her, yeah, I already know who you are because I'm an FBI agent and I've read your very intriguing file and came all the way down here to Bourbon Street just to find out if what it said was true?

Right, Beaulieux.

Luckily he was spared when a man came up to her and she turned away, sliding her arms playfully around his neck as he leaned over for a kiss.

Remi gripped his shot glass and downed the rest of the tequila in one gulp, frowning. Okay, big deal. So what if she let the guy kiss her? Her file said she liked men—the more dark and dangerous the better. What did he expect? A nun?

His scowl deepened as the man grabbed her and pulled her close. But to his surprise she broke the kiss and slipped from his grasp, laughing and urging the woman next to her to take her place in the man's arms. She left them kissing as she waved to another friend and moved on. Not that he cared.

Remi caught her eye again. This time she stopped, tipped her head and raised an eyebrow.

Dark and dangerous, eh? He could do dark and dangerous. That's why he'd done so well in his twelve-year undercover career. Remi Beaulieux *defined* dark and dangerous.

He didn't move. Didn't smile. Just swept his gaze over her in a very obvious male challenge.

Her lips parted a fraction, and even from across the room he could see her cheeks flush. Oh, yeah, she was interested.

Suddenly he wanted to kick himself. *Ça, c'est fou!* Flirting with this woman could get them both in big trouble. What if she actually took him up on his unspoken offer?

Again their byplay was interrupted by another man, and to his annoyance nearly the exact same ritual was enacted. First the kiss, then the grab, then the switcheroo, this time with a giggling friend she pulled off the dance floor.

Obviously the woman didn't like being manhandled. What was with those guys? Didn't they get that?

None of his business. She was doing fine taking care of herself. In fact, she disappeared into the crowd and he lost sight of her altogether.

Merci Dieu. Best he got out of there, anyway. He'd had no business tracking her down in the first place. He wasn't undercover yet, and this was their star witness he was messing with. He must be looking for a way to get fired. Or killed.

He elbowed his way through the throng on the dance floor, slowly easing toward the door. Bourbon Street was always a crush, and tonight was no different despite the blast-furnace heat of mid-August.

When he stepped out the door into the night, he paused for a welcome deep breath of fresh air. The smells of the Quarter made him smile in recognition: fried fish, sweet daiquiris, popcorn, the lingering tang of rotting garbage....

"Leaving so soon?"

He didn't know whether to be ecstatic or worried when he turned to find Muse leaning casually against an iron balcony pillar.

He opted for worried. He gave her a grin and said, "Almost midnight. Need my beauty sleep."

Her rose-painted lips curved up in amusement. "Oh, you wild thing, you," she drawled in a honey-sweet Carolina accent that made his pulse do a slow waltz through his veins.

He hiked a brow. "Unless you make it worth my while to stay...."

She winked. "Don't count on it, sugarcane."

Both relief and disappointment rolled through him. The proposition had been a pure male reflex, his body leading him astray in a big way. He fought the instinct to take up her transparent gauntlet, instead delivering a disappointed but accepting sigh.

"*Quel dommage.* Now, that's truly a shame."

She glanced up at his use of French. "You Cajun?"

He decided not to take it personally that she didn't pursue their flirtation but changed the subject as though his heritage was just naturally more interesting than his prospects as a bed partner. He shook his head. "Not Cajun. French Creole."

"Really? Then your family's been in New Orleans for a long time?"

He shook his head. "My people are from up the Atchafalaya River."

"Ah."

"Ah, what?"

"*Really* old money."

The woman had obviously done her research on Louisiana's archaic class system. The question was, why? "What makes you think that? There are plenty of us who are church-mouse poor."

She took in his Marc Jacobs shirt and Helmut Lang slacks and pursed her lips. "Yeah, I see that. So, where's the plantation?"

He ruthlessly deflected the knifeblade of pain reminders of Beau Saint-Coeur invariably produced, and chuckled. "You gold diggin', woman?" Wouldn't be the first one to try—until they found out he wasn't his daddy's heir.

She looked amused rather than offended. "More like iron diggin'."

"'Scuse me?"

"I'm putting together a book on old wrought-iron and cast-iron work. You know, balcony railings, gates, cemetery fences and such. I've found some beautiful examples hidden away on those antebellum plantations up there. Your place got any?"

He folded his arms over his chest and regarded her, completely baffled. He wasn't sure where he'd expected this conversation to lead, but this was definitely not it.

"You're writing a book?" Something not mentioned in her file.

"Well, photographing a book, actually. And recording the stories associated with the patterns in the ironwork. It's amazing stuff."

The surprises kept coming. "You're a photographer?"

She shrugged. "Amateur, but I do okay. So, how 'bout it?"

His brain had long ago lodged well below his neck, so it took him a moment to sort out that she wasn't propositioning him but still asking about her wrought iron. Irrationally disappointed, he forced himself to think.

"My cousin Beau's plantation has a grave on it—our great-great-great-grandmother. There's a real pretty gate on the enclosure fence with an interesting wartime legend. And my father's house has a gallery rail imported from France, with a symbol of the blessed Saint Louis."

Her eyes lit up, even in the darkness. "Really? I'd love to photograph them both. Would you take me sometime?" In her excitement she softly grasped his forearm.

Reactions burst through him like gunfire—scalding heat where she touched his skin, gut-deep bitterness at the knowledge he'd never step foot in his father's home again, sharp arousal from her invitation to a cozy trip up the river that could easily turn into much more than a photo shoot.

And warning bells in his head that he was letting this contact get way out of control.

"I'd like that," he murmured with deeper regret than he'd felt in more years than he could count. "Unfortunately, I'm goin' out of town tomorrow. Indefinitely."

She studied him for a moment. "Okay. I understand. Well—" She looked around and snagged a pen from a passing acquaintance's pocket, then with a flourish wrote her name and phone number in the hollow of his palm. "My name's Muse. When you get back, you give me a call. If you like."

He smiled, barely resisting hanging on to her hand and pulling her close, whispering in her delicate ear what he'd really like to do when he got back.

"I'll keep that in mind."

She strolled off, hailing another friend as she tucked the pen back into its owner's pocket with a wink. And then she was gone, melting into the crowd of tourists and good-timin' locals that packed the busy street.

He watched her go, taking her place against the balcony support, fighting the urge to go after her and make an improper suggestion. Or two or three. But he didn't.

It wasn't fear that she'd turn him down that stopped him. It was fear that she wouldn't.

He knew better than to start something he couldn't finish. His job made it imperative he have no ties whatsoever. No wife. No steady lover. No family that he was close to. He deliberately played up his own unhappy past, the ugly rift between him and his parents, his bad reputation as the black sheep of the Beaulieux clan, in order that those he did care about—Grandmère, Beau and his new wife, Kit, and Beau's family—would be safe from all the scumbags Remi dealt with on any given day. Though, thankfully, for the past few years he'd been able to be closer with his cousin's family.

But undercover work was always a risk. More so if there was anyone on earth who could make you lose your concentration, or your resolve.

Muse Summerville was a woman who could make him lose his concentration big-time. Especially given her unique involvement in his current assignment. The very last thing he should do is wake up in bed with her.

Aside from which, the delicious Miz Summerville was an

obvious heartbreaker. And he definitely didn't need his heart broken. There wasn't enough left of it to spare the pieces. Anyway, he wasn't interested in a relationship at this point in his life.

Just then the cell phone in his breast pocket beeped, and he tore his gaze from Muse's shapely retreating backside with a sigh. *Quel dommage,* indeed.

"Di' moi," he said, using his signature phone greeting. Talk to me.

"What the hell are you doing?" bellowed the Special Agent in Charge of the Davies case, Xavier Morris. Remi's boss didn't believe in polite social niceties.

"Research," he replied, unfazed by the realization that Morris already knew exactly what he was doing, and therefore Muse *was* being followed—by the FBI.

His boss snorted indelicately. "Sure."

"Who's tailing her?" he asked, eyeing the mass of humanity flowing around him.

"Simmons. So what's your excuse?"

Simmons was a good man, if a bit unimaginative. Probably why he got stuck with boring stakeout duty more often than not, at which he was an expert. Remi hadn't caught a glimpse of him the whole night. "I wanted to see the Summerville woman in person. In case something comes up while I'm undercover. I need to know for sure it's her if I have to bail her out of a hit."

Weak, but it was all he had. Frankly, he had no idea why he'd felt compelled to seek Muse out at her favorite haunts. And he certainly couldn't justify speaking with her.

Morris was silent for a few beats, seemed to accept the explanation, then said ominously, "As a matter of fact, something *has* come up, Agent Beaulieux. Something big."

He was following her. Again.

The fine hairs on the back of Muse's neck stood on end.

For a split second she slowed her pace, glancing behind her along the dark street. *Nothing.* But then, she seldom caught more than a glimpse of the blond-haired man who'd been shadowing her for two weeks now.

Could it be someone else? Someone from one of the bars who wouldn't take no for an answer? She loved having a good time out on Bourbon Street, dancing and flirting and chasing away the loneliness. She always walked these last couple of blocks to her apartment alone, but there was the occasional guy who just couldn't accept the fact that she preferred sleeping solo.

But no. Persistent suitors made themselves much more visible…and obnoxious.

A spurt of uneasiness flashed through her, raising icy goose bumps on her arms despite the sultry New Orleans heat. It was him all right, the man who'd been watching her. She could feel it in her bones.

Pulse thundering, she picked up her pace, the heels of her three-inch pumps clicking loudly on the pavement. The uneven French Quarter sidewalk was not the best place for running in high heels, but Muse figured breaking her neck would probably be preferable to what this guy might have in mind. Especially if he worked for Davies. Why hadn't she worn something more practical for once, like jeans and sneaks?

Not that she owned anything that practical.

She took another glance behind her.

There!

A blond male head glinted under a streetlamp, closer than before. She squinted, trying to get a better look at him between the lurching drunks that blocked her view. When this had first started she'd been certain it was Gary Fox, the boyfriend she'd just broken up with, trying to scare her back into his life. He'd been more than upset with the split, threatening all sorts of things. But she wasn't so sure it was him anymore. Gary talked a good game, but when it came to action he was a bench sitter. He wouldn't be this tenacious.

Dread seeped through her like poison. Could it be one of James Davies's real goons, sent to kill her? Or worse…

It was the "or worse" that really terrified her. She had seen what Davies was capable of when it came to traitors in his extensive crime organization—had seen it in living color and horrific stereo sound on the videotape she and Gary had stolen from him when Gary had felt the need for insurance. The beating and torture, complete with three ghoulish onlookers, had made her sick to her stomach for weeks after viewing it.

But how could Davies possibly have found out about her? As far as she knew, there was only one person in the whole state who knew of her connection to the FBI and her plans to testify against him at his trial for drug smuggling and murder.

She risked another glance backward. *Oh, God.* The man was gaining on her!

Heels be damned! She wasn't taking any chances. She hiked the short skirt of her dress up a few inches farther and flew down Burgundy Street toward her apartment. If she could at least make it to the small hotel two blocks down, she'd be safe. He wouldn't dare follow her into the lighted lobby, filled with curious tourists. She prayed.

Sweet mercy, she'd never make it. Panic made her muscles scream, yet her legs were rubbery, wanting to buckle even as she urged them faster and faster.

Suddenly she heard her name float through the hot, still night.

"Muse! Here, this way!"

A large male hand reached out, beckoning from behind one of the ubiquitous wrought-iron courtyard gates, this one just beyond the apartment building she was running past.

Thank God! Saved!

Who was it? A friend. That's all that mattered. She grabbed the man's hand and let him pull her through the narrowly opened gate. It closed behind her with a quiet metallic snick.

Relief. Talk about timing!

"Quick!" she commanded, launching herself at the man's broad chest. "Pretend to kiss me!"

It had always worked in the movies. Why not in real life?

Black hair, she thought as she swung them both behind the shrubbery, using the foliage and his body to shield herself from being seen by her pursuer. Not blond, but long, raven-black hair. And startled blue eyes. She had just enough time to register a quirk of sensually sculpted lips before they descended.

Her rescuer's mouth was warm and inviting. The timpani of her heartbeat stalled, then started up again for a whole new reason. Her throat made a small sound, her panic frozen in surprised suspension. Who *was* this guy? She tried to pull away but backed right up against a thorny shrub.

Slowly, languorously, as if there was all the time in the world, his lips began to ply their tender mercies upon hers.

She leaned into him, just a little, sighing out the rampant fear that had jolted through her just moments before, ending with a moan of halfhearted protest. Whoever it was definitely knew what he was doing.

He didn't touch her—other than his lips and a gentle hand cradling the back of her neck—a thing as unique as the rich flavor of his tongue as it slid erotically into her mouth.

"Open for me, *chère,*" he murmured, and this time her moan was of pleasure.

The warm breeze stroked over her skin, teasing her nostrils with the exotic scent of frangipani from the overflowing flower bed at their feet, and the faint, spicy musk of the man who was kissing her.

She should escape! Run away as fast as she could! But for the life of her she couldn't remember why.

Lord, oh, Lordy.

Despite appearances, she didn't usually let herself get too close to any man. A kiss or two was about as far as she ever went. Unfortunately, most men were lousy kissers, more interested in what came next than in enjoying the moment.

But this man's kiss was simply wonderful, unlike anything she'd ever experienced. It was warm as a hug from a friend on a cold night, sensual as sipping café au lait on a midnight balcony, comforting as the smell of croissants baking on Christmas morning.

Blood still pounding, she laid her hands on his chest and opened to sweet, sweet sensation.

Long moments later he pulled back a fraction, letting her up for air. Gazing into his eyes, she was struck by their clear, penetrating expression. The startlement from earlier had been replaced with a mix of calculation and hunger—a look that sent a shiver coursing down her spine.

She looked closer. The man from the bar?

"Shall I keep pretending?" he asked, drawing his index finger along her jaw.

"Pretending?" she murmured, unable to put a coherent thought together. Mercy, what he did to her insides…

His sinful lips bowed. "*Mais,* yeah. Pretending. To kiss, like you told me."

Definitely the man from the bar. His voice was that same wicked rumble of Louisiana French-accented tones, each word more seductive than the last.

She peered at the impressive man before her. Tall and rangy with wide shoulders that even filled his loose, casual shirt; muscular, athletic legs encased in black linen slacks; long, thick, pirate hair decadently skimming his collar. Even with the small scar running through his top lip and a defiantly sexy diamond stud glinting from his earlobe, the man was heart-stoppingly handsome.

"Are you following me?" she asked, and tried to take a step back. Like she needed another stalker. Though that didn't make sense. Hadn't he said something about getting his beauty sleep?

"You in the habit of asking perfect strangers to kiss you?" There was just the slightest edge to his voice.

Such impertinence. She cocked her hip and planted a fist on it. "Hardly perfect," she returned, eyeing him up and down—there was that scar, after all. "And you didn't seem to object too strenuously."

His mouth curved up and he gave her a lazy Gallic shrug. "Always glad to help a lady in need."

She just bet. "Anyway, I thought you were a friend."

His brows went up.

She opened her mouth to retort, then snapped it shut again. She didn't need to be standing here defending her actions. Okay, so she liked to kiss. So what? Considering it was the only pleasure she ever took from any of the men who constantly hounded her, she felt entitled to that simple enjoyment. Obviously, he didn't agree.

Not that this man's opinion of her mattered one whit.

All right, so maybe when she felt safe again she'd contemplate her convoluted lifestyle and see what could be done about the obvious contradictions.

Meanwhile, there were more pressing issues at hand. Such as how to get out of this huge mess she'd landed herself in with her latest brilliant idea. Who'd have thought the one truly selfless thing she'd done in recent memory could have gone so incredibly wrong? She glanced over her shoulder and out the gate to the street, suddenly recalling with a spurt of anxiety *why* she was hiding in the bushes with a man she'd barely laid eyes on and was growing less and less certain she could trust.

Time to leave.

"Thanks for rescuing me. I'll just be—"

But before she could take a single step, he grasped her wrist with a firm grip.

"*Non,*" he said, shaking his head.

Instant, irrational panic raced through her. *Omigod.* He *was* one of them. "Let go of me! I'll scream!"

She fought to free her wrist from his determined grasp—and for a second he appeared as confused as she was terrified.

Abruptly he released her and reached for his back pocket. She stumbled away, holding her wrist, putting much-needed space between them. To her dismay she saw he was now blocking the gate, her only means of escape.

"I'm sorry, Miz Summerville," he said. His expression was contrite as he produced a leather wallet which he flipped open and held up so she could read his identification.

"I don't understand," she mumbled, willing herself to calm down.

"Special Agent Remi Beaulieux, FBI," he said. "I've been sent to bring you in."

Chapter 2

Remi figured if he looked up *astonished* in the dictionary, he'd probably find a picture of Muse Summerville's face as it appeared about now—right under a picture of his own a few seconds into that amazing kiss she'd given him.

Bon Dieu, the woman could kiss like an angel from heaven above.

Muse's gaze snapped from his FBI credentials to his eyes. "You're FBI?"

"Yes, ma'am."

"Have they arrested Davies?"

Remi shook his head. "Not as far as I know."

"Then why bring me in?"

He lowered his wallet. "Orders."

"So what's changed?" Alarm flashed across her face. "He's found out about me."

Not a question but a statement. Sexy *and* smart.

"I'm not sure," Remi lied, tucking his thumbs firmly into his pockets along with his wallet.

"And Morris sent you for me?" she asked, suddenly appearing nervous—about him?

"That's right."

"Prove it."

"You don' believe my ID is real?"

"Would you?" she shot back. "In my position?"

"*Non,* I s'pose not," Remi conceded, his respect for the woman taking another upward swing. Make that *very* smart. "We better take a ride to the field office. Special Agent Morris will explain everything when we get there."

"How 'bout I call him first?" she countered, pulling a cell phone from her purse.

"*Bon.*"

Fine with him. All Remi wanted was to shuttle Muse safely to the field office as quickly as possible. His attraction to her was making him uneasy. It was a complication he didn't need right now. The sooner he delivered her to Morris, the sooner he could forget about her and her mind-numbing kisses, bow out of this retrieval gig and get back to his real job.

As she punched buttons on the phone and asked for Morris, he kept an eye on the gate in case the blond man following her came nosing around. He just hoped Simmons had seen what was going on and tailed the guy. Every lead was invaluable in tracking down Davies. It could shave weeks off his upcoming undercover work if he had a bit more to go on.

Sure enough, Muse's call had just been put through when Remi saw the man stalk past the entrance to the courtyard looking for her. It wasn't Simmons.

Lightning-fast he grabbed the phone and growled into it, "We'll call you back," while he quickly nudged her toward a nearby door well. This time he was careful not to grab her arm.

"Hide yourself," he whispered over her protest, then

ducked into the three-foot-deep alcove after her. ''He's back.''

''I didn't see him.'' Muse flattened herself against the brick, watching Remi apprehensively. He couldn't tell if it was because her pursuer was back, or because she still didn't trust him.

''I'm on your side,'' he assured her. ''One of the good guys.''

Attempting to lean past him to peek around the corner, she muttered, ''That's what they all say.''

He gave her a grin and barred her way. At least she hadn't lost her sense of humor. ''*Mais,* yeah, but I really am.''

Damn, she was pretty, jumpy and all. Mere inches separated them, sandwiched as they were into a few square feet of door well, giving him the opportunity to study her closer. She had an unusual face, not classically beautiful, but the blue eyes, high cheekbones and shapely lips formed a combination that had his woefully disobedient body humming with appreciation.

She glanced up. ''All right, then, Mr. Good Guy, get us out of this.'' Her big blue eyes were all wide and worried, and he felt an overwhelming need to reach out and pull her close.

Just to reassure her.

Not to steal another of those bone-melting kisses.

He pushed his fingers back into his pockets. ''I'll see what I can do. But let's give it a few minutes first, in case he's still out there.''

''Can I call Morris back? If I talk real soft?'' She gnawed on her plump lower lip and he made himself look away.

''Sure. Go on ahead.''

Closing his eyes for a slow count of ten, he fought to get his perspective back. The first kiss hadn't been his fault. She'd caught him off guard that time.

But it wouldn't happen again. He was on official assignment here.

Temporary official assignment.

There would be no more kisses.

Non.

Absolument not.

"What's wrong?" she said, interrupting his inner lecture. The phone was nowhere in sight and he realized she must have finished her call.

Oops.

He flashed her a smile. "*Rien.* Not a thing."

She may be a smart, intriguing party girl and exactly his type, but anything between them was completely out of the question.

Impossible.

She'd be gone from his life by tomorrow. Morris was setting it up right now. She would be stashed away with a 24/7 bodyguard, somewhere far away from Davies. And just as far away from Remi, who'd be deep undercover, getting next to the very man who was trying to kill her.

Dangerous even to fantasize.

"What did Morris say?" he asked.

"You were staring at me."

"He did?"

Rolling her eyes, she gave an impatient wave of her hand. "He wasn't at his desk, but his secretary said we should come in immediately."

Remi grunted. "Then let's go."

As he stuck his head out from their hiding place to check the scene, she repeated, "Why were you staring at me?"

He lifted a shoulder as casually as he could manage. "*Une jolie femme*—a pretty woman like you, what man wouldn't?"

"You weren't looking at me like that."

He glanced back at her. "Like what?"

"From the neck down."

He chuckled. "*Non?* I must be slippin'." He perused her from the neck down. Thoroughly. "That better?"

When he looked up, she was blushing. Now, that was *really* unexpected.

"No. I prefer the first way."

Personally, he thought both had merit.

"Stay here," he said, to prevent her from stepping out of the safety of the doorway. And himself from leaning in for the unruly kiss that was desperately trying to break loose from the grip of his resolve.

He eased up to the front gate and searched in both directions. After a full minute of careful observation, he was satisfied the blond man wasn't in the vicinity any longer. Nor did he see Simmons.

"Okay, we're clear." He signaled Muse to come out, and together they quickly walked to Decatur Street, where they found a cab.

She went along with him willingly enough, but she still seemed mighty jumpy.

Not that he blamed her. Having one's life threatened by the biggest gangster Louisiana had seen since Reconstruction would do that to any sane person. What amazed him more was that she'd lasted as long as she had spying on the New Orleans crime boss. She had to have nerves of steel. Six months was a hell of a long time to play that game, even for a seasoned undercover agent like himself. And he had the whole FBI organization to support him, if needed. All she'd had for backup was her low-life boyfriend, Gary Fox.

Big help he'd have been—Fox, whose main job was to deliver Davies's messages and fetch his café au lait and beignets every morning. At least it had been, up until some weeks earlier.

Davies had gone to ground several weeks ago, followed

by Fox and a handful of others a few days later. According to her file, Muse had seized upon that circumstance to give the little prick his walking papers, saying she didn't want to disrupt her life by disappearing with him.

Had she really grown tired of Fox? Or maybe the pressure had just gotten to her, but she was really still in love with the guy. After all, she had been with him for six months.

The agent in Remi warred with the man in him. Nobody had a clue where Davies and his cohorts were holed up. If Muse had chosen to go into hiding, she'd have reported back their whereabouts by now. Remi's undercover gig tomorrow would most likely have been unnecessary.

But then she'd still be with Fox.

For some reason, thinking about her together with a scumbag like Fox bugged the hell out of him.

Was she insane or what? Fox might be a good-looking guy on the surface, but the man was *bien mauvais draigille*—totally bad news. Not only a criminal, but from all indications, not a very astute one. A sharp woman like her didn't belong with a man like Fox. She belonged with—

None of his business, that's who.

Remi settled into the back seat of the cab, letting Muse handle the directions, and tried to reel in his badly wandering focus.

It was a damn good thing he was only the deliveryman for this package. He'd known the second he'd laid eyes on her that anyone in close proximity to Muse Summerville was in for a crazy ride. But how could he have ever guessed how strongly he'd be drawn to the woman himself?

Merci Dieu. Thank God it wasn't him who'd be babysitting her at the safe house until they could put Davies behind bars.

That would be nothing but a pure disaster.

Muse was able to control her dread over what Morris was about to tell her enough to sign in at the New Orleans FBI field station with a fairly steady hand and follow Remi down the halls to the conference room where Morris was already waiting.

"Miss Summerville, I'm so glad you made it in safely. I see you've met Agent Beaulieux," he said, shaking her hand.

Morris cordially invited her to be seated, pouring her a cup of coffee. Remi leaned a hip against the end of the massive, polished mahogany table, where he quietly contemplated them both.

Muse took a deep breath. "Agent Beaulieux says you want to put me under FBI protection. Is that true?"

"Yes, it is," Morris said. "Didn't he explain, when he made contact?"

She looked from Morris to Remi, mildly flustered at the memory of how she'd attacked him in that courtyard—hardly giving him a chance for explanations or anything else. And he'd already clarified that he hadn't known about this development when they'd spoken the first time.

"Um—"

"We didn't really have a chance to discuss the whys and wherefores," Remi interjected smoothly. "Trying to avoid the guy trailing her."

"I wasn't thinking too clearly at the time, anyway," she admitted. She'd been too busy going into shock from that kiss.

Remi held her eyes, and her pulse skittered. Against her will, her gaze slid to his lips. A slow smile lifted the very corners of his mouth, warm and meltingly seductive.

So, he was remembering, too.

"Are you saying you want to put me in some kind of a witness protection program?" she asked, breaking the thick silence.

She and Morris had talked about it a few times during

the half year she'd been spying for him, that it might one day become necessary. But the idea of turning her life completely upside down, giving up her job, her apartment, her friends, even for a few weeks, made her miserable just to think about. Not to mention the panic if Davies wanted to kill her.

"Afraid so. I know this isn't what you wanted—"

"Don't you think we may be overreacting?" she ventured, latching on to a last straw of hope. "I mean, we don't know for sure the blond man intends to harm me. We don't even know he works for Davies. It could just be some kind of joke one of my friends is playing."

"Trust me, this is no joke," Morris said. "I've had you watched for a couple of weeks now—"

"You *what?*" she exclaimed. "You mean all along this guy following me was your agent?"

"Agent Simmons isn't blond, Miss Summerville. There was at least one other person watching you, and we think there was even a third for a day or two."

A *third?*

"Was Simmons able to follow the man after Muse lost him tonight?" Remi broke in.

"Yes." Morris tapped his fingers on the table, then stood. "The suspect went straight back to his office, and Simmons was able to find out his identity. I just got off the phone with him."

That got her attention. "Who was the guy?"

"A PI working for an anonymous client. He gave us good reason to believe his client is James Davies, mapping your movements in preparation for—"

His words cut off, and she felt her face drain of blood.

"Davies must have found out you've been helping us," Remi said gently, breaking through her rising dread. "We can't risk your safety any longer. You have to accept FBI protection, at least until Davies is behind bars."

As he talked, Muse sank back into her seat, terror creeping up her spine like a large, malevolent spider. ''You really think he knows about me testifying?''

''I'd say that's a given,'' Remi confirmed.

''How long will it take to arrest Davies?''

He shrugged. ''Hard to say since we don't know where he is at the moment. A few days if we're lucky. More if we're not.''

She massaged her forehead for several seconds, trying to gather herself, then sighed. ''There's no alternative?''

''Trust me, Miz Summerville, none you'd care for.''

No choice. ''All right, I guess I can do it. For a few days.'' Sitting up straight, she asked, ''So what happens now? Will I at least be able to go back to my apartment and pack some things?''

Morris gave a quick nod. ''I think we can manage that. Then you'll be taken to the safe house until Davies is caught and put in jail.''

''Don' worry,'' Remi said sympathetically, and if they hadn't just met she might believe the look on his face was one of true concern. ''Special Agent Sylvia Delgado is in charge of the safe house. She'll take good care of you.''

Morris cleared his throat. ''Unfortunately, there's a problem with Delgado,'' he said.

Obviously surprised, Remi said, ''What kind of problem?''

Morris grimaced. ''She's in the hospital. Appendicitis.''

Remi's eyes narrowed and his next words were laced with a distinct flavor of suspicion. ''So who's taking over?''

Morris hesitated a fraction, and Muse could almost feel the room closing in. *Please, no.*

''You are, Beaulieux.''

''What!''

Remi jumped away from the conference table, and Muse's consternation skyrocketed.

"But I'm going undercover tomorrow," Remi said, his voice a low but unmistakable growl. "How are we going to find Davies if I don't—"

"He knows," Morris interrupted, and Muse's stomach plummeted.

"Knows what?" Remi ground out.

"You've been made. I don't understand how, but Davies found out about your cover, the plan, the whole operation."

Remi spit out a harsh oath. "You're sure?"

"Hundred percent. The PI mentioned it, hoping the info would dispose us to not serve him with a subpoena at Davies's trial."

Muse blurted out, "All this isn't necessary. I'll leave town instead. I can disappear completely—"

"Ain't gonna happen, *chère,*" Remi shot back. "Regardless of who's guarding you, we need you here. To testify, remember?"

"I remember," she said, straining to sound composed. "I…I just don't think it's a good idea for you to be my bodyguard."

Morris folded his arms and drilled her with a sharp look. "May I ask why not? Has he done something?"

"Yes. No! I mean no." She averted her eyes, unwilling…unable to explain that her motivation ran so much deeper than a simple kiss in a courtyard—as unsettling as that kiss was. "It's complicated."

"I see," Morris said slowly, causing her to meet his knowing gaze. "Look, Special Agent Beaulieux is a professional. He would never do anything to compromise you, himself or this case. Isn't that right, Agent Beaulieux?"

Muse swallowed. It didn't matter how professional Remi was. She knew men, and she knew very well what they all thought of her.

Yes, it was her own fault because of the outward image she had long ago chosen for reasons that were no one's business but her own. And true, so far Remi had been a breath of fresh air compared to most men. But it wasn't as though he'd had a chance to show his true colors in the few minutes they'd known each other.

If they were thrown together in a safe house, twenty-four hours a day, he would be no different from the rest of them. Of that she had no doubt. And honestly, she did not have the energy to deal with men and their base urges right now.

Especially when a part of her was actually trying to convince herself that this man could be different.

Lord, how gullible could you get?

Luckily Remi was enough of a gentleman to admit to his fundamental male nature. "She's right, Morris. This is a bad idea. Seriously."

"Find someone else. Please," she added to his appeal. "Anyone else."

Morris studied them silently, then addressed Remi. "Just fetch her things, get her to the safe house and stay put. I'll see what I can do. Give me a few hours."

"You okay?"

Muse glanced up when Remi pulled out her chair and helped her stand.

"I guess so." She raked her fingers through her hair and realized her hand was shaking. Damn. "I can't believe this is happening."

One day she was a happy, if underpaid, paralegal thinking she was doing society a big favor, and the next she was yanked out of her busy life because a madman wanted her dead.

"Believe it, darlin'."

"Thanks. I needed to hear that."

Lightly touching the small of her back, Remi guided her from the conference room through the hallways of the FBI building and into the parking garage.

He paused as he unlocked a dusty classic Porsche convertible. ''Don' worry. We're not going to let him get to you.''

Taking in his broad shoulders and strong, confident air, she believed him. Still… ''How can you be sure? You don't know this guy—''

''Trust me, we know him,'' he said as he helped her into the low-slung, leather passenger seat. Lowering onto his haunches next to the door, he grasped the metal end of her seat belt. ''For five years we've been working to lock him up for good. We know exactly what he's capable of, and that's why we're putting you under guard.''

He watched her with concern, almost intimately, yet his eyes held a powerful gleam of determination. She gave an involuntary shiver at the intensity of purpose she saw in their depths, and felt a brief moment of gratitude she was not the object of that potent resolve.

''Well, thanks for taking me to the safe house.'' She smiled tremulously. ''And thanks for rescuing me from that PI following me.''

A grin sneaked across his lips. ''My pleasure.''

Before she could protest, he leaned over her and snapped the metal seat belt hook into the catch. Muse sucked in a reflexive gasp, shrinking away from the sudden, unexpected confinement. His body didn't touch hers but they were nearly nose to nose, his large frame completely filling the small space in front of her seat. She had to hold her breath to prevent her breasts from pressing into his chest.

She swallowed heavily against an instinctive panic.

''We'd better go,'' she rasped, striving to control her totally inappropriate reaction. After all, this man had shown her nothing but consideration. Not to mention given her the most tender, delicious kiss she'd ever experienced. He was not a—

He sat back on his heels. ''There a problem, Miz Summerville?'' he asked, appearing somewhat puzzled by her mercurial demeanor.

She forced a smile. Her personal neuroses were not something open for discussion. Besides, he was on her side, not out to… She shook her head clear of the last dregs of the ancient fear, and smiled wider. ''No. Of course not.''

''Sure?''

''Sure.'' She nibbled on her lip. ''Listen, about what I said in there—''

He waved her off. ''*C'est rien, ça.* I feel the same way.''

''So you know it's nothing personal.''

He chuckled softly. ''*Mais,* yeah, it's personal. *Too* personal. And that's the trouble, *non, chérie?*''

Without thinking, she tucked a long strand of midnight-black hair behind his ear, then brushed down the side of his face with her fingers. ''Yes. It is.''

His smile changed character as he regarded her, his shadowy gaze dipping to her lips. ''We should go to your apartment now…to pick up your things.''

She knew what he was thinking. It was there in his dark, half-lidded eyes, in the way he held himself, in the very way he breathed.

''We'll have to be careful,'' he continued. ''Your apartment is the first place they'll look.''

He was wrong about her, but she didn't mind because she knew she was safe with him, at least for now.

And it was all part of the intricate dance between man and woman. Despite everything, she did love flirting. Loved how Remi was looking at her now. Loved the heady, butterflies-in-the-stomach feeling of being wanted by a man like him. She definitely loved his kiss. Too bad she could never—

But, no. Things would never get that far. Morris had promised Remi's only assignment was to drop her off at the safe house, then he'd be gone. And as for her apartment, she'd gather her things and they'd be out of there before he had a chance to try anything.

Much.

But what could it possibly hurt if she flirted a little with the man? Or gave in to another one or even two of his divine kisses?

She warmed inwardly, a reluctant anticipation swirling through her insides.

"Then we'll just have to make it quick," she whispered.

Chapter 3

"This is it," Muse said, pointing to a narrow courtyard off Burgundy Street. "My apartment's down at the end."

Remi pulled into a no-parking zone in front of the apartment building he'd already known was hers, turned off the Porsche and did his best to shore up his faltering resolve.

"Coming?"

He hadn't had time to put a careful plan into motion, but if Davies was having Muse watched, her apartment would be the first place he'd stake out after losing her last night. And if Remi gave in to the temptation he was feeling, they might not get out of there for a while.

"Agent Beaulieux?"

Like maybe a week or two.

A plan.

That's what he needed. He never did anything without a carefully thought-out plan with several escape routes. The reason his undercover work always succeeded was because he made it a point to be one step ahead of every possible situation. He always had a plan. Always.

Except now.

"Remi?"

And the first item needed in the plan was how the hell to get her in and out of her apartment without laying a finger on her.

"Is everything okay?"

No kissing.

No touching.

No falling into bed.

He stifled a groan. Definitely no falling into bed.

"Everything's jus' dandy," he croaked at her worried look.

Yep, he had to come up with a good plan. And fast. Then he had to stick to it—or risk putting both of them in danger.

He got out of the car, walked around and opened the door for her, all the while searching for a sign of anyone observing them.

"Thanks, sugarcane," she said, glancing up and down the street.

In and out. Period. Hands firmly in pockets.

Sounded like a plan.

Remi followed Muse through the overgrown courtyard and up the stairs to the second-floor landing.

"Wait here," he admonished, and went through the door first, weapon drawn. After checking out the tiny two-room apartment for intruders, he gave the all-clear and closed the door behind them.

"This lock is a joke," he remarked, shaking the wobbling entry doorknob. He made a mental note to have Morris get it changed before she moved back in.

"Really?" she said, and scurried quickly into the bedroom. He heard a closet open and a suitcase being unzipped.

"A child could break in," he called, wandering around the cozy living-room-dining-room-kitchen combo. "This is nice."

Simple but nice. A few pieces of pale plush antique furniture, old glassed-in bookcases and wooden kitchen table, an entire wall of flowing white sheers covering floor-to-ceiling windows and French doors. Long strands of Mardi Gras beads hung everywhere, a distinctively New Orleans splash of color in the otherwise subdued decor.

"Yeah, I like it," she said above the rustling of hangers.

He spotted some framed black-and-white photos above the sofa and walked over to take a closer look. "Wow, these are great," he said, studying the incredible prints of iron lace patterns, stark black against a variety of settings. There was one particularly moody photo of an ancient gate hanging by a single hinge backdropped by a dilapidated antebellum mansion, and covered with rambling roses. "Beautiful," he murmured.

"Thanks."

He turned. Muse was standing in the bedroom doorway, leaning against the doorframe. The expression on her face melted his heart—uncertain, hopeful, yearning, yet with a flush of pride that was unmistakable.

"They're yours," he said. And then his attention was snagged by what she was holding. A sheer, red, baby-doll nightie.

Instantly his imagination dropped what it was doing and filled the lacy scrap with her generous curves.

"Do you really like them?"

This time he did groan. "Don' do this to me, *chère.* Not unless you intend to change into that thing—" *no falling into bed* "—which would probably not be a good idea just at the moment."

Her gaze dropped to the nightie. "Oh!" She whipped it behind her and backed into the bedroom. "Sorry, I didn't mean— I mean, I don't— That is, I—" A drawer slammed shut. "I'm not bringing that."

He let out a long breath. "Not a problem, *chère*. But maybe we should hurry this up a bit."

"Sure, I'm almost—" she looked up and froze when he prowled over and stopped just inside the bedroom door "—done."

They stared silently at each other, and he was surprised lightning didn't strike from the electricity in the air.

"What is happening here between us?" he murmured, thick desire constricting his throat.

"I believe it's called chemistry." Her wobbly voice was barely above a whisper.

"No kidding. So what are we going to do about it?"

He could swear he saw a shadow of fear flit though her eyes. "I, um—" Her gaze darted to the bed. The large, ornate wrought-iron bed, draped in satin sheets. Just as quickly it darted back to him. "I don't—"

Black satin sheets.

"Definitely not," he agreed. He shook his head determinedly. "That would not be…"

"…a good idea," she finished. "For many reasons."

"Right."

"Right."

But neither of them moved, not body nor eyes.

He'd never desired any woman quite so badly in his entire life.

But he couldn't have her.

For many reasons. Not the least of which was that someone might even now be waiting downstairs to kill her.

"You could kiss me," she suggested softly. "A goodbye kiss. Since you'll be leaving me at the safe house with someone else and we probably won't ever see each other again."

His pulse stalled at the thought of kissing her, then stopped altogether at the thought of never seeing her again.

A kiss? Tempting. *Too tempting.*

He shook his head again, not trusting his tongue to form the words he must say.

"No, huh?" she said, unable to cover her disappointment.

Merde.

"We'll see each other again," he said with all the conviction of a federal judge. "And when we do, I'll—"

He cut off, not wanting to go there. Maybe by then he'd have driven this crazy attraction clear out of his mind and his blood.

She backed up, just a fraction, but her eyes widened. Her tongue peeked out, sliding erotically over her bottom lip. Again.

He blinked. *Saloperie!* Damn, damn, *damn.*

He took a step forward, then halted.

He shouldn't. He shouldn't even *think* about kissing her again. Neither of them should.

"*Non.*" It was the hardest thing he'd ever had to say. "No kiss."

"Okay," she whispered.

She turned and hurried into the bathroom. He moved instinctively after her, thinking she was going to cry. But instead she grabbed a *necessaire* and began busily filling it with makeup and other things from the bathroom counter.

"I'll be just a minute," she called.

He raked a hand through his hair. Maybe he was wrong. Maybe she didn't feel it as strongly as he did, this…whatever it was that drew him to her. Maybe he was just another of the multitude of men who desired her and had no special effect on her heart or her temperature. Just another mouth to kiss. Pick a number for her favors.

The notion annoyed him immensely. Unfortunately, there was nothing he could do about it at the moment. Not even find out if it was true.

"Do me a favor?"

He clamped his jaw. "Sure."

"There's a safety-deposit-box key in the nightstand. Can you get it for me?"

He stalked to the nightstand, yanked open the drawer and just stared. It was filled to overflowing with condoms, of every type and variety. He didn't know what he wanted to do more, kill her or fling her onto the bed and slowly work his way through the entire stash.

He heard her suck in a breath behind him and turned.

"Wrong nightstand. The other side."

He grunted noncommittally and stalked around the bed, jerked open the drawer and rooted for the key. He grabbed it and turned to find her standing between him and the windows. She was watching him with a strange expression, somewhere between nervousness and defiance. But no guilt.

"They were all given to me. I didn't—"

"None of my business," he interrupted, his annoyance spiking dangerously.

"Whatever," she said, taking the key. Turning to the window, she lifted the curtain rod from its moorings and dumped the whole wall of silky curtains into a heap on the floor.

"What the hell are you doing?"

"Since I'm going to be away, I thought I'd take the curtains to the dry cleaners. Could you get the ones in the other room?"

"*Are you out of your mind?* Davies could be here any second and you're worried about *curtains?*"

She ignored him, and started rolling up the endless yards of fabric into a neat bundle.

He knew enough about women to recognize the stubborn set of her jaw, so he didn't fight her but stalked into the living room and pulled down the curtain rod. There had to be a hundred yards of the stuff. When he was finished, his bundle wasn't nearly as orderly as hers, but he was too irritated to care.

Women.

"Ready?" He hefted the two enormous rolls onto his shoulders. Damn. How would he hold his Beretta and the curtains, too?

She glanced at the door, then hesitated. "I really need to call my sister."

He gritted his teeth. "You know I can't let you do that."

"I swear I won't tell her anything. Just that I'm all right. Please…?"

He squared his stance and tried to look as menacing as was possible toting a hundred pounds of diaphanous silk. "No doubt Davies already knows about her," he said, "probably even where she lives. But if she's the last call you make before dropping out of sight, he just might get the idea she means something to you."

He held her eyes for the several seconds it took for comprehension to finally flood them.

"I understand," she said hoarsely, and picked up her bulging overnight bag.

He strode out the door and waited for her to lock it, wishing he could have spared her that little slap of insight. Wishing she had asked to phone one of her many gentlemen friends instead of an innocent sister in Carolina. He might even have let her make the call.

"Have you ever handled a weapon? A gun?" he asked.

She glanced up. "This year's top-ranking woman at the gun club in rifle marksmanship."

His jaw dropped. "Top ranking?"

She grinned. "As in number one."

"What about pistols?"

She made a rueful face. "Only number four. But I was having a bad day."

He snapped his jaw shut. "In that case, take the Beretta from my shoulder holster."

She looked at him blankly, then gave his torso a once-over. "What shoulder holster?"

Sacré— He took a cleansing breath. "Under my shirt."

She looked closer. "Oh."

She set down her suitcase and wiped her hands on her dress. He noticed it wasn't the same outfit she was wearing when they'd gotten there. She must have changed while she was in the bedroom. This one was a brilliant magenta, short and breathtakingly—

Her fingertips touched his skin and he nearly leaped out of it.

"Sorry," she murmured breathily, and moved her hands up his midriff under his shirt.

"Muse..." he warned, clenching his teeth.

"Sorry," she repeated, her fingers skimming over his hardened nipple as she sought his weapon. Using both hands she unsnapped the strap holding it secure and lifted it from the leather.

"Careful."

One way or another she was going to be the death of him.

"Put the gun in your bag and leave it unzipped."

"Isn't this against some kind of regulations?"

"About a hundred," he ground out. "But don' worry, it's my spare. And I want you to use it if you have to."

She did as he asked, and he prayed they wouldn't run into any trouble. He didn't want her involved in a shooting. He knew he could dump the curtains, get to the other Beretta tucked in the back of his waistband and drop whoever was threatening them faster than most people could blink, but it was nice to have a little backup. Even if she was only ranked number four.

Incroyable.

He made her stay behind him until he was satisfied the courtyard was empty, and as they walked down the street he practically pinned her against the buildings with the long columns of fabric on his shoulders. He wasn't taking any chances. Thank God the dry cleaner was just around the corner.

"Of all the nutty ideas…" he muttered as he hurried her back to the Porsche after depositing the curtains with the dry cleaning attendant.

He flung open the door and tried to hand her into the car.

"Wait! I just need to put the cleaning ticket in my briefcase upstairs."

Before he could object she was through the gate. He bit down a curse of frustration. Tapping his foot, he swung his head back and forth scanning for trouble until she ran out again.

"Okay, done!"

He helped her in, jumped into the driver's seat and screeched out of the parking spot, irritated as hell at her potentially dangerous dilly-dallying.

But she just smiled, her eyes glistening in the morning sun, her blond hair flying in every direction.

"Nice ride," she commented, and he couldn't help but smile, too, his annoyance dissolving just from the sheer joy of looking at her.

"Confiscated from a tax accountant who was embezzling money from little old ladies across three states," he said. "I've threatened to cut off the obscure Italian car magazines I'm supplying the Bureau garage super with if he checks out this baby to anyone else."

She grinned. "Oh, you ruthless man."

"You bet." He grinned back. "Don' forget it."

"Mmm." She snuggled into the butter-soft leather seat looking like a cat in cream. "If this is one of the perks, maybe I'll become an FBI agent, too."

He sifted carefully through the various reactions that suggestion hit him with—doubt, alarm, protectiveness, but in the end chose the honest truth. "You'd make a good one," he said, and she cut him a surprised look.

"You think?"

"Sure." Remi sighed inwardly. The good guys were having a hard enough time dealing with her… "The bad guys wouldn't stand a chance."

"Thanks." Muse gazed at him in amusement, no doubt suspecting she was being teased, but seemed pleased with his compliment nonetheless. "I think."

"Why don't you grab a short nap while we drive to the safe house? How long have you been up?"

She glanced at the old-fashioned dashboard clock that showed nine-thirty. "Over twenty-four hours." She let out a sigh, and weariness washed visibly over her. "How far is it?"

"About an hour away."

"In that case," she said over a yawn that involved her whole body wriggling deep into the seat. "Maybe I will."

Muse's eyes sprang open, totally disoriented. The Porsche was spinning in a one-eighty, rubber screaming against the pavement. A gunshot rang out, then another. She screamed and a whole volley burst around them like wind chimes in a hurricane.

"Get down!" Remi yelled, shoving her head below the level of the dashboard just as she heard a pop and a rip of canvas from the ragtop.

No time to shake the grogginess from her brain. Acting on pure instinct, she grabbed the Beretta from her overnight bag and peered over the rim of the passenger door, scanning for the shooter. Cursing in unison with Remi, she whipped down the window just as she spotted a man with a semiautomatic rifle crouched behind some bushes.

"What in blazes are you doing?" Remi yelled.

"Shooting back," she snarled, and blasted the guy.

"Jeezus, Muse! Stop!"

She missed. But felt an enormous satisfaction at the astonishment in the creep's face as he dropped and rolled.

She lowered the Beretta, knowing the man was out of range by now. Remi had the Porsche on the straightaway, flooring it down a seemingly everyday suburban neighborhood street.

He swore an even more potent oath. "I can't believe this. He's made the safe house, too!"

"Davies?"

"I can't imagine who else would be shooting at us." He took a corner on two wheels. "Help me watch for kids and dogs."

The silence was spring loaded as he sped down peaceful, tree-lined avenues, occasionally pulling into a hidden driveway to watch for a tail. Thankfully, if there'd been one, they'd lost it.

After about fifteen minutes of evasive maneuvers, he pulled into an alley and shut off the engine. She only realized she still had the Beretta clutched in her hands when Remi pried it from her fingers.

"I can't believe you returned fire. What were you *thinking?*"

"What was I supposed to do? Let him kill us?"

Remi's mouth formed a thin line. "You could have hit an innocent bystander."

She bit her lip. "Oh." She hadn't thought of that. "Sorry."

He shook his head. "In the future, save any shooting till I give the order."

She glanced up sharply. "You think there'll be more?"

He gave a wry half smile that didn't come close to his eyes. "God, I hope not. I'd better call in."

After setting the weapon back into her overnight bag, he dug in his pocket for his cell phone. As he flipped it open, she stared at the gun in the bag, torn between horror at actually having shot bullets at a real live person and the overwhelming urge to go back and finish the job.

How dare anyone shoot at them! Anger gushed through her. And violation. And lastly, profound fear.

At first it had been almost a game, the spying. When she'd shortly understood how evil and detestable drug dealer James Davies truly was, she'd gotten serious about gathering information to put him away for good, choosing to work for the FBI when they approached her.

The notion of getting hurt had been remote and theoretical…until she'd viewed the videotape she and Gary had stolen from him. That's when she realized just how much trouble she was in if Davies found out about her.

Luckily the tape had also been her ticket out. By then her relationship with Gary had become more than uncomfortable. She'd long since wanted to call it quits but hadn't had the heart to disappoint Agent Morris by cutting off his most reliable source. However, with the video, in addition to the other evidence she had already provided, she knew the FBI could lock Davies up and throw away the key. So she'd stolen it from Gary before breaking up.

Of course, she hadn't told Morris about the tape. As long as he thought he needed her alive, he'd do everything in his power to protect her from the bad guys. With the video in FBI possession, her value as a witness would go down, along with her long-term chances of survival—especially while Davies was still at large. So at the moment it was hidden in her safety-deposit box at the bank, her ace in the hole until Davies was behind bars.

She'd hidden the safety-deposit key in a place her sister, Grace, would be sure to find it, if something happened. She knew without a doubt that Grace would come to find her if she disappeared, and she wasn't taking any chances. Muse was determined that Davies would spend the rest of his life in jail, even if she wasn't around to put him there.

But now she was safely in FBI custody. Maybe she should tell Morris about the tape? Or Remi?

"Someone on the inside must be dirty," Remi said speculatively, interrupting her thoughts. He was still holding the phone in his hand, undialed.

"What?" A chill swept through her, raising goose bumps. "You mean inside the FBI?"

"It's the only way Davies could have found out about both my undercover setup and the safe house. There's no other explanation. He's gotten to someone in the field office."

Fear spiraled down her spine. "So I'm a walking dead woman."

"Not if I have anything to say about it."

She smiled bleakly, tipping her head to size up the bullet hole in the roof. "I appreciate that. But if he has a paid informer inside the FBI tracking our every move, I doubt you can stop him."

"I wouldn' be so sure," Remi said, starting the Porsche with a roar. "I have a plan."

She turned to him as he shifted smoothly into first. "And what would that be, Special Agent Beaulieux?"

He fixed his determined gaze on her. The one that, just a short hour ago, had made her shiver with its intensity.

"Do you trust me?"

His simple question jolted through her.

Her life was undoubtedly in danger, yet there was an even more unnerving aspect to this whole situation. She took in the handsome face, so calm and resolute. Remi Beaulieux was, without question, just as dangerous as James Davies. Oh, yes. Especially to her heart. Certainly to her peace of mind.

Did she trust him?

"Do I have a choice?"

The scar above his lip twitched. "No."

"So, what is this plan of yours?" she asked with growing dread. A dread that had nothing to do with dying.

The car leaped forward and spun onto the thoroughfare heading south. "Simple. We don't tell them where we're going."

"But that means…

"You're in my hands now, Miz Summerville. You don't eat, you don't sleep, you don't even blink without me there watching. From this moment on, you don't leave my sight until I'm satisfied you're safe."

Oh, God. She squeezed her eyes shut.

"Any questions?"

Yeah. A really big one.

In his hands Muse might very well be safe from James Davies. But…

Who on earth would protect her from Remi Beaulieux?

Chapter 4

It wasn't until they were deep in bayou country that Remi figured he could relax a bit. At least for now. In the tiny village they found themselves in around noon, he doubted anyone would pay them any notice. Just another couple of tourists on a leisurely tour through picturesque Cajun country.

"You want me to drive?" Muse offered from the passenger seat. "You look like you're about to fall over from exhaustion."

"More likely from tension. I'm not a big fan of improvising on the run." He gave her a weary smile as he pulled into an ancient mom-and-pop filling station, complete with an ancient sign that had probably been in use since before cars were invented. "I'll just run in here and get another cup of coffee."

She put a hand on his arm. "What you need is some sleep. I could use some, too."

He looked into her dog-tired face and realized he wasn't

the only one who could barely keep his eyes open. ''It'll take us another hour or two to get where we're going.''

''And where is that?''

''A friend of mine's place. I just hope he's not off on a job.''

Though it was unlikely Guy de Valein was anywhere but ensconced in his hidden shanty home in the middle of a South Louisiana swamp. ''Dev'' didn't get out much, even for work. He was strictly a virtual man these days.

Muse sighed and glanced around. ''Sugar, I'll never make it another hour or two. Especially if I have to be civil when we get there. Look, there's a cute bed-and-breakfast across the street. Please can we stop for a nap?''

Remi glanced over at the quaint old Victorian house. A hand-painted sign hung from the rose arbor entrance, Chez Noisette B&B.

He swiped a hand over his gritty eyes. He was used to being awake for days at a time on stakeout, but not the mental exhaustion of being in a situation without the safety net of a solid plan to follow when his brain cells stopped firing on all cylinders. He didn't like the exposure, but they could both definitely use some shut-eye.

''All right,'' he reluctantly said, checking his watch. ''We can get in a few hours of rest and still make it to Dev's before dark.'' Finding the out-of-the-way property after sunset was not an option.

Remi parked the Porsche behind the B&B, hidden from the main road, and they went in. He was so out of it, he didn't blink when the proprietress informed them the only room she had available was the elaborate bridal suite.

''That's fine,'' he said, smiling at Muse's consternation. He could well afford the pricey room. He was carrying even more cash than usual because he'd been expecting to go undercover for a long time.

"Is that all your luggage?" the woman politely asked, indicating the stuffed bag Muse clutched to her chest.

He nodded, hesitating over the register before signing Mr. and Mrs. David Brown. John Smith was *so* yesterday. "Just an afternoon siesta."

"Ah. Well. I'll send up your champagne at once," she said with a prim smile, and handed him an ornate metal key. "All the way up, to your left."

"Champagne?" Muse asked in an oddly raspy voice. Come to think of it she was awfully pale, as well. She really must be exhausted.

"Complimentary with the room," the woman said. "Can I get you anyth—"

"We're all set," Remi assured her, took the bag from Muse and guided her to the staircase with a hand on her backside.

"Remi," she whispered, pausing on the landing.

"David," he whispered back. "Shall I carry you over the threshold?"

"What? No!" she said. "Don't be— Oh, my God," she murmured when he flung open the door to the suite. "It's beautiful!"

All he could see was the bed. Big. Fluffy. Comfy. Inviting. He let out a long, heartfelt sigh. "I'll say."

With that he kicked off his shoes, dove onto the feather comforter, closed his eyes and passed out.

A loud rumbling noise shook Remi from a deep, drugging sleep. He snapped awake, instantly sitting up, Beretta in hand and pointed at the door. He checked Muse, who was lying next to him on the bed. Her worried eyes met his, silently confirming she'd also been awakened by the ungodly racket.

Suddenly both their stomachs rumbled in unison. In the tense quiet, the sound was deafening.

Their eyes widened, then they both burst out laughing.

"Lord have mercy," she said, catching her breath. "I thought we were dead."

"Apparently just from hunger." Remi chuckled. Neither had eaten since yesterday. He glanced at the waning light through the lacy curtained window and let out a curse. "Damn, no wonder. We must have slept for hours. It's almost dark."

She rubbed her eyes and sat up. "Is that a problem?"

"Dev lives in the middle of a swamp. The trail he laughingly calls a road is barely wide enough for a car to drive on. I don't even want to think about what would happen if the Porsche went off the path."

"Stuck in the mud?"

He snorted, his heartbeat slowing to normal, and he lowered his Beretta to the nightstand. "That would be the best foreseeable scenario."

Probably not wise to mention the gators. Or the booby traps and motion sensors rigged all along the road. Even though he'd helped set them himself, he would never remember where they were placed, not after five years.

Sinking back onto the downy quilt, he watched as Muse raised her arms above her head and yawned, her whole body involved in the motion. Her hair was delightfully mussed, her magenta sundress rumpled and twisted around her generous curves. As she stretched, its hem rode up dangerously high on her long, sleek thighs.

Mmm. She would be so sweet under him.

No falling into bed, Beaulieux.

But they were already in bed.

Bien. Maybe just a quick repeat of that unbelievable kiss?

He sighed. *Non.*

He'd been through this before. The FBI had rules. He could be severely reprimanded, even fired, for kissing Muse Summerville again—let alone anything else—regardless of how willing a participant she was. She was a witness, and it was his duty to safeguard her—not attack her himself. Besides, it would be unfair of him to imply he was interested in pursuing a relationship of any kind.

He realized she'd turned and was regarding him carefully. "We should eat," she said, her voice thready.

"Yeah," he agreed, firmly tamping down on his wayward thoughts. "But I don' see how. We shouldn' let ourselves be seen outside."

"Surely we could risk it in a dinky town like this?"

She crossed her arms under her breasts, emphasizing how incredibly round and perfect they were. His pulse zinged into double time and he knew he was in one big, X-rated heap of trouble. Because the fact was, he wasn't sure he cared if he got fired.

One more taste of her might just be worth the risk.

Le bon Dieu mait le main. God help him resist this woman. He surely didn't have the strength himself.

Just as he was about to reach for her, she slid off the bed, brushing down her dress with her palms. "Should we try?"

He swallowed. *Oh, yeah.*

She looked up. "I remember a diner just down the road..."

Diner. Food.

Not sex.

His stomach rumbled again, together with an inner groan. "All right, you win. But we'd better be extra careful."

He pushed off the bed and headed for the bathroom where he dunked his head into the sink and turned on the cold-water faucet.

"Still tired?" she asked, hanging back at the door.

"Just shaking out the cobwebs." And the overactive hormones.

"I could sleep for another twelve hours. That bed was

wonderful.'' She ventured in and handed him a towel when he groped at the rack for one.

It was a nice-size bathroom complete with clawfoot tub and a huge antique mirror, in which she watched him rub his hair dry. It smelled faintly of old roses.

''You may get your wish. Looks like we'll be stuck here overnight. No use setting off before dawn.''

''Think we'll be safe?''

''I'm here to protect you,'' he said, holding her eyes in the mirror.

She gave him a brave smile. One tinged with fear and anxiety, but filled with trust. ''Thank you,'' she said. ''I know this isn't what you signed up for.''

She slid her arms around his waist from behind and rested her cheek against his back. Luckily the damp towel dangling from his fingers prevented him from turning around and pulling her into an embrace.

''Thanks aren't necessary. It's my job.''

''I'd never forgive myself if anything bad happened to you because of me.''

He took his time placing the towel carefully back on the rack, tugging out every wrinkle and making it hang exactly square.

''Nothing bad's going to happen,'' he assured her. ''Davies shouldn't find us. Not unless we give ourselves away. Remember, no credit cards, no traceable phone calls, no using our real names in front of anyone.''

''I understand.'' She slid away from him and reached for her toothbrush. ''What about Morris? Won't he send out the troops, thinking something's happened to us? He's got to know about the shootout by now.''

''No doubt.'' He grabbed his comb and raked it through his wet hair. ''I have a prepaid cell phone in my undercover gear in the car. We'll have to use it to call him. Hopefully he can place you out of state, somewhere Davies isn't able to compromise. But until then…''

''We'll be on our own,'' she said, facing him for the first time since leaving the bed. Worry blazed in her Caribbean-blue eyes.

''Just you an' me, darlin'.'' He set aside his comb and pushed back a lock of her thick golden hair. ''Don' worry. It'll be fine.''

She gazed up at him with such uncertainty, it took all his willpower not to lower his lips to hers, just to show her how fine it would be.

''Anything happens to you happens over my dead body. That's a pure, damned certitude,'' he murmured.

But what had him a whole lot more worried was what might happen *with* her…over his very much alive body.

''Remi—'' she whispered.

''Let's go make that phone call,'' he said, before it had a chance to happen right then and there.

''You know as well as I, getting involved with a witness is against Bureau policy.''

''Yes, I do know. But these are special circumstances.''

Remi was speaking with Morris on the phone and he simply couldn't believe what he was hearing. ''Especially a witness I'm supposed to be *guarding,*'' he added for emphasis.

''Get it through your head, Beaulieux. There's no one else available. It'll take several days to authorize an out-of-state transfer. Hopefully by that time we'll have Davies in custody. Until then she's all yours.''

''But I told you, we've already kissed. Tonight we'll be sharing a—''

''Keep the details to yourself, Agent Beaulieux,'' Morris said. ''I'm only interested in results. I want her alive for trial and I don't care what you have to do to accomplish that.''

Remi sighed. His reputation for wild living while undercover was finally doing him in. Praying other arrangements could be made, he'd confessed twice now to the sizzling attraction between him and Muse, warning Morris where it was surely heading. But given Remi's history, Morris wasn't buying his objections to playing Romeo to Muse's Juliet. Normally he'd be right. But not this time. She just hit him too close to home to slip comfortably into that role.

Besides, he didn't care for the way the play ended.

''Muse Summerville is a difficult-to-manage witness with a well-documented defiant streak.'' Morris said. ''Both our careers are in the balance with this one. I'm counting on you to keep her in line and the case on track.''

''She's not difficult to manage,'' Remi objected. *Much.*

''You said it was Miss Summerville who returned fire at the safe house. Stunts like that could easily get her killed.''

''And bury our hopes for a conviction against Davies along with her,'' Remi conceded morosely, knowing he wasn't going to win this argument.

''Settle her down and gain her trust. But above all, make her obey orders.''

''You'll work on the out-of-state transfer?''

''Meanwhile, do whatever you have to do. Remember, we need her alive.''

Muse was terrified.

What on earth would she do?

As much as she liked Remi, there was no way she could spend the whole night with him in that bed. Or maybe it was because she *did* like him so much. Or maybe it was because they were stuck together for an undetermined amount of time and the last thing she wanted to deal with was sex. Whatever the reason, she could not sleep with the man.

Not that sleeping with him—actually sleeping—wasn't absolutely wonderful. When he'd tumbled onto the big canopied four-poster and nodded off within seconds, she'd been astounded, and elated. That meant she'd been able to curl up behind him and savor his cozy warmth and his delicious male scent, his strong, steady heartbeat lulling her into a soothing sense of comfort and security. Without all that other stuff.

She hadn't slept so well since, well, since that time she was dancing with a friend on Bourbon Street and he'd had a few too many and she'd felt obligated to tuck him into bed after he passed out. He'd felt warm and cozy, too, when she'd enjoyed a few stolen hours of closeness in his bed, sleeping next to his solid back, then sneaking out before he awoke the next morning.

No, sleeping with Remi would be fine. It was the other…complications, all the things he'd expect her to do before falling asleep, and enjoy, that was the problem.

Her only possible reprieve was the phone call Remi'd just made. Maybe the FBI would send her to Alaska or somewhere else, far away from the temptation of Special Agent Beaulieux's skillful kissing.

"So what did Morris say?" she asked, trying not to look too hopeful.

Across the diner's dingy red-checkered tablecloth Remi studied his coffee cup, looking calm and composed. No, on second thought, looking agitated but attempting to appear calm and composed.

"We're on our own," he said.

Her heart stalled. "What about the transfer?"

"It'll take a few days to arrange."

"What about Davies's inside informer?"

"I didn't tell Morris where we are or where we're going, and he didn't ask. I think it's someone lower down."

"So I'm safe."

"As long as you're with me." He glanced up, meeting her gaze. The diamond in his ear glinted in the garish fluorescent lighting.

Oh, God, she was in trouble. Unless… "So, I guess this calls for a drink." Or maybe ten. "How about a beer?"

His lips tipped up wryly. "Are we celebrating or drowning our sorrows?"

She shored up her faltering courage and flashed him her best flirty smile. She could do this. "What do you think?"

He leaned back in the cracked vinyl booth and tipped his head. "I think we better eat hearty. We'll need our strength later."

Her pulse stalled. What had changed?

Before, he'd seemed to fight their attraction—like in the bathroom when he'd ignored her embrace, though she knew darn well he'd wanted to return it. But now, it was as though some barrier had been lifted and he felt free to pursue it, or rather, her.

She leaned back, too, careful not to let panic sneak through her facade. "What happened to 'this isn't a good idea'?"

The scent of red rice and hush puppies wafted over from the next table as the sounds of the busy diner receded. The clinking of forks and china, the conversations around them, the waitress calling up her orders, all became a low buzz in the background.

Remi watched her, his gaze steady. "It still isn't a good idea. But we're going to do it anyway, aren't we?"

Before she could jump up and shout "No, no, a thousand times no!" the waitress appeared at their table, pad in hand, chattering on about blue-plate specials and how nice the bed-and-breakfast was and how her uncle Earl had helped with the renovations and how long were they staying? By the time the woman had scribbled down the order Remi gave for both of them it seemed like they'd been acquainted for years.

And the subject of Remi and her sleeping together had been dropped like a done deal.

She should bring it up again. Explain things. She could be honest with him; it wasn't as if he was her boyfriend or even her potential boyfriend. Despite their instantaneous attraction, there was no interest in that area on his part. He'd made it clear from word one he was an FBI agent doing his job. That was his sole interest in her—other than the purely physical, which was simply him being a guy. He'd understand that her refusal was nothing personal.

Or would he?

It was times like this when her lifestyle came back to haunt her in the worst way. He'd seen her behavior, the way she dressed, heard her suggestive comebacks, no doubt gotten detailed descriptions of her Bourbon Street antics from that thick FBI file kept on her down at the field office.

How could she convince him she always ended up in bed alone? That it was all a pretense?

She couldn't. She was too good at it. Had kept it up for too long.

Her sister, Grace, the psychologist, said acting the part of a bad girl was Muse's way of seeking the love their good-timing, wastrel father had never given them. Muse thought her sister was delusional. She just adored flirting.

But she had to admit there might be merit to Grace's repeated warnings of repercussions. This was a golden example. And if Muse lived through the next few weeks, she made a vow to start changing her image. Move to a place they didn't know her and start over.

In the meantime she must deal with Remi.

"How's that *étouffée?*" he asked, interrupting her quandary.

"Great. But I'd really prefer to order for myself."

"And what would you have ordered?"

She huffed out a breath. *"Étouffée."*

He looked smug. "I knew that."

"How?" she challenged. After all, they'd known each other all of a day.

"In the car." At her raised brows he went on, "When we talked about the restaurants we like in the Quarter. Wasn' too hard to figure out you like Cajun food. I jus' listened."

He just listened.

To her.

To what she liked. And he actually remembered.

"I always make a point of listening to the woman I intend to make love to."

She closed her eyes and tried to stem the tide of feelings that flooded through her at his low-spoken statement. Amazement. Longing. Bewilderment. *Desire.*

How long had it been since she'd felt desire?

Had she *ever* felt desire?

She opened her eyes to find him draining his beer.

"Remi—"

"*Vien.* Come, let's get out of here. I saw a place where we can dance."

Another thing he knew she liked.

"Remi, I—"

"Unless you'd rather go straight back to the room?"

She shook her head, unable to put the truth into words. How could she tell this man she couldn't…didn't want to… "You don't think it's too dangerous?"

"Being seen in public, you mean?"

"Y-yes," she stammered. *Coward.* That's not what she'd

really wanted to ask. She'd really wanted to ask if he was feeling as threatened by her as she was by him.

But of course that was impossible. All he was feeling was a healthy male anticipation for the coming night.

She had to do something. To stop it.

Like go back to Plan A. Forget about telling him the truth. That was just too complicated.

"I think we're okay for tonight. Davies's men would have shown up by now if he knew where we were."

"Great," she said. "Guess we better eat, drink and be merry while we can."

With emphasis on the be merry.

Plan A: get Remi drunk. So he'd fall asleep or pass out. Then everything would be okay. Tomorrow, in the bright light of day, she'd tell him how things stood. When she didn't risk frustrating him. Or worse, angering him.

He paid the bill and escorted her out of the diner, coming close to her side when they began walking. His arm went up, and assuming he was about to sling it around her shoulders, she braced herself. But instead, he brushed lightly at her sleeve, showing her a ladybug before he sent it flying on its way.

"I hear ladybugs are good luck," he said with a smile, then took her hand, tucked it in the crook of his elbow and led her toward a bar with a flashing neon sign in the window.

"Let's hope so," she murmured.

She could use all the luck she could get. In outrunning Davies.

And in outwitting Remi.

Chapter 5

"I got you another," Muse said.

Remi accepted the tequila from her. His third. He and Muse had talked for over an hour, sitting at a microscopic Formica-topped table in the murky bar. His back was to the wall and hers was to a small wooden dance floor where nobody was dancing to the jukebox that blared a popular country tune. But it was still early, only about nine.

Between the shots, the beer chasers and the few hours of sleep he'd gotten, Remi was feeling a whole lot more relaxed. Maybe too relaxed. Because he was starting to think sleeping with Muse Summerville was actually a good idea—a sure sign of some form of diminished capacity.

"Thanks," he said and put it to his lips, taking a tiny sip of the liquor. No sense going overboard. He wanted to have all his faculties intact. "But I'd better slow down."

Her gaze cut to his. "I thought you said we were safe?"

He shrugged. "Still best to be careful. Besides, I wouldn' want to pass out on you." He gave her a wink. For a split second he thought she blanched. Must be the neon lights.

He pulled a yellow pack of gum from his breast pocket, methodically drew a stick out and folded it into his mouth, enjoying the sweet fruity taste that contrasted with the sour tequila on his tongue.

"That is so disgusting," she said, wrinkling her nose. "How can you stand that combination?"

He grinned. "Just think of it as an instant margarita."

She made an even more disgusted noise. "Gross."

"Don't knock it till you try it." He jerked his chin at her. "*Vien ici.* Come, give it a taste."

He'd been wanting to do this since waking up next to her. He leaned over the table and captured her lips before she could protest. Not that he thought she would. Even though she'd been acting a little peculiar since they left the diner, he knew she'd been thinking about kissing him just as much as he'd been thinking about kissing her. He could tell by the way she kept looking at his mouth.

He gave her a quick taste then pulled back. "See?"

She looked surprised, and he couldn't decide whether it was because she liked the strange combination or that she'd expected him to keep going.

Off balance. That was a nice change. Up till now it had been him struggling to stay upright. Much better this way.

"Pretty good, *non?*"

"Very good," she agreed, and again he wondered if she was talking about the gum or his kissing. She licked her lips and he smiled inwardly. He was betting on the latter.

He leaned back, savoring the hint of her that lingered on his tongue. "So, tell me about your sister."

"Grace?" Her focus shifted and she gazed into the distance. "I moved away from home when I was eighteen, but she's still my best friend."

"You miss her."

"A lot." She smiled wistfully. "We call each other every

week, but it's not really the same. I wish..." Her words trailed off.

"You understand why I can't let you contact her, right? We have to assume Davies knows about her. Especially if someone at the field office is feeding him information."

"You think Davies is watching her? Or tapping her phone?"

"It's a possibility. We don't want to take any chances."

She nodded bleakly. "The last thing I want is to put her in danger. But I'm really concerned."

"About?"

"We have this pact."

"What kind of pact?"

"To come to the rescue. If we don't hear from each other on our regular calling day, that means one of us is in trouble and needs help. The other is supposed to come at once. It was the only way I could get her to stop worrying about me when I moved away."

"And your regular calling day is...?"

"Wednesday. Tomorrow. What if—"

"Has either of you ever actually come to the other's rescue?" he asked, trying to assess how big a problem this could turn into.

"Grace has. Three times."

Big enough. He frowned. "Get into scrapes that often?"

She tore the edge of a napkin, avoiding his eyes. "It happens."

"What kind of scrapes?"

She tore another strip. "Men mostly. I have terrible judgment when it comes to them."

More information than he wanted. But he couldn't resist asking, "You including me in that evaluation?"

"You're a man, aren't you?"

He decided not to pursue that topic. He had the distinct

feeling it would just annoy him. "Does Grace still live in Charleston?"

Muse nodded. "She's a school psychologist. She stayed home while I wandered back and forth across the country."

He regarded her through the smoke-filled dimness of the bar. The ca-chink of quarters being fed to the jukebox echoed across the room, followed by the whirr of machinery and finally the strains of an old Merle Haggard tune.

"Looking for what?" he finally asked.

"Nothing in particular. Why would you think that?"

"Because I left home and wandered back and forth across the country, too."

Of course, he hadn't been looking for something, he'd been running from it. *Alors,* from a couple things.

"And what were *you* looking for?"

He gave her a lazy smile. "A woman who tastes like you."

Her gaze dropped to his lips. "What a coincidence."

"So you like the Juicy Fruit and tequila."

"It's growing on me."

He tossed his gum in a nearby bin, put his fingers under her chin and gently guided her face close to his.

"Let's make sure." He covered her mouth with his.

He felt her hesitate, so he slid his tongue past her lips and languidly caressed hers. Coaxingly. Undemandingly. She moaned softly, and he felt her arms wind around his neck. Then she melted into him and his long, thorough kiss.

She tasted so good.

After several minutes he pulled back slightly. "Everyone's staring. Maybe we should get a room."

She closed the tiny gap between their lips and kissed him back. "Let 'em stare," she whispered. "Besides, you haven't finished your drink."

With reluctance he drew away and threw it down. "Now I have. Let's get out of here."

"Don't you want another?" she asked as he rose to his feet.

"I need to get my gear from the car, anyway. There's a bottle in it. And don't forget, iced champagne comes with our bridal suite." He gave her a disreputable grin.

"Yes. Okay," she said, her tone strangely reluctant for a woman who'd just been kissing him like she never wanted to stop.

Obviously the lady was not ready yet. Which suited him just fine. He enjoyed sex, but what led up to it could be even better, if a man put some effort into it. Nothing beat a good, slow, mutual seduction beforehand, for a mind-blowing experience when you finally made it into bed.

He touched her fingers to his lips, then laced his through them as they walked back to the Chez Noisette parking lot, fetched his duffel from the Porsche, then headed for the B&B.

"You seem nervous," he remarked, wanting to know if her reluctance went deeper than wanting to be wooed.

"Terrified."

"Of me?"

She smiled, looking as fragile as he'd ever seen her. "Of everything. The whole situation. Davies. Running for my life."

"And me?" he pressed.

Her eyes glistened in the glow of the old-fashioned gas-lights lining the walkway to Chez Noisette. "Especially you."

"Mr. and Mrs. Brown. I hope you enjoyed your dinner," the B&B's proprietress greeted them when they got inside.

"Our plans have changed," Remi told her after chatting for a moment. "We'll be spending the night after all."

"And I still owe you a bottle of champagne. I came up with it after you checked in, but there was no answer when I knocked."

"Sorry. We fell right to sleep," Muse said with a quick smile. "Could you make that two bottles? Just put the extra one on our bill." She gave the woman a conspiratorial wink as she disappeared to the kitchen.

"Two bottles?"

"We're celebrating, remember?"

When they got to their room, he popped one open and poured golden, bubbly liquid into two crystal flutes that stood waiting on an ornate silver tray on the dresser. He spotted an antique radio on the nightstand and turned it on.

"That actually works?" Muse asked, walking out of the bathroom and coming over to admire it. "Looks like art deco."

"Mmm," he said, glancing at her. He'd half expected her to have slipped into something more comfortable, as they say, but she was still wearing the sundress. Not that he was complaining. She looked fantastic in it. He found the radio station he was searching for, and the strains of an old jazz tune softly filled the room.

"That's nice," she said.

He handed her one of the flutes. "To us," he said, and her eyes went soft.

He wanted to pull her into his arms and kiss her like there was no tomorrow. Which, for them, there wasn't. Hopefully not literally, but certainly in all else. Tomorrow they'd be hidden where Davies's gang couldn't find them, and the crime boss would, with luck, be in custody soon.

Which would mean Remi's time with Muse would be over.

No tomorrows. Not long-term, anyway.

That was his rule.

He touched his glass to hers, producing a pure crystal tone. They drank deeply, silently toasting each other.

But tonight they were together, so he intended to make it good.

Slowly.

He remembered her reaction to the men on Bourbon Street who'd put their hands all over her. She'd pulled away. He wasn't about to make the same mistake.

However, she did like to dance.

Muse refilled their glasses and let him draw her into a one-handed dance position, his hand on her hip, her arm around his neck, as they sipped.

"Tell me about Remi Beaulieux," she said as they spun slow circles around the room. "You know all about me. I want to know about you."

He chuckled. "Fair enough. But there's not much to tell. What you see is what you get." One of his cousin Beau's favorite phrases. Of course, with Beau it was actually true.

"Somehow I doubt that," she said.

He took a slug of champagne. "As I mentioned, my family's up around Verdigris, Louisiana. I don't see them much."

"Why's that?"

He gave her a lopsided grin. "Black sheep and all that. You know the drill."

"Don't I ever." She touched her flute to his and sipped again.

He drained his and set it aside. "Figured you would."

"I'm lucky, though." She smiled broadly. "They love me anyway. How 'bout you?"

He kept his own smile firmly in place. "Best friends with my cousin Beau. And Grandmère is my favorite lady in the world. Present company excepted," he added, nuzzling her ear.

She slid out of his arms, refilled his flute, handed it to him and slid back into the dance before he had a chance to tell her he didn't care for any more to drink. He'd obviously had enough. He never talked about his family. Never spoke of them, never answered questions about them. Ever.

"What about your parents?"

Especially them. "Anyone ever tell you you talk too much?" He moved his hand from her hip to her bottom and pressed lightly, bringing her closer to where he wanted her. So she couldn't miss how he was feeling.

He put his lips to hers to prevent further questions. And because he could kiss her all night. The woman sure knew how to use her mouth. Not that it was any great shock. What surprised him more than her skill was the pure, sweet emotion he felt in her response to him. Emotion he'd never have expected from a woman like her.

A woman so like himself.

A few moments later she broke the kiss and lifted her glass. "Drink up, sugarcane. It would be a shame to let this fine champagne go to waste."

"Not much for the stuff myself." He set his own down on the dresser tray. "Don' really like to mix my poisons, either."

She gave him a look he couldn't decipher and slid away from him. "In that case I'll get the tequila from your duffel bag." She hurried over and unzipped it. "Here it is. I'll just grab a glass from the bathroom."

"Don' go to all that trouble. I really don'—"

"It's no trouble. I hate to drink alone."

"I'm sure we could find something better to do than drink," he suggested with a crook of his finger.

She nibbled on her lip and handed him a tumbler half filled with his favorite tequila. He always carried it with him because the imported brand was sometimes hard to find, but at the moment he was cursing his habit.

What was going on?

She was nervous as hell, and if he didn't know better he'd think she was either trying to avoid him…or get him drunk?

Non. That wasn't possible. Why would she avoid him? It

was obvious she loved kissing him, enjoyed being close to him. They'd already shared the bed and she hadn't had a problem with that. Hell, they'd even *talked* about making love. Sort of. And by all accounts she wasn't the kind of woman who would suddenly develop moral qualms.

As for getting him drunk, what would she possibly gain from doing that?

"You know," he said, hooking her waist so she came back to him, dancing to the slow jazz with their bodies barely brushing. "You don' have to get me drunk to take advantage of me. I'll come willingly."

A smile crept over her lips. "But will you do what I want?"

Excitement purled through his loins. "Anything at all, *chère.* Just name it."

"Right now I want to dance and finish my champagne."

"D'accord." He was in no hurry. He set aside his ridiculous doubts and moved with her to the music. But just in case, he poured the contents of his glass into a potted fern as they swayed past the plant stand in the bow window.

He lost count of the songs that played softly in the background as he savored the feel of her arms around him and tasted every corner of her sweet mouth while testing the curves of her body with the angles of his. He even managed to rid them of their drink glasses—to her murmured protest.

He loved how she ran her hands over his back and sides and arms, feeling every muscle and sinew. With iron discipline, he held her hips lightly, only very gradually, millimeter by millimeter, inching his hands up her torso until his thumbs rested just under her breasts. He itched to touch them, caress them. Put his lips to them and taste her creamy skin and the taut, puckered nipples he could feel poking through the fabric of his shirt.

For the dozenth time he brushed his arousal against her abdomen, and felt her tremble. Each time she would clutch whatever part of his body her hands were exploring, and softly whimper.

He'd never wanted any woman as much as he wanted her now.

Slowly he traced the fingertips of one hand around and up her back, lingering at the top of the zipper to her dress. He didn't think he could wait another minute. He had to have her now, silky and naked and moaning his name.

He slid down the zipper.

"What are you doing?" she murmured.

He smiled. "Taking off your clothes."

She pulled away, her hands fluttering like nervous birds. "Wouldn't you like another drink first?"

"Non." He pulled her back, fitting her body to his like two pieces of a puzzle. "I want *you.*"

Her fingers clung to his biceps. "Remi, I…"

He paused. "What is it, *chère?* Is something wrong?"

"No, I…that is, I…"

She looked up and he held his breath. Praying she hadn't changed her mind. *"Chérie?"*

"I…I… I think I'd like a shower first," she said in a rush.

Relief crashed through him. His pent-up breath tumbled out on a laugh. "Of course. Damn, I'm sorry. After two days on the run I'm probably not at my freshest."

"Remi, that's not what I meant—"

He gave her a lingering kiss. "All I could think of was how good you smell, not how bad I must."

"No, I love the way you smell," she refuted softly, burying her face in the crook of his neck. He felt her inhale. "All musky and spicy and…like a man."

"Well, in that case—"

"Oh, no." She stepped away from him and reached for the bottle of tequila. "You go first while I get my things together. Here's one for the road.'' She handed him his glass.

He took it and headed for the bathroom where he closed the door and promptly poured the tequila down the sink.

That clinched it. Something was not right here. She was definitely stalling and trying to get him drunk.

But why would she want to do that?

And, more importantly, should he pretend she'd actually succeeded?

It wasn't working.

Or was it?

For the life of her, Muse couldn't figure out if Remi was flying high or just pleasantly buzzed. Not that it mattered. As long as he fell asleep before she got out of the bathroom, he could be stone-cold sober as far as she was concerned. There was just a higher probability of that happening with a good dose of alcohol in his system.

She stepped under the blast of hot water from the showerhead and counted his drinks in her mind. Hmm. Could go either way, depending on his tolerance. She'd have been under the table long ago imbibing as much as he had. But she'd only sipped on her own drinks, managing to consume very little as she always did.

Still, better give him ample time to fall asleep. Just in case. She stuck the plug in the clawfoot tub. Yep, a nice, long bath should do the trick.

Because if it didn't, she'd be forced to choose.

Either face her darkest fears…

Or drive away forever the one man she'd ever truly respected. Or wanted to get to know better.

The man she was falling for fast.

Chapter 6

When the bathwater went shiver cold for the fourth time, Muse figured it was safe to venture out into the bedroom. Surely Remi was asleep by now.

She toweled herself off and reached for her nightie. And halted in midmotion. What had she been thinking? The filmy pink baby doll she'd brought was far too suggestive to wear. Even if Remi was asleep now, there was always a chance he'd wake up later; she didn't dare put it on and expect him to keep his distance. That's when she spotted his duffel bag sitting unzipped in the corner. Well, why not?

Choosing a light blue button-down shirt from the bag, she slipped it on and rolled up the sleeves so they didn't hang over her hands. Definitely better. The solid fabric was cool but covered her completely, the tails reaching well down her thighs. For good measure she pulled on the silk panties that went with the baby dolls. Their protection was more psychological than real, but she felt much less exposed.

Hopefully it wouldn't matter. The man had to be asleep.

As quietly as possible, she opened the door to the bedroom and peeked in. Sure enough, Remi lay on one side of the huge canopied four-poster, half buried in the fluffy feather bedding. A lacy quilt covered his lower body, but his chest was clearly visible in the soft light from a Tiffany lamp on the nightstand.

He was nude.

At least his upper half was.

She glanced at his face. His eyes were closed. Thank God.

Still, she turned and searched the room for alternatives. Maybe she should sleep on the settee. Or the window seat. He looked far too big and male and naked to take a chance on—

"I thought you might have gone down the drain with the bathwater. What took you so long?"

She jumped and whirled to see Remi lounging on the big bed, one hand under his head, watching her.

"I, um…I, um…"

The corner of the quilt flipped over in a perfectly clear invitation.

"Coming to bed?"

"Um, sure."

"You're wearing my shirt."

"My nightie was—" She stopped just short of blurting out "too sexy."

He lifted a brow.

"Torn."

His eyes roamed over her appreciatively. "You look good in it. Better than I ever did."

She smiled nervously and took a tiny step toward the bed. "I thought you might be—" Her words crumbled as he patted the mattress beside him.

"Asleep? Not a chance."

Oh, no. She ached with the need to crawl in beside him

and cuddle up to his broad back, surrounded by his soothing scent and the steady sound of his breathing. Did she dare?

She took another small step. "Are you sure this isn't against some kind of FBI rules?"

"It's against *all* the FBI rules."

"Won't you get in trouble?"

"You're talking too much again."

A special panic oozed out between the cracks where she kept it locked up, deep inside her, in her own private Pandora's box. She slammed the lid back down.

Remi was different. He'd be gentle.

She clasped her hands together to keep them from shaking and walked determinedly to the bed. She slid in and turned to face him.

She could do this.

It wouldn't be so bad. She really didn't have to stop what was happening. Or tell him…anything. That would be far too humiliating, having let things go this far. She'd be fine. Really. After all, this wasn't the first time she'd done it since— It would be over soon and then she could savor his closeness for the rest of the night. Which she wanted more than anything in recent memory. Far more than she was afraid.

Afraid? No. Her therapist had said she was cured long ago. This wasn't fear, just nerves. It had been years since the last time.

She felt his hand stroke down her arm and realized she'd squeezed her eyes shut. She forced them open and smiled. "Why don't you kiss me?" she whispered.

He smiled back. "My pleasure."

Her whole body trembled as he took her in his arms and kissed her, and she had to fight back tears of gratitude and relief when he just embraced her and let his mouth caress hers, not demanding more. At least for now. And he wasn't completely naked. Thank God for small favors.

Winding her arms around his neck, she held him like a falling angel clinging to the gates of heaven.

As always, his kiss was incredible. Slow and sweet and filled with the promise of as much time as she needed. She shuddered out a breath, wanting this blissful feeling to go on forever and ever.

"Somethin' wrong, *chère?*"

She shook her head. "No, nothing."

His hand smoothed up her thigh and she sucked in a breath.

"You like me to touch you?" he murmured, easing his hand over her hip. It was a strong hand, long-fingered and powerful, confident and unwavering in its movements. It was a hand that could give a woman untold pleasure, or if it chose to, unspeakable pain.

"So far," she replied faintly, unwilling to lie. Remembering the pain. But wanting so much to experience the pleasure. Even just once.

He chuckled. "Do I hear a challenge?"

"Maybe."

"You're a hard woman to pin down, Muse Summerville."

She ran her tongue over suddenly parched lips. "I hate being pinned down."

His hand skimmed over her stomach and her skin flinched. She forced herself to relax, getting used to the feel of his touch. He was gentle, seeking in his movements, rather than the groping and grabbing she was used to from men.

He kissed her, then drew back a fraction. "Do you want me?"

She closed her eyes and kissed him back. "Hurry," she whispered.

"Ah, *chère,*" he murmured and canted over her.

She froze. She couldn't help it. The sudden weight of

him, the pressure of his body on hers, being unable to escape, it all closed in on her like the lid of a coffin. She couldn't move. She couldn't speak. She couldn't even breathe.

"What is it, baby? Muse?"

She opened her eyes. Composed herself. "Nothing. Honestly," she added when he looked skeptical.

"Darlin', there's been something wrong all night. One second you're melting in my arms, the next you're frightened as a lamb. Now, tell me what's going on."

She should have known he'd be too smart, too intuitive to fool. She cleared her throat delicately, stalling for time. She had no choice but to tell him.

Heat crept up her neck and blazed through her cheeks. "I, um… Well, the thing is…I don't like sex," she softly confessed.

The disbelief in his eyes sent a dart of pain winging through her. Not his fault.

"You don't like sex."

"Not really."

He lay perfectly still, half straddling her. She could feel his heart beating, his arousal throbbing against her thigh.

"Why?"

"Why?"

He nodded.

No way was she getting into all that. Besides, she was *over* all that. She simply didn't care for sex. Some women didn't. She was one of them.

She shrugged. "It's messy, and not all it's been cracked up to be, in my opinion."

His eyebrows shot into his scalp.

"*Sacré,*" he muttered after a long pause, and rolled off her onto his back. She remained silent, waiting for the inevitable words of anger and frustration to erupt. Instead he said, "And here I thought you were enjoying yourself."

She turned on her side to face him, her heart breaking. "I was enjoying myself. Up to a point. You're a wonderful kisser and I loved dancing with you. I just don't like…the rest. It's not you, Remi. It's me."

He jetted out a breath, turning a scowl on her. "Then why the hell did you get into bed with me? You only had to say no. I would have respected that." Amazingly, she believed him.

"Because," she said, looking anywhere but into those blue eyes filled with confusion and betrayal. She'd expected him to be furious. But not hurt. "Because I want to sleep with you."

"Jeezus," he said, flinging up his arms. "Make up your mind, woman!"

"No, I mean *sleep* with you. Really sleep."

"Sleep? But no sex?" His expression was incredulous.

She nodded bleakly.

He laughed once, then twice, then couldn't seem to control his mirth. *"Chacun à son goût,"* he finally said, shaking his head. "To each his own. Me, I love sex."

"I'm sorry," she said, wondering what to do or say next. His reaction wasn't like anything she'd ever expected. Maybe—

"Good night, Miss Summerville," he said, and settled back onto his pillow with a long sigh.

"Please don't be angry, Remi."

"I'm not angry. I'm just…a bit frustrated. Maybe I should find somewhere else to sleep."

"No! Please stay with me." She leaned over him, put her hand on his chest. "We could just kiss," she suggested.

He chuckled wryly. "There's no way I could just kiss you. Not now."

"I see," she said, and let out a shaky breath. "I really don't mind if you want to—"

He gently set her aside. "I don't think so."

She crept back to his side. "I don't want you to hate me."

"I could never hate you, *chère.* Thanks for the offer, but I'd rather not."

She raised up on an elbow and studied him. She couldn't believe he actually meant it. "Really?"

"Really."

She lay back on the pillow, folding her hands on her abdomen. She pleated her forehead in confusion. "So you don't want me?"

"Only a dead man wouldn't want you, Muse. And even that's not a certainty."

"Why, then? I thought you liked sex?"

"I do. A whole lot. But you don't."

She glanced at him. "Does that matter so much?"

He gave her a tender look and pulled her into his arms.

"Yes, it matters," he said in his low, bayou-flavored voice. "It matters a great deal. I think sex—making love—is like two people exchanging presents. Each giving the other a wonderful gift of delight and pleasure and the joy of mutual satisfaction. If one person doesn't like her present, well, it rather defeats the purpose, don't you think? Leaves both unsatisfied."

She stared at him for a long time, thoughts whirling by so quickly she couldn't grab on to one. It was as though he had just explained some difficult mathematical formula which up until now had eluded her understanding. Light flared through her Pandora's box, revealing the empty blackness inside.

"Maybe I'd like it with you," she finally whispered.

He smiled, an oddly tormented twist to his lips. "Why would you like it with me and not the dozens of other men you've been with?"

Pain razored through her heart—that he would believe

such a thing of her. That the reason he believed it was her own doing.

"There haven't been dozens," she said quietly, laying her cheek on his chest so he couldn't see the silent tears well up. "And, anyway, you're different."

"I'm not different." He kissed the top of her head, and she breathed in the warm, musky scent of him. "I like all the same stuff those other guys liked. Want to do the same things to you, with you, that they did. I'm not different. The only way you'll change your feelings about sex is if something about *you* is different."

She gazed up at him, wanting, needing him to reveal the secret that could make her whole again. "Like how?"

The words slipped from his lips in a low whisper, bewildering and unexpected.

"Like if you're in love."

The next morning Remi made sure he was up and dressed well before Muse woke.

Que diable! He couldn't believe the things he'd said last night. He'd practically given permission to the woman to fall in love with him. *Great move, Beaulieux.*

Despite the temptations, getting romantically involved with an attractive, available woman would only spell trouble for him.

Non. The last thing on earth he needed was to get close to a woman like Muse Summerville—someone he'd have a hell of a time leaving behind when the time came. And it would come. It had to. He didn't have the lifestyle to support any type of commitment. He didn't even have a decent apartment in New Orleans to invite her to. Hell, even if they kept it casual, she would no doubt prove to be a major distraction while it lasted.

He let out a sigh. And in his business, *any* distraction could prove deadly. Especially on this case.

On the other hand, what was he supposed to do?

Muse was a gorgeous woman who aroused him just by breathing. The boss had given him carte blanche in how he handled things as long as he did his job. Yet if he made a move on her, knowing what he did, he'd be the biggest jerk on the planet.

Yeah, he was good in bed. Damn good. But he didn't delude himself that his lovemaking would be able to effect any sudden, amazing cure for Muse's dislike of physical intimacy.

What had happened to make her feel that way? Remi suspected something deeper than her shrugged explanation of "It's messy." But it wasn't his place to pry. He was just the bodyguard, not the analyst. Muse's sister, Grace, could hold that honor with his blessing.

He hadn't meant to say those words last night, to plant such a suggestion and let it grow between them. He didn't want anyone falling in love with him. Especially her. Because she already had him dreaming of too many impossible things.

Things like getting back into that big, inviting bed and teaching her to enjoy the feel of a man holding her, the feel of him moving inside her.

As he quietly packed his things, set them by the door and tucked the Beretta into its holster under his shirt, he let his gaze wander over the woman sleeping peacefully in his bed.

Why was it, after just two short days, he felt as if he'd known her a hundred years?

Was it because she reminded him so much of himself? That she kept her hurts and disappointments hidden and mysterious, living only for today, never thinking of the future, never looking back?

Was there something awful in her past, as there was in his, that had left its mark so indelibly on her soul and character that the outward life she lived was so obviously in conflict with who she really was inside? He thought so.

Last night she had slept tight up against his back, snuggled close as a second skin. Yet each time he'd made to turn to her, she'd scooted to the edge of the bed, even if she didn't awaken. Only to creep back and mold herself to his spine when he resumed his unthreatening position. He hadn't gotten a wink of sleep. He'd wanted her so badly he'd ached with it. But he wouldn't have touched her in that way. Not if she didn't want it. He'd only thought to hold her.

Fearing he might actually climb back into bed and try again, he slipped quietly out the door and went downstairs to the deserted dining room where a samovar of fragrant chicory coffee and a tray of hot buttered croissants and other assorted delicacies beckoned from an antique Victorian sideboard. The long-forgotten sweet aromas of fresh bread and roses mingled in his senses, luring him back to times gone by when he lived in a house even older and grander than this one.

Shunning the memories, he helped himself to a modest breakfast, then pulled out the map of Louisiana he'd tucked in his back pocket and took a seat in one of the plush velvet chairs with a good view of the staircase, so he could see anyone coming or going.

Spreading the map, he sipped coffee and worked out a few escape routes and alternatives to Dev's place, in case things didn't go as expected. He was feeling a bit less uneasy about being on the run with no prior plan—if they themselves didn't know where they were going how could Davies?—but his need for order and covering all contingencies was too ingrained to ignore. It had saved his life too many times. It was the only way he worked.

Which was probably why he felt so out to sea with Muse. She defied all attempts to put her into a safe, orderly category, such as: a witness to protect, a brief love affair, someone he'd spend a few days with and never see again, a flirt who didn't intrigue the hell out of him, a woman he'd give anything to get to know better.

Non. Scratch that last one.

He was still trying to hammer her into a predetermined box when she came running down the stairway at full speed. Spotting him, she came to an abrupt halt at the foot of the stairs, just outside the dark-paneled entry to the dining room.

"There you are," she said, sexy and disheveled in a short red skirt and old-fashioned white camisole that was barely buttoned up the front.

"Good morning," he said, thinking she looked like she'd just come from some man's bed, then remembered with a start that it had been his own. "*Vien.* Coffee's great."

She gripped her hands together in front of her. "I thought—"

He wrenched his sight from her delicious body to her anxious eyes.

They held uncertainty and a slight edge of panic.

"You thought I'd left," he said, not moving a muscle, unable to believe— How could she think he'd leave her?

"I woke up and you weren't there."

"I would never just leave," he said, clearly, distinctly, so there would be no question of his seriousness.

Her shoulders relaxed slightly; the panic receded. "No, of course not. Your job—"

"Has nothing to do with it," he said, cutting her off, but refused to be personally offended by her rationalization. She still didn't know him, or she'd never say such a thing. "I've given you my word that I'll protect you. I always keep my word."

"Good to know." Her lips formed a shaky smile. One that spoke volumes of past betrayals. A smile he recognized on a visceral level. No wonder she'd thought he'd gone.

"I'm not like him," he assured her without thinking.

The smile vanished. "Who?"

"Whoever left you," he said, "and hurt you so badly."

Her chin lifted slightly. Tellingly. Her gaze went to the Oriental carpet, tracing the intricate pattern at her feet.

"Was it Fox?" he asked, though it was none of his business, and didn't make sense anyway.

She glanced up, surprised. "Gary? No. I left him."

"Why?" he demanded, suddenly wanting to know everything about her former boyfriend, the bastard who'd gotten her into this whole mess in the first place. The man she'd been with for six whole months. And presumably shared his bed for most of them.

Jealousy ripped through him at lightning speed, sharp and shockingly ugly.

Then suspicion and anger. Maybe that was why…

"Did he hurt you? Physically?"

Her mouth opened. Then shut. She still hadn't moved from the doorway. Her blond hair was held up with a simple claw barrette, stray strands and curls escaping every which way about her face. Her eyes were wide, and he was struck by how very young and vulnerable she looked when she wasn't trying so hard to be something else.

"Why do you ask that?"

"Somebody did."

Her tongue peeked out. Disappeared. "Just because I don't like sex?"

"Because of the *way* you don't like sex. You love kissing, touching, cuddling. What you *don't* like is being grabbed, manhandled, held too tight, being pinned down. That adds up to just one thing in my book."

She turned abruptly and walked to the sideboard. Very carefully she poured herself a cup of coffee and buttered a croissant, spooned a daub of jam on her plate just so. Without looking at him, she came over and took the seat opposite, on the other side of the low parlor table.

''Despite what you might think,'' she said at last, taking a shaky sip of steaming coffee, ''deep down, Gary's a pretty decent and likeable person. He's made some really bad career choices, and is certainly messed up in some ways, but he's not violent. No, Gary's not the reason I don't like sex.''

Remi didn't know if that made things better or worse. ''Then why did you leave him?''

She sighed, still avoiding his eyes. ''I'd just met Gary a week before when the FBI contacted me. Morris wanted me to spy on Gary's boss, James Davies. Gary was pleasant and…convenient. But I only stayed that long because I wanted Davies put away for good. Toward the end Gary started getting very possessive, and pressuring me. So as soon as Morris said I'd gathered enough evidence for a conviction, I left.''

''Pressuring you how? Physically?''

''Emotionally.'' She finally glanced up, looked Remi right in the eyes. ''I'm not big on ties. Not the type for a picket fence.''

They were words Remi could have spoken himself. *Had* spoken himself too often to count, just before kissing some woman he'd met the night before goodbye.

So why did he feel like he'd just been slapped?

''What about sexually?'' he pressed, perversely unable to let it go. *Leave it alone.* Muse's relationship with Gary Fox was none of his business. Had no bearing on the present situation. Knowing would only amplify Remi's irrational thoughts and faltering resolve to leave this woman be.

Her eyes didn't waver even a millimeter. ''There *was* no sexual. Gary Fox is impotent.''

Chapter 7

"So, tell me about this Dev person," Muse urged as she set up another shot with her Hasselblad camera.

She'd managed to talk Remi into taking a small detour on the way to Dev's to find a certain old antebellum plantation, long overgrown and abandoned, that she'd heard about third hand and had always wanted to visit as part of the research for her book. The remaining wrought-iron fences on the property had been reported as being spectacularly lovely.

The reports turned out to be true. She'd spent the better part of an hour meticulously photographing the fallen balcony railings, rusting cemetery fence and broken-down front entrance gate they'd found as they worked their way around the dilapidated plantation buildings, wading through man-high weeds, choking vines and God-knew-what hidden slithery creatures. She was covered with scratches and mosquito bites, and her white sandals were completely ruined, but she'd gotten some fabulous photos.

"What do you want to know about Dev?"

She focused in on an iron fleur-de-lis surrounded by black curlicues. "Whatever you want to tell me."

Remi held back a branch of bramble she pointed to, having fallen into the role of photographer's assistant without even a blink.

"There is only a handful of people I'd trust with my life," Remi said. "Dev is one of them. His name is really Guy de Valein." He pronounced Guy in the French way to rhyme with *see.* "He's a computer whiz, and a frequent consultant for the FBI. He lives and breathes security. He's the best…but a bit of an eccentric."

She took another shot. "How so?"

"He lives by himself way out on the bayou, where he runs a multimillion-dollar computer security software company from a…*bien,* a shack on stilts in the middle of a swamp."

She swung the camera lens to him. "You're kidding."

"What can I say?" he said, and she snapped a picture. He made a face—too late. "Dev doesn't like people much."

"But he likes you."

Remi grimaced. "I worked with him on a particularly nasty case, once, involving computer kiddy porn. We burned the bad guy together and in the process became good friends."

"And you think he won't mind sharing his shack out in the middle of the swamp? Will he have room for us?"

Remi chuckled and she snapped another picture of him.

"He also owns a bunch of small houses that aren't quite so primitive, scattered around the wilderness. He lends them out free of charge to environmentalists, artists and just plain people down on their luck who need a place to stay. We'll be handed a key, no questions asked."

She paused for a second, then snapped a final picture, capturing the suggestive, bad-boy expression that slowly crept over his face. The man definitely had mischief on his mind.

Ever since she'd spilled Gary's secret, Remi's mood had improved markedly. She could only imagine what he thought that fact gained him.

On second thought, she'd rather not know. Whatever it was she wasn't ready for it. He might think she was, but she wasn't. She would never be.

''Remi,'' she ventured, taking her time changing the lens on the Hasselblad, replenishing the film, then tucking it safely back into the camera bag. ''I think we need to talk.''

He held things for her, handed them back and took the bag when she'd gotten everything squared away, lifting the strap onto his shoulder. ''About?''

''Tonight.''

He was silent for a moment, and she watched him turn and take in the decaying beauty of the old plantation spread all around them. The fecund green foliage spilling over tumbled brick walls and leaning ionic columns, formerly white but now streaked with emerald moss. The rich smells of humid earth and sweet honeysuckle and jasmine. The soft, sultry breeze stirring the blades of grass and the ends of their hair.

''Reminds me of home,'' he murmured. ''*Beau sans coeur.* Beautiful but rotten.'' He looked up. ''What about tonight?'' he asked.

She filed away his puzzling comment and let out a sigh. ''I think we should ask Dev for a house with two bedrooms.''

He turned to her, expression unsurprised. ''If that's what you want.''

''It's not what I want. But it's for the best.''

He shook his head. ''*Non.* I think you're ready.''

She gave him a cheerless smile. ''I don't think I'll ever be ready,'' she said, and started walking toward the Porsche.

"Do you want to talk about it?" he asked, following.

She decided not to deny the obvious. What was the point? The man saw far too much. "Not especially."

"It might help to talk."

"Already done that."

"With…?"

"My sister and my shrink. I'm over it."

"I noticed."

She couldn't help laughing at his wry tone, despite the painful subject. "Look, I just don't like sex. I'm sorry. Believe me, I wish I did. Never more than last night."

He gently caught her arm from behind and swung her around to face him. His expression was dead serious now, filled with the hard determination that sent shivers down her spine every time. Not of fear, but of recognition that this man would lay down his life to protect her. And wouldn't accept anything but complete honesty in return.

"Tell me what happened," he quietly demanded. His fingers slid down her arm and laced with hers. "Tell me what he did to you."

She hadn't even told her mother, just Grace and the psychologist her sister had referred her to a few years later when Grace had started her psych major at college.

Could Muse trust this man, with his dark good looks and seductive tones and the ability to strip back her defenses like an orange peel?

She didn't even have to think about it.

She took a steadying breath. "We were on a date. In high school. He was a football player. Very popular. Very big. He wanted to. I didn't. He held me down and did it anyway. End of story."

In the quiet morning, birds twittered overhead, bees buzzed by on their never-ending quest for nectar. She swore she heard the hushed rasp of an orange slowly being stripped of its peel.

"Not end of story. Not by a long shot."

She scowled. She didn't know what she wanted to do more, smack him silly or fall into his arms and sob.

In the end he decided. He pulled her close, holding her as the unwanted tears of frustration welled, kissing her temple and rubbing her back as she unwillingly purged herself of the horrible memory of that awful night, wiping the wetness from her cheeks when she was finally able to drag herself back into that safe place she'd carved from the loneliness and guilt so long ago. Only to find she was no longer alone.

"Feel better?" He handed her tissues from the camera bag.

"Feel like an idiot."

"Why? Because some creep violated you and took something precious he had no right to?"

She gazed up at the man who'd spoken so fiercely, unable to stop one last hot tear from trickling down her face.

His jaw set. "Who was it? I want a name."

She'd never uttered it since that night, and wasn't about to start now. "Why?"

"So I can kill him."

He looked so angry and ferocious she actually believed him. Her hero. She sent him a watery smile. "Too late. Drive-by shooting. The suspect was never convicted, but I heard he'd had a sixteen-year-old sister."

Remi hissed out a long breath, then took her face in his strong hands and pressed his lips to her forehead. "Better than the bastard deserved." He held her there for a long time. She felt his body slowly relax, muscle by muscle. Finally he said, "Let me help you."

She swallowed, terrified by what she thought he meant. "Remi, I don't—"

"Wait, hear me out," he interrupted. "It's obvious you're

attracted to me. God knows I'm attracted to you. Have you been with anyone since…it happened?"

She glanced away. "I've tried a few times. It wasn't all that great."

"And yet last night you trusted me enough to give me permission, even though you'd get no pleasure from it."

She leaned her forehead against his shoulder. "Not many men would have turned me down."

"My greatest pleasure lies in seeing yours. Let me give you that pleasure."

She turned away, ashamed. "It's no use. I'm frigid."

He cupped her face in his hand, large and comforting and wet with her own tears, and made her look at him. His smile was both tender and reassuring. "Darlin', no woman who kisses like you could possibly be frigid." The corner of his lip curved. His fingers slid into her hair. "You jus' need a man who knows what's going on."

His boundless self-confidence was endearing…and heartening, if misplaced. She smiled back. And was unable to resist teasing him. Just a little. "I thought you said to enjoy it I'd have to fall in love."

His eyes widened. Just a little. Then he recovered, dropping his hand. "Ah, *non.* What I said was, to enjoy it, something about you had to be different. Falling in love was just one example."

Suddenly she felt more lighthearted than she'd felt in years. Since…high school. She tucked her arm under his and led him toward the Porsche. "So you aren't suggesting I fall in love with you?"

"That would not be recommended," he said, and cleared his throat. "Neither of us are interested in that kind of relationship. Right?" He glanced at her for confirmation.

Her heart stopped, and for the briefest second she thought she might blurt out, "Wrong!"

Totally against her will, of course.

Because lighthearted or no, she *wasn't* interested in that kind of relationship. Even if she somehow miraculously learned to enjoy sex—which wasn't going to happen—there was still that basic personality defect, inherited from her worthless father, preventing her from falling in love. Grace said it was because she was afraid of being abandoned again by a man she loved. But that wasn't true. Muse was simply unable to settle down, unable to commit to one person for the rest of her life. She liked being unattached and on the move. She was too restless, too rootless, to stick around. Just like her father.

"Right," she affirmed, and prayed Remi hadn't misinterpreted her slight, meaningless hesitation. "No love involved."

"Alors," he continued, "so you can give the physical a try with me and not have any pressure. If we don't succeed—" he shrugged in that peculiarly Gallic way "—no harm done, because our relationship doesn't depend on it coming off." He looked at her hopefully. "As it were."

She blinked. Then burst out laughing.

When she recovered, she said, "Lord have mercy, Remi, you really know how to sweep a girl off her feet."

The grin that crept over his face was pure devilment. "*Mais,* yeah, *chère.* But that part comes later."

She was just about to set him straight on that small detail when a loud voice from next to the Porsche boomed, "Step into the clearing and put your hands in the air."

Swift as a snakebite Remi stepped in front of Muse and assessed the situation. Older cop. Blue cruiser of local jurisdiction. No weapon drawn.

Remi raised his hands as relief poured over him. The self-recriminations would have to wait. At least he'd be alive to invoke them.

"What's the problem, Officer?" he asked.

"I'd like to see your ID, please," the cop ordered. "The lady's, too."

Not if he could help it. He was about to produce his FBI wallet from his pocket when Muse flounced her way past him waving her camera.

"Hi! Are you a Louisiana State Trooper?" she asked, adopting the flat nasal accent of a Yankee tourist—and ignoring the local city police emblem big as a satellite dish plastered on the cruiser door.

Apparently the officer was as dumbstruck as he was, and Muse continued blithely without interruption, "I'm so glad you came by! I'm a photographer and my fiancé here—he's from New Orleans, you know—well, he told me about this old place and I just couldn't resist coming by and snapping a few pictures since we were in the neighborhood, could I, sweetie?" She extracted the pack of Juicy Fruit from his breast pocket, gave him a peck on the lips and offered a stick to the officer. "Gum?" She whisked it away before he'd even had a chance to move. "We've been enjoying some good South Louisiana hospitality, haven't we, pumpkin? And now we're headed back to New Orleans. You know anything about the history of this place? It's so romantic! I'd love to hear about it."

She took a breath and the cop managed to squeeze in, "Well, I s'pose I might know a bit—"

She interrupted, saying, "Say, would you mind if I got a picture of you standing with me in front of this cute old cookhouse? That would be great—" she turned to Remi "—wouldn't it, pumpkin?"

Remi tried in vain to react to being promoted to fiancé and being called "pumpkin" all within the same minute, but the whole situation had him frozen to the spot. What the hell was she doing? Lying to an officer of the law!

"Honey pie, why don't you take a picture of the nice

policeman and me?'' she urged, shooting him a get-with-it-or-die look as she tucked the gum back in his pocket.

She thrust the camera into his hands so he was forced to do something other than stare at her as if one of them had lost their mind. Just which one he wasn't sure. He started snapping shots to hide his consternation. And to cover up that he had no earthly idea how to keep things from deteriorating even further.

''Who did you say built the place?'' she asked the cop as she flirted shamelessly with him and for the camera.

The poor guy didn't stand a chance. Nor did Remi. Every time he tried to take control of the situation, she snatched it back and got them in even deeper. Luckily the cop never noticed he was being led down the garden path.

A half hour and two rolls of film later Remi'd heard as much as he ever wanted to know about local history and this run-down pile of rubble in particular, but the officer was finally pulling away in his cruiser.

Never mind he'd never gotten around to checking their IDs, Remi was ready to strangle the woman.

He let out a string of Cajun invective, right after he let out the breath he was pretty sure he'd been holding the entire time.

''What the *hell* was that all about?''

Muse glanced up in surprise. ''I was getting us out of trouble.''

This was no doubt exactly the kind of stunt Morris had in mind when he'd said Muse was hard to manage. He should have listened.

''You lied to a cop!''

She looked indignant. ''I did not lie! I just charmed the man.''

''Your 'fiancé'?''

She lifted her chin in mock affront. ''Well, if you don't want to marry me, the wedding's off.''

He rolled his eyes. "He could have arrested us!"

"For exaggerating about being engaged? I doubt it. Besides he can't arrest you. You're with the FBI."

He didn't bother to set her straight. "Why didn't you just let me tell him that in the first place?"

She stuffed the camera back into the bag and zipped it shut. "I thought we were supposed to be incognito. What if he'd written us up in a report or something? Davies could get wind. I could get dead."

"That's not going to happen," he gritted out. "It's my job to take care of you. *My* job. So from now on, let *me* handle things." To drive it home he added, "*I'm* the FBI agent, *you're* the helpless witness." He nearly choked on the words. She was about as helpless as a swamp cat. He tapped his chest with a finger. "*I'm* in charge. Got it?"

She planted her hands on her hips. "And what would you have done differently, Mr. Federal-Agent-in-Charge?"

He clamped his jaw. "That's not the point. The point is, you do as I say."

Her lips thinned. "Oh? And does that include tonight in bed?"

He jerked back in disbelief. Like he'd been slugged in the gut.

"Separate rooms, remember?" he ground out. Grabbing the camera bag, he stalked to the car and yanked open the passenger door. "Get in," he growled. When she slid in he reached down and jammed her seat belt home with a quick stab, mumbling, "Sorry," when she gasped at the unexpected gesture.

"Do you always buckle your passenger's safety belt for them?" she snapped when he slid into the driver's seat and fired the engine with a roar.

"Only the women I want to order around in bed," he answered curtly. He was a gentleman, so sue him. He made a mental note to let her buckle her own damn belt in the future.

She crossed her arms under her breasts. He averted his gaze.

"I'm sorry," she said, actually sounding repentant. "You didn't deserve that comment. It was awful of me, and I didn't mean it."

He kept his mouth shut and drove. He was overreacting and he knew it. He just couldn't help being irritated. *Bien,* hurt.

This was exactly why he didn't get close to people. No matter how much you tried to please them, they only ended up hurting you.

A timely reminder that he was letting his guard down way too far with Muse Summerville.

"I was only trying to help," she murmured, then stared out the window for the rest of the trip, all the way to the cutoff to Dev's place, embracing his silence.

"This is it," Remi said, slowing the Porsche to take a sharp turn off the highway onto a dirt track winding just inches above still, black swamp water. He stopped the car, recognizing the rusting black mailbox and dilapidated newspaper receptacle hanging off it by one nail. An old shotgun-blasted board on a nearby tree declared in a dark red scrawl, Private Property. Trespassers Will Be Shot.

Very atmospheric. All for show, of course. The only mail Dev got was e-mail, he also read his newspapers online. Anyone trespassing would no doubt be blown to smithereens well before coming within gunshot range of the somewhat antisocial Mr. de Valein.

"Nice," Muse commented with obvious sarcasm. "Very welcoming."

"I told you he doesn't care for people."

Remi glanced over at her, warring with himself. She'd

apologized to him; he should apologize, too. Even though he knew he was right, it hadn't been necessary to come on quite so strong about being in charge.

On the other hand, the gaping distance his firm scolding had established between them was a good thing. He'd been crazy even to consider sleeping with the woman, let alone designing a detailed plan of attack as to how he could teach her to enjoy the finer points of physical love.

C'est fou, ça. Just plain crazy.

From now on the woman was strictly off-limits. And in consequence this assignment would be a hell of a lot simpler.

He gave the orders. She followed them.

Simple.

Smacking aside the persistent, niggling urge to make things right between them, he pointed from the gravel road to the mailbox post and back. "I want you to memorize this entrance," he said. "In case you need to find it again and I'm not with you."

"Why wouldn't you be with me?" she asked, peering over at him in alarm.

"I don't know," he said matter-of-factly. "But one should always have an escape route and a backup plan. If anything ever happens to me and you need help, come to Dev. He'll take care of you."

After a short pause she said, "And what do you think might happen to you?"

"I'm counting on nothing happening to me," he assured her. "But you never know. Running into that cop was a wake-up call. Better we're prepared for any contingency than to be taken by surprise again."

"Thanks to you I *am* prepared."

He followed her eyes when they lowered to the overnight bag, which sat unzipped at her feet. His spare Beretta rested on top of her clothes, right where he'd told her to put it yesterday when they'd left her apartment.

"Davies will have to get through me if he wants to hurt you," she said with such calm he thought she was joking, except for the look in those blue eyes when he glanced up in surprise. She turned away to study the road and mailbox. "I think it's time I started fighting my own battles."

"Not necessary," he countered. "That's my job."

"I'm well aware of what your job is," she said quietly, opening the passenger door and getting out before he could stop her.

The tension between them was thicker than the mud oozing at the edge of the narrow road. He sat behind the wheel watching her for a moment as she wandered a few yards down the track, past the mailbox—tripping the silent alarm on the console of monitors in Dev's living room. Her short red skirt and bright white camisole top stood out in brilliant contrast to the muted greens and browns of the cypress swamp behind her. Just as she did among the drab bureaucrats and the shadowy criminals that populated his usual world. His body quickened at the mere sight of her, so luminous and tempting, reminding him of the unbelievable need he'd felt for this woman since the first time he'd laid eyes on her.

His *mind* reminded him that's all it was. Simple lust. Nothing more. Except he was beginning to understand that nothing about Muse Summerville and his relationship with her was simple and never would be.

Davies will have to get through me if he wants to hurt you.

Meaning what? That *she* intended to protect *him?*

Talk about unbelievable. Nobody'd ever protected him, or even tried, except on the rare occasions his cousin Beau had stalwartly defended him against some perfectly legitimate accusation of youthful infraction. But there was no one else on earth like Beau.

Remi must have misunderstood Muse's meaning.

He slid out of the car and caught up to her; he pointed up into the old oak tree the No Trespassing sign was nailed to. "There's a small camera up there in the branches," he said. "Smile and wave." He gave it a wave himself and a thumbs-up. She just stood staring.

"Now he knows we're coming and won't set off any of the unpleasant surprises awaiting unwanted visitors."

"My God, this guy's a psycho."

"I helped him set everything up," Remi informed her wryly. "Several years back."

She regarded him. "Figures. What now?"

"Now we go meet him."

"I can hardly wait."

He could hardly wait, either. Hopefully, he'd be able to contact Morris safely from Dev's place and find out what in blazes was going on with the case. With any luck Davies had been located and was already in custody. And Remi could turn the Porsche right on around and take the confounding woman back to the French Quarter of New Orleans where she belonged. Never to see her or think of her or touch her, ever again.

Not a minute too soon as far as he was concerned. He didn't like the confusion raging in his mind and body, tearing him apart.

He didn't apologize to anyone for doing his job the best way he knew how. And he certainly didn't apologize just because she had abandonment issues and obviously thought he was out to rid himself of her at the first possible convenient moment.

Because he wasn't.

Bien, all right, he was. But not for the reasons she thought.

She thought it was because she wouldn't sleep with him. Nothing could be further from the truth. The truth was, it was because he wanted to sleep with her so badly he was willing to go to just about any lengths to change her mind.

Big difference. One that could get them both killed if he didn't get his head screwed on right. Or something.

And *that's* why he had to rid himself of her at the first possible convenient moment.

Not because one more night with her might just kill him, before Davies ever got the chance.

Chapter 8

Muse glanced around as Remi brought the Porsche to a halt, parking next to a black Mercedes that sat in a soggy patch of sawgrass at the head of a stick-built jetty. Far out at the end of the crooked pier stood a tiny shack perched on a deck on stilts right above the surface of the motionless bayou. It looked like something straight out of *Deliverance.*

Muse suppressed a groan. Swell. This should be comfy.

"*Comment ça va,* you ol' bastard! How the hell are you?" The man who must be Guy de Valein shouted the greeting as he emerged from the shack and came toward them.

Remi answered in kind and went to meet him, going through the usual male bonding rituals, with a French twist to the lingo. She followed behind, dragging her feet. Why men couldn't just hug and say "Good to see you" like normal people, she'd never understand. Any second now would come the comments about her.

"Your taste in women is improving, Beaulieux. Aren't you going to introduce me to your *jolie femme?*"

"Muse Summerville," she said, sticking out her hand. She plastered a curve on her mouth but was surprised into a genuine smile when Dev bent over her hand and brought it to his lips.

"Guy de Valein."

This was the computer geek hermit?

The man looked disreputable as hell. Too-long black hair, a day's worth of stubble covering his jaw, a sinful sparkle in his eyes as he watched her reaction to him. He was just the kind of man that usually got her in the mood to dance the night away.

"Forget it, Dev," Remi interrupted with a glare, cutting short their mutual assessment. "She's a Bureau witness. Under *my* protection."

Dev chuckled richly. "I understand. Well, *mademoiselle,* would you care for a sweet tea while my friend tells me how I can be of service in your protection?"

"That would be lovely," she answered, gratified by the deep scowl that affixed itself to Remi's forehead, hopefully permanently, when Dev ignored him, offered her his arm and escorted her down the uneven jetty toward his home. She was feeling more cheerful already.

Dev casually quizzed her about the events that had led them to his doorstep. She figured if Remi trusted the man with his life, it was all right to trust him with the details of the case and their flight. So she did. With hardly any embellishments or evasions at all.

Remi stalked along behind them, wordlessly for the most part, but occasionally tossing out a short addition to her narration. Dev opened the front door and ushered them into the cool interior. For all its rundown exterior, it was amazingly clean and comfortable inside. A huge bed covered in designer linens dominated one corner, and various simple but elegant pieces of furniture were grouped around the room so it was naturally divided into kitchen, living and sleeping areas.

Dev handed them glasses filled with chilly amber tea, his grin getting wider and wider as she related how she'd managed to distract the police officer from checking their IDs at the plantation. Remi remained stoically closemouthed during the whole story.

''Mais, sacré bleu, mon ami. Ça va brute, non?'' Dev said to Remi with a laugh, whose scowl just got deeper. Dev clicked her glass with his. ''My friend here, he likes havin' things his way. But it sounds to me like you handled the situation jus' fine. Be extra sweet to him tonight, he'll get over it.'' He winked.

Muse felt heat rise in her cheeks. ''Miracles do happen,'' she muttered and headed for the front door. ''You two probably have things to discuss, so I'll just make myself scarce.''

She got no argument, so she walked back out onto the deck that circled the small house. To hide from Remi's scowl.

And to figure out just what the hell she would do now.

It was obvious he regretted his actions last night and had decided to pull back in a big way from any closeness they'd formed by sharing secrets and a bed.

Of course, it had only been *her* secrets. He hadn't confessed things he'd never told another living soul. It had been all her.

Inwardly she cringed. She didn't blame him for withdrawing. What normal man would want a woman with her problems? Certainly not one who could have his pick of friends and lovers, as Remi undoubtedly could.

She sighed. It was a blessing in disguise, really. He was saving her a heartache of major proportions by putting an end to things now, before she got even more emotionally involved. Because, whether it came today or next month, whether he was the one to leave or she was, she knew very well the end would be the same.

She'd be alone again. As always.

Remi watched Muse's retreating figure and the door closing behind her with a strange mix of emotions. Relief to be rid of the woman and the confusion within him that always accompanied her nearness. Dread at the inevitable ribbing he was in for from Dev—his friend knew him too well to miss the symptoms. Worry that his personal involvement with Muse could lead to her being harmed or worse. An instant craving for her immediate return.

''So, *mon ami,* you've finally met your match,'' Dev said with a chuckle.

''More like opposite,'' he answered, choosing to address the less uncomfortable of the phrase's two possible meanings. ''The woman is driving me insane.''

''I can see that. *Très sympathique.*''

Again with the double meanings. ''I appreciate your sympathy,'' he said, knowing full well Dev had meant to say he'd seen their attraction. And approved. Like he hadn't noticed. ''Feel like taking her off my hands?''

Dev let out a bark of laughter. ''No way, man. I have no desire to be hunted down by a lovesick federal agent. Besides, you know how I feel about women.''

Sidestepping the lovesick crack, Remi remarked, ''Didn't seem to have any trouble being friendly to this one,'' sounding like a petulant teenager even to his own ears. ''I could have sworn you were flirting.''

Dev grinned. ''I knew I was safe. She only has eyes for you.''

Remi snorted. ''Yeah. Listen,'' he said, downing the last of his iced tea and deciding it was time to change the subject. ''I need to phone the field office. Securely. Any chance your computers can route me through Outer Slobovia via the Antarctic so my call's untraceable?"

Dev shook his head. "Not a hundred percent. E-mail's safe, though, if that works for you."

He'd known he could rely on Dev. They trooped over to the built-ins that lined one entire wall and flipped up the garage-style door of a long console cupboard, revealing the bank of computer monitors Remi had helped install when his friend had decided to give up the high-society life of New Orleans for this quieter venue. Something about a series of bad love affairs, as he recalled. At the time Remi'd thought the never-shy Dev would last maybe six months, tops, way out here in the back of beyond. That had been over four years ago. He shouldn't be surprised, though. Remi, of all people, understood the devastating power of crushed emotions.

Another good reminder of his present foolishness.

As Dev booted up an impressively nondescript desktop computer which Remi knew damn well had to rival the capabilities of the best Pentagon hardware, he glanced along the line of security monitors, several of which showed split views of the shack and surrounding deck, the jetty and the road in. He zeroed in on the one that showed the object of his protection.

Muse was sitting in a patch of shade, lounging in one of several Adirondack chairs that littered the deck. Her legs were slung over one chair arm, her red miniskirt riding dangerously high on her thighs. She'd undone one of the few remaining buttons on her camisole so her breasts were in imminent danger of spilling out of the flimsy garment. Her head rested on the chair back, face tipped up, eyes drinking in the surrounding swampland like she didn't have a care in the world.

Every time she moved, the camera adjusted its angle on her, seeming to zoom in closer and closer each time. Remi had to fight the urge to leap up, charge out there and wrap a blanket around the woman. He growled with frustration, then deliberately turned away from the monitor. Peripheral vision was just fine to keep tabs on her.

Dev did a pretty good job of hiding his knowing smirk as he set things up for the secure e-mail, but Remi swore he'd flatten the guy if he made a single comment—or so much as glanced at the monitor. Luckily he didn't.

After several minutes Dev finally gave him the go-ahead on the e-mail. Remi marshaled his concentration and typed in an oblique message to Morris asking for news on Davies and clicked Send.

"How long before he gets it?" Remi asked.

"The rerouting really slows things down," Dev answered with a puckered brow. "Might take as long as forty-five seconds."

Remi chuckled. "Jeez, as long as that?"

Dev looked up and threw a pencil at him. "Smart-ass. Want a beer while you wait for the answer?"

"Sure, why not?"

"I assume you guys need a place to stay for a while." Dev said as he fetched a couple bottles from the fridge.

"Depends on the reply to my e-mail," Remi said with a sigh, praying Morris had good news. "Hopefully Davies is in custody."

"Don't get your hopes up. I keep on top of breaking news, and there's been nothing about an arrest that I've heard from any source."

Remi had noticed one of the monitors was tuned in to CNN, and another seemed to be tapped into a highly classified government site with a running ticker of intelligence from around the world.

He jerked his chin at it. "Is that legal?"

Dev smiled. "Doubtful."

God knew what other government secrets his friend had

ready access to. Not that he was worried. Dev was one of the good guys.

A chime pinged and Dev's fingers flew over the keyboard. "Mail's in. It's for you."

Another chime pinged. Dev turned to the bank of monitors. "Excuse me."

Remi read the short message from Morris.

Our friend is still on vacation, so why don't you extend yours for a little while. Watch your back. M.

He uttered a succinct oath.

"Anywhere in particular you have in mind for your little love nest?" Dev asked, ambling back from whatever had attracted his attention.

"It's not a love nest. I'm protecting her," Remi insisted. "We'll need two separate bedrooms."

Dev's lip curved. "If you say so."

"Preferably a place with security and countermeasures installed," Remi went on. "If you've got something available."

"I've always got something available. I think I know just the house. Two separate bedrooms, huh?"

Remi nodded, trying not to appear grim or frustrated or any of the other 150 things he was feeling at the news he'd indeed have to spend at least one more night with the exasperating Muse Summerville.

"Definitely two separate bedrooms."

If he lived to see morning without being seriously unmanned, it would be a pure damn miracle.

He glanced back at the monitor with the Adirondack chair. And frowned.

She was gone.

"What the hell!" Remi leaped to his feet, searching the other screens for any sign of her. Nothing. *"Where is she?"*

Dev looked over. ''She got up a few minutes ago. I assumed she was going for a walk.''

''And you didn't tell me?'' he demanded, drawing his weapon from its holster and sprinting for the door. ''Davies's men could have found us and taken her.''

''If anyone comes within ten miles of here, I know about it,'' Dev called after him as Remi hit the dock running. ''Nobody's taken her! Check the—''

But the rest of his words were muffled by the sound of Remi's footsteps pounding down the wooden planks. He had to find her. If anything happened to her, he'd never forgive himself. He should have been watching that monitor like a hawk, not ignoring her just because he couldn't keep his own unruly hormones in check.

He burst onto the path through the sawgrass at the end of the jetty just as the Porsche door opened. Skidding to a halt, he saw Muse crawl backward out of the back seat.

''What in blazes are you doing?'' he demanded.

She turned to him, her camera dangling from her fingers. ''Getting the Hasselblad. I thought I'd take a few pictures. Why?''

He grasped her arms, barely resisting giving her a shake. ''Don't you *ever* do that again!''

''What?''

''Run off like that. I need you in my sight every second.''

She tugged on her arms. ''I've been out of your sight for the past hour, and you didn't seem too concerned.''

''No,'' he corrected hotly. ''There are security cameras. I've been watching you the whole time.''

She glared up at him, but behind the irritation a spark of vulnerability flared in her eyes, deflating his anger. ''We've been through this before. You have to do as I say so I can protect you.''

Suddenly he didn't want to fight but to hold her.

"Ah, Muse," he murmured, and pulled her stiff body into his arms. "What am I going to do with you?"

She sighed and he felt her soften against him. "I'm sorry. I'm used to making my own decisions. I guess I don't take direction well."

"And I'm being an overbearing bastard."

"Yes, you are," she agreed, and he smiled into her hair. "Come on, let's go see Dev. He's got a place for us to stay."

"Did you contact Morris?" she asked as they walked back toward the house.

Remi nodded and gave her the bad news. "They still haven't picked up Davies. Morris wants us to lay low for a while longer."

"What about the out-of-state transfer?"

"Still working on it," he fibbed.

The fact was, neither Morris nor he had mentioned the transfer. Frankly, the more Remi thought about it, the less he liked the idea. If Davies really was paying someone from the field office to tip him off, Remi didn't want anyone there having a single clue as to Muse's whereabouts.

"What about Grace?"

"Grace?"

"Was he able to contact her, to let her know I'm all right?"

Damn. He'd forgotten about that complication. "He didn't say. But I'm sure he's gotten in touch with her. Today was your calling day, right?"

She nodded.

"Don' worry. I'll e-mail him a reminder."

Dev was waiting for them, lounging against the door-frame with a crooked smile on his face. "Found her, I see."

No doubt he'd witnessed their embrace and read a multitude of misinformation into it. Never mind. In a perfect world, all his assumptions would be correct—all except that part about being lovesick, of course.

"I need to send one more e-mail, then we should be going."

Dev talked them into staying for lunch, a spontaneous feast of shrimp gumbo and home-baked bread, after which he handed them a key and told them how to find the cottage he was letting them use. He also gave Remi a rundown of the security measures he'd installed there: motion sensors around the perimeter of the property; silent alarms at all points of entry; security cameras strategically placed; and all the doors, including the garage door, were specially built and maintained to open and close noiselessly.

"Sounds like an armed camp," Muse remarked.

Dev shrugged. "In my line of work it pays to be prepared. But it's all well hidden. You'll never see any of it."

"Just another country cottage," she murmured.

"That's right. And you don't have to worry about the locals, either," Dev assured them. "I grease the wheels regularly in the village, so anyone staying at the cottage is treated like kin, and any strangers asking about them are treated as hostiles."

"Sounds perfect," Remi said gratefully.

"Stay as long as you like. Just mail me the key when you get back to New Orleans."

After saying their thanks and goodbyes, Remi pointed the Porsche back to the main road. For the first time since the bullets started flying at the safe house two days before, he felt like he'd caught up with his plan. Thank God for Dev. The man was a bit of an eccentric, but friends didn't come any better.

Another hour and Muse would be safe from the long reach of James Davies.

He just wished he could be equally certain she'd be safe

from the rather short reach it would take for Remi Beaulieux to get his hands on her.

He'd made up his mind, resolved to keep her at arm's length, off-limits. But thinking he'd lost her, then holding her close again, feeling her warm, soft breasts press into his chest, seeing that hint of vulnerability in her eyes, knowing how she struggled against appearing weak despite her fear, everything about her made it difficult not to want her like crazy. And made it almost impossible not to reach for her and soothe her fears by giving her a few moments of intimacy with a person who really cared for her.

And he did care for her. Too much for his own good.

He wanted so much to make her forget all the bad things that had happened in her life. Show her that not all men are out to hurt her.

And to give her the pleasure she so deserved.

He could do it. He knew he could. It would take some time and patience, but she trusted him. That was the key. And he'd already planned it out in detail, how to ease her into the pleasure without triggering her anxiety.

The question was, did he dare?

He was already feeling far too emotionally involved with Muse for comfort. She wasn't part of his plan. His job demanded no ties, no relationships to compromise his effectiveness.

And once they'd crossed that line of being together, there was no going back. Muse wasn't like the other one-night stands he'd indulged in over the years. Would he be able to have a short fling with her, lasting only as long as they were in hiding, and then leave her?

He didn't know. But he had the sinking feeling he wouldn't be able to just walk away.

And that was dangerous. More dangerous than anything Davies could throw at him.

He wanted her like he'd wanted no one and nothing else in his life. But was the price they'd both have to pay too high?

The cottage was lovely.

Muse grabbed her things from the back seat of the car and wandered up the uneven brick path toward the front door, taking a deep breath of rose-scented air. Despite the oppressive heat of the summer sun, the garden was a riot of color. Perennials of all description crowded the flourishing flower beds on either side of the entryway, and every inch of the white picket fence enclosing the yard was draped in pink rambling roses.

A perfect spot for a honeymoon hideaway.

Remi strode up to meet her, carrying his duffel bag on his shoulder, looking tall and dark and enchantingly masculine in contrast to the romantic femininity of the garden. Her heart sighed. Too bad this wasn't their honeymoon and he wasn't her groom, about to carry her over the threshold and into a wonderful new life.

For a split second she felt a twist of pain deep inside because she would never have any of those things.

She pushed the pain aside. It was her choice. As much as she'd like to have a normal life with a normal husband, it wasn't going to happen. She wasn't a normal woman, and it was useless to wish it were otherwise.

Besides, she enjoyed her life as it was. Truly. She had a good job as a paralegal, lots of friends, a nice place to live, a loving sister and a terrific mother. Yes, things sometimes got a bit wild, with too much dancing, too many parties, too many people who didn't see her as she really was. But that was going to change. As soon as she got out of this current mess, she was definitely going to simplify her lifestyle. Give up the craziness and work on becoming more respectable. More responsible. Maybe she'd even move back to South Carolina for a while. It would be good to be with her family, have their support, as she struggled to shed the layers of the past and emerge a better person.

Maybe if she got through all that she could consider what Remi had proposed.

Or maybe not.

Meanwhile she could surely enjoy the view.

"Pretty cute, huh?" Remi said as he stopped next to her, looking around.

"You sure are, sugarcane," she answered with a smile, and stood on her tiptoes to give him a quick kiss. Pretending she didn't see his astonished look, she walked up the stairs to the front door, juggling the things she was carrying. "Open up before I drop all this stuff."

"Don't move!" Remi said, his voice suddenly urgent. "Stay right where you are."

She froze. "What is it?"

He slowly lowered his duffel to the ground and drew his weapon.

"Remi, what's wrong?"

"Behind you. A snake. A really big snake."

Ho-kay. Cautiously she turned her head to check it out.

"Don't move," he repeated, "I'm going to shoot it."

"No!" she cried, spying the giant black reptile coiled peacefully in the sun, regarding them with passive alertness. "It's just a harmless water snake."

She glanced back at Remi, who was squinting at the snake with an expression of grim distaste. He inched backward. "It's huge. Let me get rid of the thing."

"By killing it? No way." She couldn't believe— "Oh, my God! You're afraid of snakes!"

"I am not afraid of snakes," he muttered. "I just don' like them."

She grinned, shuffling the things in her arms. Her purse dropped, causing the snake to lift its head, then quickly slither off. "Well, apparently the feeling is mutual," she said, absurdly pleased that she'd found a weakness in the otherwise perfect man.

Unlocking the door, he frowned at her, no doubt half in embarrassment. ''If he gets in the house, *you're* taking him out.''

''Baby,'' she chided with a wink and went inside as he held the door open.

''Very funny.''

''He might have friends. Maybe I should check all the rooms before you come in.''

She heard Remi's duffel drop to the floor right before her own things were lifted from her hands. ''You are really askin' for it, woman.''

Suddenly she was in his arms and he was chuckling and tickling her and kissing her all at the same time.

She squealed in surprise and batted at his hands and laughed and struggled and threw her arms around him and kissed him back, and it wasn't until much later that she realized she hadn't once felt afraid of his hold on her. She was too busy enjoying the taste of him, the smell of him, the feel of his fingers in her hair and her own on his muscular backside, thankful the awkwardness between them had dissolved.

He moaned, kicked the door shut and leaned against it, bringing her with him so her back was to the room as their kiss deepened. His body trembled when she ran her hands up his chest. His grip was gentle but insistent as he held her, his fingers edging up her body, slowly, slowly, closer and closer to her breasts. Their tongues tangled, her nipples ached, the air deserted her lungs, her blood pounded. And panic seeped into her, claiming her inch by inch, as surely as Remi's mouth and hands.

She pulled away. Out of his arms.

They stared at each other, breath coming in gulps.

''I'm sorry,'' he said.

"So am I," she whispered. "I wish—" Her voice broke and she tried again. "I wish I could give you what you need."

He shook his head. "I wish I could take away your fear."

"You do," she said, and moved back to him, rested her head on his shoulder. "More than anyone ever has before."

"I feel like I'm pressuring you. That's the last thing I want to do."

"Grace says change only happens under pressure," she murmured without thinking. "Maybe you should keep it up."

He lifted her chin with a finger. "You really want that kind of change?"

"More than anything," she finally acknowledged aloud. To him. To herself. "I just don't think it's possible. It would take a miracle."

"Are you giving me permission to try?"

Her blood slowed to a stop. "I don't know. I'm so afraid."

"Of me?"

She closed her eyes, and a wave of tremors shook her body. "No. Never of you."

"Then what?" he asked softly.

And suddenly she knew with blinding clarity. It wasn't Remi she was frightened of, or his touch, or even if he failed to change her feelings of panic to pleasure. What scared her most was something quite unexpected.

"I'm afraid of what will happen if you succeed."

Chapter 9

Muse spent the rest of the afternoon avoiding Remi.

What had gotten into her, saying those things to him?

She *didn't* want to change. She *didn't* want him to pressure her. She *was* frightened of him, of his touch, of the pleasure. Terrified, in fact.

And he wouldn't succeed, anyway, so any concerns she might have about afterward were moot.

Choosing the smaller of the two bedrooms, she went in and slowly unpacked her few things, stretching out the time as long as possible. Sitting on the bed, she picked up the gun that had lain atop her overnight bag and contemplated it for a moment. Should she carry it around with her? She felt safe enough. Dev seemed more than trustworthy to keep their whereabouts a secret, and out here in the back of beyond the threat of James Davies finding her seemed remote. She placed the gun under her pillow.

She wandered around the cottage a bit, exploring its nooks and crannies, and realized that Remi had gone outside. He was busy conducting a tour of the cameras and motion detectors. Dev was right, you could hardly spot them even if you knew what you were looking for. It was obvious Remi did, for he had little trouble locating the small electronic gadgets hidden in each of the corners of the property.

Not that she was following him, but she decided to go out, too, and take a look at the garden. Going in the opposite direction from Remi, she spent a couple of hours examining every single one of the many flowering plants someone was taking meticulous care of. She'd never had a yard of her own because she'd always lived in apartments. But she'd always dreamed of having one just like this.

The brick pathway meandered among drifts of green and pink and purple, full of sweet scents and buzzing insects and teeming with sunny optimism.

After running out of plants, she climbed the stairs onto the back verandah and sank onto an old-fashioned wooden swing, pretending to rest her eyes. But she was really peeking out from under her lashes, watching Remi as he ambled back and forth, testing the cameras and motion detectors and checking out the results on the monitors in the cottage. It seemed from his casual pace he was doing it for lack of anything else to do more than from any real need.

Every time he passed by the verandah, he gave her a lingering look.

It was unnerving. In fact, she'd never been so petrified in her entire life.

She knew he would never hurt her, so she couldn't understand the quaking in her limbs. But this wasn't her normal knee-jerk reaction when a man cornered or manhandled her. It was far worse. It was a gnawing, numbing trepidation deep inside the most hidden parts of her. Places that hadn't felt anything for half her life.

She didn't know whether to jump in the car and drive like hell until she got clear to the Yukon or to throw herself on the ground in front of him and cry, "Take me now and get it over with!"

At least then she wouldn't have this horrible kind of anticipation. Not knowing what he intended to do—or if he intended to do anything at all.

"You plannin' to avoid me forever?" his voice interrupted her quandary. The sun was going down. She must have fallen asleep on the swing.

Remi was leaning against the porch rail, holding two glasses of wine. His black hair had been brushed back from his face, emphasizing the strong, masculine angles of his square jaw and long, straight nose. The diamond in his ear gleamed bloodred from the sunset light as he tipped his head awaiting her response.

"What do you mean?" she stalled, noticing the trim lines of his tall, lean frame, his slim waist and muscular thighs encased in a pair of well-fitting slacks. The man was killer handsome.

Not only that, but he was a good person, sensitive and thoughtful, protective, and as much as it annoyed her, being organized wasn't really a bad trait in a man.

She was crazy not to want him like crazy.

Except she *did* want him like crazy. Just not like *that.* And surely not for a relationship. She didn't do relationships.

So what did that leave?

"Feeling confused?"

It was uncanny how he always seemed to be able to read her mind.

He offered her one of the glasses of wine. She took it, glad for something to do with her hands besides wring them.

"Yes. Very confused."

"*Dis moi.* Talk to me." He indicated the swing and walked over to join her.

He sat but she preferred to stand. ''It was a mistake. What we talked about earlier. I can't do it.''

He took a sip of wine. ''Because you're afraid I'll succeed.''

''No. Yes.'' She shook her head. ''No. You won't succeed.''

''You didn't sound so certain earlier.''

She looked down at him in quiet desperation. ''You won't. But let's say for argument's sake a miracle happens and I like making love with you. What then?''

He took another sip. ''Then that's a good thing, *non?* It's nothing to be afraid of.''

''Yes, it is. Because what happens after that?''

''We do it again?''

She couldn't help smiling at his predictably male response. ''Be serious.''

He smiled back. ''I am.''

She kicked his shoe, then sat down beside him. ''No, I mean it. You're so big on having a plan for everything. So what's the plan for us?''

''We do it as many times as we want for as long as we're together.''

''And then we say goodbye?''

''We say *au revoir.* New Orleans is my home base. I get back there every so often, between assignments.''

She pushed out a breath. ''And that's it.''

There was a short silence, then he said, ''And that's it. But you won't be afraid any longer. Someday you'll meet another man, the right man, and you won't have to go through all this again.''

She folded an arm across her stomach and looked away, taking a swallow of wine without tasting it. ''What if I don't want another man?''

This time the silence was much longer. ''Has something changed since this morning?''

"No." She got to her feet, paced a few steps away. Turned. "No. I don't want a relationship, I'm not the kind of person—" She closed her eyes. "It's just—" She opened them and gazed at him pleadingly. "I've never wanted a man before. What if you actually do this thing, take away my dislike for intimacy and give me pleasure? I'm a woman, Remi. After that, *any* woman would want you. Want to *keep* you. And that would just complicate both our lives."

His somber expression said he hadn't thought about that. "It would," he agreed quietly. "And I don't want to hurt you." He held out his hand. *"Vien ici."*

She felt weak and at sea and wanted nothing more than to run. Run like hell, away from this situation, away from Remi, away from her whole messed-up life. But she did as he asked, went to him, and he guided her to stand between his knees, took her wineglass and set it along with his on the verandah railing, then linked his fingers with hers.

"I wish I could offer you more than these few days together. But my job makes it impossible. It would be too dangerous for both of us. Besides—" his mouth turned down in a thin, humorless smile "—if you really knew me, you wouldn' want me for long. I'm one unlovable bastard, and that's the plain truth."

"I don't believe it for a minute," she protested, wondering why he'd say such an awful thing. "You're the most amazing man I've ever met."

His smile turned wry. "Which isn't to say I'm lovable. Don' worry, I've worked hard all my life at being anything but."

"And why's that?" she asked, recognizing a defense tactic when she heard one.

He slid his arms loosely around her hips and pulled her near. "It's a long, boring story."

She touched his shoulder, his hair, lifted a raven lock

behind his ear. "And we've got all night with nothing to do but talk."

He tugged her closer still. "But we were talkin' about you."

"I think we've used that subject all up."

"*Mais, non,* I don' think so."

He looked up at her, his eyes moving over her body all the way up, and suddenly she was acutely aware of what she was wearing. The thin cotton camisole, barely buttoned and showing acres of cleavage, had never seemed immodest before. In fact, modesty had never been an issue with her at all before. She was proud of her body and didn't mind showing it. She'd even been known to earn a necklace or two down on Bourbon Street. It was part of her image—flirty and sassy and a little bit wild.

But with his smoky eyes on her, his face so close she could feel his warm breath on her skin, his arms holding her there between his powerful legs, she suddenly felt naked. And vulnerable.

She inhaled deeply to keep the usual panic at bay and felt a whole new kind of panic. One of wanting him to peel away the covering of her camisole and let his life breath pour over her breasts in a hot current, touching her yet not, letting her feel the sweet heat of him without the choking confinement.

His lips brushed a kiss between her breasts, and she shuddered out the air from her lungs unevenly.

"Easy, it's all right," he murmured, loosening his grip on her.

She stumbled back a step. "I want—" Torn, she didn't know what she wanted more, to rush in and put on a turtleneck sweater—

"What do you want, *chère?*"

—or to unbutton the last two buttons of her camisole, open it and beg him to breathe on her some more.

As a rose-scented breeze stirred the leaves of the trees and flowers, covering her in a rash of goose bumps, she imagined it was his breath. A lone cricket chirped in the dusking night. Remi gazed up at her, willingness written in his eyes, so she knew she could ask anything of him, anything at all, and he would give it to her.

But courage failed her. She couldn't.

"How about some supper?" she asked instead of what she really wanted.

Because the sad, honest truth was, she didn't know *what* she wanted anymore.

"Tell me about your family," Muse said and leaned back in her chair.

Remi gazed at her over the remnants of the meal they'd just shared. It must have been that second glass of touchy-feely California wine that gave him the impulse to actually give her a straight answer. He wasn't used to the stuff. He should have stuck to tequila. Safer by far. A real drink. Not prone to making a man spill his guts about things better left buried deep inside.

To show he was stronger than the wine, and the memories, he took another swallow and said, "Spent most of my childhood with my cousin Beau on their plantation, Terrebeau," then proceeded to entertain her with tales of growing up a very bad boy in Verdigris, Louisiana, in the company of his terminally good cousin, Beau, and how his only supporter was his equally feisty paternal grandmother known simply as Grandmère. No reason to bring up Beau Saint-Coeur and all that other stuff.

But at the end of the stories, instead of laughing heartily and rolling her eyes at his youthful antics, Muse gave him a sad smile and asked, "What happened to them?"

"They're both still living at Terrebeau, along with Beau's new wife, Kit."

''No, I mean your parents.''

He froze, his third glass of wine halfway to his lips. He set it down. ''Nothing. Why would you ask that?'' He hadn't mentioned his parents. Not once.

''They must have hurt you very badly to make you do all those things.''

He was too stunned to move, too taken aback to respond except to say, ''I don't talk about my parents.''

''I noticed.'' Her liquid blue eyes gazed softly into his. ''I don't talk much about my father, either.''

It took several moments for her statement to sink in. His eyes narrowed of their own volition. ''What did he do to you?''

''He left. And came back. And left. And came back. Just often enough to give us hope, then snatch it away again.''

Remi's jaw set. ''Bastard.''

''Grace was always the good sister. I was the bad one. That's how I know. About you, I mean.''

He closed his eyes, understanding what she was saying. And recognized a kindred soul on the deepest gut level possible.

''Why were you the bad cousin?'' she asked.

He let out a single, heartfelt oath. And looked at her. ''My father thinks I'm a bastard. Literally. He's always believed I am a product of my mother's indiscretion. She denied it, of course, from the beginning. But she was a weak woman and went along with his decree that I was to be treated as a bad seed. Me, I just fulfilled their expectations. The really ironic part is I have an illegitimate half brother whom my dear father showers with his affections. No doubt the will is drawn up accordingly.''

''Oh, Remi,'' she said, sighing, and took his hands across the table. ''I'm so sorry.''

''Don' be,'' he said, shrugging off the old agonies and outdated sorrows. It was all ancient history now. ''I never wanted to own a plantation, anyway. And my juvenile delinquent background's served me well in my undercover work.''

Enough true confessions for one day. He rose and gathered their plates. ''Let's clean up and go out on the verandah for some stargazing.''

Moments later they were snuggled together on the porch swing, looking out at the sparkling night canopy over the inky darkness of the garden. They spoke for a long time in hushed voices about the twists and turns fate had put into each of their paths, about how they'd pulled themselves out of the negativity and built something good of their lives despite their rocky beginnings. Muse managed to get in a few more questions about those bad old days with his parents at Beau Saint-Coeur and, amazingly, he was able to answer them before changing the subject. Muse just seemed to invite confidences. She listened to him, really listened and instinctively understood the turbulence of his childhood.

They had a lot in common, Remi realized. A whole lot. No wonder he felt like he'd known her his whole life. He just wished—

Non. No sense going there. Keeping Muse for longer than the term of this case would take some major changes in his life. His living arrangements, for instance. Being undercover for most of his career, he hadn't put any time or energy into a place to live. Four bare walls in a seedy part of town, something that blended in with the people he ran with, that's all he possessed in the way of a home. Why bother when he didn't see it for months at a time?

For the first time ever, he paused to consider his dangerous job and self-imposed nomadic lifestyle. Was he willing to give it all up for her, buy a place and settle down, even if she wanted him to?

Could he?

Though he seldom dwelled on it, he was fully aware that

his avoidance of love and commitment was not based solely on his job.

Because of his childhood, he'd always been ultrawary of family and any kind of emotional commitment. Intellectually Remi knew his mother loved him, but in his whole life she never dared show him more than a glimmer of that love, choosing to reject him in favor of cowering to his father's bitter imaginings. If a mother's blood ties to her own child could be so thoroughly betrayed by a father's jealousy and suspicion, how fragile must be the simple bonds of love between two strangers?

If Remi fell for Muse, changed his whole world for her, could he trust that she would not make a similar, hurtful choice, breaking his heart all over again in the process?

No. He couldn't.

Better not to take the chance.

During the last decade of his life, Remi had managed to let go of the pain of his past. Learn to see the disappointments in perspective. Understand that what had happened to him as a child was not his fault.

But he didn't think he could go through that process again as an adult. Not and remain sane.

Still, that didn't mean he shouldn't see where things led, on a strictly physical level, as long as they were together. Muse was the most attractive, exciting woman he'd ever met. If she was up to sharing his bed in any way, there was not a chance in hell he'd kick her out.

He just had to make damned sure when she got up to leave, she didn't take his heart along with her.

Someone was watching him. From the bedroom doorway.

Vaguely surprised he'd actually fallen asleep, Remi lay perfectly still in his bed and let his senses tell him who it was.

Muse.

He could smell her. The hint of soap from her shower, the sweet perfume that clung to her hair, the unmistakable scent of her warm woman's body.

Moving only his eyes, he checked the clock on the nightstand, illuminated by the blue light of the computer monitor on a desk across the room. It said 3:42 a.m. The low, intermittent tones of the security system beeped softly without interruption. All was quiet.

Except his heartbeat.

Had she changed her mind? *Dieu,* he hoped so.

After their long talk, they'd shared a lingering kiss or two on the verandah swing. Or maybe it was three or four. He'd lost count, but she must have sensed he was about to act on his serious need to touch her and had pulled away, saying they should get some sleep. With that she'd slipped from his arms and gone to her room.

He'd felt her reluctance to leave him and could probably have talked her out of it. But for a single instant he'd hesitated. His reasons for wanting her were incredibly selfish, he'd told himself. And before he could think of all the reasons they weren't, she'd gone.

But now she was back. Watching him in the dark.

What did she want? Him? Or was she just looking for company, unable to sleep?

Either way, he wanted her in his bed.

She moved away, toward her room.

He started to hum, harmonizing to the tone of the security monitor beeps. An old bump and grind tune, popular years ago. An invitation to sleep with him.

''Voulez-vous coucher avec moi,'' he sang in a low rumble, *''ce soir? Voulez-vous coucher avec moi?''*

She stopped, turned back. He could see her better now, cast in the pale-blue monitor light. She smiled, amused. She was wearing his shirt. The same one she'd worn to bed the night before. She looked sexy as hell.

He hummed another verse, then whispered, "I'm naked under this blanket," knowing instinctively it wasn't the sight of his body she was afraid of.

Her smile widened and she said, "Prove it."

"Come on over and prove it yourself," he dared with a grin.

The smile slipped a fraction. He could see the sassy wild child wrestle with the frightened victim within.

"No. I don't want to lead you on," she finally said.

"You won't. I think I know the score by now," he assured her and stretched, then crossed his arms under his head, letting the blanket slide down his chest.

He could feel her eyes on him as tangibly as if her hands were stroking over his skin. Her gaze caressed the coarse black hair on his chest, his pebbled nipples, his face and shoulders.

"You don't mind?"

He shook his head.

"How do you put up with me?" she quietly asked.

"It's my job," he answered. Evading her real question.

"And this?" she said, indicating the bed where he lay wishing like hell she would just shut up and slide in next to him.

He sighed. "You're the sexiest, most beautiful woman I've met in a long, long time. Is it so strange I'd like you in my bed?"

"Yes. Under the circumstances."

"Circumstances change," he said as she walked slowly closer. "We have plenty of time."

When she stood right next to the bed, she said, "You're so patient with me. How do you do it?"

"I wouldn't count too much on that patience," he said, patting the mattress at his side. "Hop in."

She licked her lips. "You won't try anything?"

He gave her a half smile. ‘‘I’m probably gonna try a whole lot of things. But I’ll stop if you say no.’’

She didn’t move for so long he thought his words had pushed her too far. He’d known it was a risk, telling her he wouldn’t sleep politely next to her as though he were impotent, like Gary Fox. He would never be content to do that, so he’d taken a chance. It was part of his plan, to push her relentlessly verbally, then go very slowly with the physical. That way she’d be expecting him to demand much more of her, when in reality he would ask for very little. That should make her more and more at ease with him for every passing night.

Provided they had a few nights to spend together.

‘‘All right,’’ she said at last. ‘‘I can live with that.’’

As Muse slid into bed beside him, Remi had the fleeting thought that it might not be such a bad thing if it took several weeks for his colleagues at the Bureau to track down James Davies.

She looked up at him, her eyes filled with a poignant blend of apprehension and uncertainty. But mostly with trust.

Did he say weeks? *Dieu,* make that several months.

Now all he had to do was figure out how the hell he was going to find the strength not to roll her onto her back, jump her and relieve this incredible need he felt to thrust himself deep inside her, claim her and command her to love him as much as he was growing to love her.

Somehow he had to find the willpower to go very, very slowly.

And the good judgment to ignore the fact that he had just admitted to himself he was falling hopelessly in love with the woman.

Chapter 10

Muse listened to the soft burr of Remi sleeping next to her and couldn't quite figure out if she was in heaven or in hell.

Surely it was heaven. Because she was in bed with the man of her dreams, her body nestled up to his back. He was naked in her arms, they'd kissed and cuddled for ages, and he hadn't even tried to make love to her.

No, it had to be hell. Because she was in bed with the man of her dreams, her body nestled up to his back. He was naked in her arms, they'd kissed and cuddled for ages, and he hadn't even tried to make love to her.

And for the first time ever in her life, she wanted more. Could she be experiencing sexual frustration?

Impossible. Muse Summerville didn't want men. Muse Summerville was frigid.

And yet there it was, a sharp hunger lodged deep inside her, between her legs, in her belly, making her breasts ache. A hunger only Remi's touch could satisfy.

How had this happened?

The man was from Louisiana. Obviously he'd put some kind of voodoo spell on her.

She tried to imagine what it would be like if she woke him up, told him she was ready to give it a try.

He'd be gentle, of course. He'd kiss her tenderly, roll her onto her back and climb on top of her, lever himself between her legs. She braced herself, imagining the weight of him pressing down on her, onto her breasts and stomach. The strength of his knees pushing her thighs apart.

Squeezing her eyes shut, she took a deep cleansing breath, told herself it wasn't real, she was just imagining. And tried to get back the feelings of hunger and desire.

It was no use.

She licked her lips, tasting salt.

It was a good thing he hadn't tried to make love to her. She would never be able to enjoy it, even with a man as wonderful as Remi Beaulieux.

She placed a tiny kiss on the back of his shoulder, mourning the loss of that brief flare of hope.

Ah, well. She'd known it would be this way, despite what he believed. She would survive this disappointment, too. Hadn't she always? This time it might take a bit longer to recover, like about eighty years....

In the meantime she'd savor the warmth of his body sleeping next to hers, the smell of him on her skin, the feeling of perfect safety in the circle of his protection. So she'd remember.

Yes, it was heaven after all.

Muse awoke to the smell of bacon and coffee. Remi's side of the bed was cool and empty, his weapon gone from the nightstand. The strains of a Cajun squeeze box tune wafted in from somewhere, accompanied by French lyrics in a deep baritone she recognized from the night before.

The split-screen monitor across the room caught her eye, and she realized one of its screens showed the kitchen. Remi was in front of the stove dressed in perfectly tailored black slacks, a white muscle shirt, and his shoulder holster and gun. With his long black hair and diamond earring, he looked more like a gangster than an FBI agent. No wonder he did so well in his undercover work.

She fluffed up her pillow and settled back on the bed with a smile, enjoying the sight of her man singing and flipping bacon to the rhythm of an old-time Cajun waltz. She almost fell off the bed when at the end of the song he turned to the camera and pointed his spatula at her.

"Get up, you lazy bones. Breakfast is ready. You've got five minutes to get your butt in here."

With a laugh, she bounded out of bed and ran to the bathroom to brush her teeth and jump into some clothes. She made it to her seat at the table with twenty seconds to spare.

"That's what I like. A woman who follows orders." He gave her the once-over approvingly. "And looks good doing it."

She'd put on the first thing her hand had hit in the closet, a baby-blue sundress with a clutch of spaghetti straps, a low-cut front and a high-cut hem.

She liked Remi's reaction to its sexiness, but she made a mental note to tone down her wardrobe at the same time she reinvented her image. She never wanted another man to look at her with the desire she saw in Remi's eyes as they moved over her. After Remi, she didn't want another man to look at her at all. She'd have to consult Grace. Her sister was a master at dressing to avoid men's notice.

Of course, turnabout was fair play.

"You're not so bad yourself, sugarcane," she said, taking a second gander at the muscle shirt that stretched over his pecs and abs like a second skin. The raw maleness of it, along with his sophisticated black trousers, made a surprisingly sexy statement. "Where'd you learn to dress like that? Mafia U?"

Remi chuckled. "James Dean and Philip Noiret. Beau and I used to devour old film noir movies growing up. I guess the look stuck with both of us."

"Works for me." She bit into a piece of bacon, fried to perfection. "Mmm. Now, that's what *I* like. A man who cooks," she said, and winked. "And looks good doing it."

"Show me your black lace."

Remi sidled up to Muse on the sofa where she sat several hours later fiddling around with the photos for her book. He nuzzled her ear with his lips. "I want to see all of it."

She turned to him uncertainly. "Excuse me?" She didn't remember packing any black underwear, and even if she had—

He smiled and kissed her, a slow, thorough kiss, one that both asked and claimed in one long, delicious persuasion.

"Sorry, got distracted by your…dress," he murmured, and she completely forgot the topic of conversation. He took his finger and pushed one of three thin spaghetti straps off her shoulder, placed a kiss where it had been, then dragged off another, kissing where it had been, too. She held her breath, waiting for him to slide the last one from its place.

He looked up and said, "Well?"

She blinked. "Well what?"

"Your wrought iron?"

She glanced down at the coffee table, littered with her photos of iron fences and railings. "Black lace" fences and railings. Comprehension finally slogged its way through her muddled brain.

She stared at him openmouthed. "How do you do that?"

He settled back in the sofa. "Do what?"

"You kiss me and make me forget my own name, you

touch me and make me forget the project I've been working on for three years, you whisper in my ear and all I can think about is sex.''

The corner of his mouth curled up disreputably. ''Really?''

''It's madness. I don't even like sex.''

The other corner joined the first. ''You're wrong, darlin'.''

She frowned at him. ''I'm not wrong.''

''*Mais,* yeah. I told you. It's not sex you don't like. It's the feeling of being forced.''

Her mouth parted. She wanted to deny it, to say she disliked everything about sex, but found herself thinking hard about his words.

Could he be right?

He pinned her with an intense gaze. ''I'll never force you, *chère.* To do anything.''

''I know you won't,'' she said, knowing to the marrow of her bones it was true. ''I trust you.''

He just smiled. ''Show me your pictures.''

And for the next hour she forgot all about sex and James Davies and everything else, and told him about the project of her heart, born of an early-morning walk in the French Quarter when she'd met an old woman who'd shared a remarkable story about the wrought-iron centerpiece of her balcony rail. From then on she'd always taken pictures and asked people about the origins of their home's iron-lace elements.

It was amazing how much of Louisiana's history was packed into those intricately designed pieces of architectural art. Hopes and dreams, love, hate, desire and betrayal were all woven into gates, railings and cemetery enclosures in the form of symbols, crests, flowers and stylized body parts.

''I had no idea,'' he murmured, sifting through the photos she had shown him. ''Tell me which is your favorite.''

''Oh, I don't know,'' she said. ''That's like asking a mother who her favorite child is.'' She winced inwardly when his jaw ticked at her analogy, and hurried to say, ''There are better photos, but I guess this has to be my favorite story.''

She pulled out a moody picture of a grand entry gate in front of an elegant plantation in obvious decline.

''In the center of this gate is a big, gnarly oak, which symbolizes the patriarch of the family back in the eighteen hundreds. He was said to be cruel and brutal, both to his slaves and the young bride, Julia, whose debt-ridden father had sent her over from France at age seventeen in an arranged marriage. She did the design.''

He grimaced. ''Cheery.''

''Patience,'' Muse admonished. ''They say Julia took refuge from her abusive husband in her gardens, symbolized here in the flowers below the tree.''

Remi looked closer at the photo, then remarked, ''There are two of every flower.''

She smiled. ''You should be a detective.''

He grinned. ''You think?''

''The story goes, after her first year of marriage she'd withdrawn so far she didn't speak at all, except to sing softly when she was in her garden. It wasn't until after the old buzzard died it came out that Julia and the estate's handsome young gardener had fallen in love, right there under the old man's nose.''

''Ah. And I suppose that's what the weeds growing all around the outer edge of the gate symbolize. The wild, upstart gardener.''

She laughed and smacked him on the arm. ''They are not weeds. It's a rose and a briar, entwined together for always. The rose for her, the briar for him.''

''Briar being because he was long and thorny…or should

I say horny?'' He pulled her close. ''Remind you of anyone?''

She giggled. ''You are so bad.''

But she kissed him anyway.

She wasn't relaxed. Not completely. But being in Remi's arms made her feel she could forget the troubles of the outside world and just melt into his chest and let him take care of her, and everything would be all right.

''I can't believe I'm here with you because I'm running in fear for my life,'' she murmured. ''All that stuff with Davies and Gary Fox seems so far away.''

He slipped an arm around her shoulder. ''Hopefully it'll stay that way.''

''Do you really think we'll be safe here?'' she asked, fear never far from the surface.

He kissed her forehead. ''For a few days at least, I think we can count on Davies not finding us.''

''I'm still worried about Grace, though. Morris did say he'd call her, didn't he?''

She didn't care for the pause before Remi answered, ''I suppose we could go back to Dev's tomorrow and send Morris another e-mail. Just to make sure he actually followed through.''

''It would make me feel a lot better, knowing he'd gotten ahold of her.''

''I understand.''

''I just don't want her coming to New Orleans. Davies might mistake her for me, and…'' Muse's words trailed off as all the horrible possibilities flashed through her mind.

Remi frowned. ''Why? Does she look that much like you?''

''We're identical twins.''

''Identical twins?'' Shock stamped itself on his features and he muttered something ugly-sounding in French. ''Why wasn't that in your file?''

"Morris never asked."

"We'll go to Dev's first thing," he stated firmly.

She let out a sigh and leaned her head on his shoulder. "Thank you. I know you think I'm being a worrywart, but you don't know Grace. She really will come to my rescue if she thinks I've disappeared. I'd die if she got hurt."

"Don' worry. Morris'll make sure she doesn' get anywhere near New Orleans."

The rest of the afternoon they spent in quiet conversation, listening to the radio and reading last week's Sunday paper, which had been included in the box of groceries Dev had ordered in from the village market before their arrival yesterday.

It was like trying to melt a glacier, but as they talked, Muse was slowly able to get Remi to open up even more about his childhood and his parents. Not that she specifically tried to pump him for information. But instinctively she felt he could use the opportunity to vent some of the emotions he'd kept carefully in check, deep inside, since he was a small child.

He didn't say all that much. He didn't have to. But from the few things he told her, she could tell it had been awful.

He hadn't been beaten or abused. But was being ignored for sixteen years any better? Ignored by a father who believed him to be the result of marital infidelity and a mother who was so dispirited and spineless she'd caved in to her husband's bitterness rather than stand up for the child she knew was his—a child one only had to look at to see the unmistakable family resemblance.

Remi had shown her an old, creased picture from his wallet of Beau and himself at sixteen, a few months before he'd run away to join the Navy, standing along with their *grandmère*. It could have been a mother and her twin sons.

How could a father be so blind?

She wasn't sure which was worse, a father who willingly claimed you as his then left for greener pastures, or a father who kept and fed you but refused to acknowledge you as anything more than an offensive reminder of sin.

Was it any wonder neither of those children wanted or trusted lasting commitments?

He was being a selfish bastard. That, on top of being completely out of his head.

Standing at the rail on the back verandah, Remi was ostensibly doing a last check on the property and motion detectors before bedtime and making sure the gate was securely latched. All of which he had meticulously done.

However, the real reason he was out there was to try to talk himself out of spending another night in the same bed as Muse Summerville.

If they shared a bed tonight, there wasn't a doubt in his mind something was going to happen.

Something hot. And tactile. And highly pleasurable.

But did he have the right to take her places she was so obviously hesitant to go? Simply because he wanted her so much he'd do just about anything to convince her she really wanted to?

His plan was working brilliantly.

He'd known it would. Muse didn't hate sex any more than he did. It didn't take a psychologist to understand that in order to conquer her remaining fears all she needed was a man with patience and respect, who took the time to show her she was in complete control of every situation with him.

He'd understood that instinctively, because of his own background, having also battled against the controlling hold of a man who'd only wanted to hurt him.

But she wasn't in control. Not really.

Remi was.

Just as he would be when the Davies case was over and he walked out her door.

Was it fair? To her?

What about to himself?

He glanced around the midnight garden, thought about a young, abused bride singing softly to her lover, and wondered briefly what had become of that pair after the patriarch's death, so long ago. Had Julia donned respectable widow's weeds and sailed back to France, never to see the young gardener again? Or had they defied society, married and raised a passel of kids? Maybe moved out west, to California, far from the memory of that Louisiana iron gate and the equally rigid strictures of the Victorian social order?

Remi smiled, watching a lone firefly blink in the humid darkness, floating all by himself like a tiny beacon among the sweet-smelling flowers and trees. Where was his mate?

The back door quietly opened and closed.

"Here you are."

Remi turned, and Muse was standing there in a puddle of moonlight, her blond hair shining like a halo around her face. Once again she was dressed for bed in his shirt, sleeves rolled to her wrists. And nothing else.

His breath caught in his throat. She was so damn beautiful.

He held out his arms and she came to him. Willingly, without hesitation, she slid into his embrace.

He was careful not to squeeze too hard, but *Dieu!* he wanted to crush her to his chest, to hold her as tightly as he possibly could, to chase out the depressing thought that this moment was fleeting and would never, could never, become forever.

"What are you doing out here?" she softly asked.

Having a nervous breakdown.

"*Rien,*" he said. "Jus' making sure everything's as it should be."

"And is it?"

His lips formed a cheerless smile. "Yeah."

She kissed him and whispered, "Want to sit on the swing and neck for a while?"

He closed his eyes and fought the impulse to laugh hysterically. She was actually asking him to get physical with her. Everything was going perfectly according to his plan. Except he no longer wanted it to.

"Muse," he said, resisting when she slipped from his arms and attempted to tug him toward the swing. "We better not." At her puzzled look he added, "I'm pretty tired. I think I should—"

"All right," she said quickly. "We can go to bed."

His body gave an involuntary lurch at her choice of words. *Damn, damn, damn.*

"*Chère*, I, uh, I think… Listen, you were right all along. We shouldn't sleep together. In the same bed, I mean."

Even in the moonlight he saw her face grow pale. "Why?"

He heard a hundred questions in that single word. And he couldn't answer a solitary one.

He struggled to come up with an explanation that wouldn't hurt her or ruin their growing friendship.

Or come close to the real reason.

"It just isn't a good idea," he said lamely. "Things are getting too…complicated."

Her hands sought his arms, her fingers gripped his flesh. "Please, Remi. Let me sleep in your bed. What I said last night, I was wrong. I won't try to keep you. I promise."

"What if I want to keep you?" he ground out before he realized what he was saying.

Her mouth dropped open in astonishment. "But…but that's impossible, you said so yourself." Her voice took on a desperate edge. "Your job won't let you… And me, I'm not the settling-down kind. You know I take after my father.

No roots, no…'' The flow of words stopped abruptly. ''You're just kidding. You didn't mean it. Right?''

Apparently, he didn't. Faced with such overwhelming arguments, his better judgment took over.

''Right,'' he forced himself to say. ''Temporary insanity. I'm better now.''

But the truth was, he wasn't sure he'd ever be better again. Not in this lifetime. Not without her by his side.

Maybe it was time to do some serious thinking about his life and what was important in it.

''You had me worried for a minute there.'' She kissed him tenderly. ''Now come to bed. I have something to ask you.''

It was strictly curiosity about what she wanted to ask that got him to slide in under the covers with her in the big bed in his room.

It had nothing to do with itchy fingers or throbbing body parts or the sweet memory of her taste in his mouth. None of those things had any part in his decision to renege on his earlier determination for separate sleeping arrangements.

Persuasive as those things were.

What was much more persuasive was her unmistakable aversion to their relationship getting serious.

What a relief.

And here he'd started to worry about her getting too emotionally involved with him. Hurting her if he left. *When* he left.

He should have known. Should have remembered. It was all in her FBI file. She was a wild party girl who'd never shown any signs of wanting anything other than her vivacious lifestyle in the French Quarter.

Yeah, he'd found a lot of depth hidden behind her untamed ways, some major intelligence, a lot of vulnerability and a few shocking secrets.

But she'd never once let on that she desired any kind of long-term relationship. Not with him, not with anybody.

On the contrary, she'd just reminded him she wasn't the type.

As he wasn't.

Perfect.

Now he could think about those throbbing body parts with a clear conscience.

Bien, fairly clear, anyway.

He turned to her on the mattress, reached for her hands under the covers. And was surprised when he realized she was lying there watching him nervously. She hadn't objected when he'd come out of the bathroom completely naked from his shower to join her in bed, so that couldn't be it.

"*Comment?*" he asked. "What?"

Her tongue slid over her lips. "I was just wondering..." Her words trickled to a halt and she bit her lip.

He lifted a brow. "Wondering...?"

She shifted a little closer. Not close enough so they were touching, but almost. She cleared her throat.

"Spit it out, *chère.*"

"Last night," she said, hesitated, then went on, "when I came into your room..."

He casually closed the gap between their bodies, putting his arm over her hip, around her back. "I seem to recall that, yeah."

"You said...you said you were going to try all sorts of things with me."

"Mmm-hmm." He toyed with the back of her sleep shirt. Waiting.

"But you didn't."

"*Non.* I didn't want to push you."

"Oh."

He brushed his hand slowly down her back, then up

again. "Why do you ask? Did you...*want* me to try things?"

"No!" She bit her lip again. Exhaled. "No. I just wondered. Why you hadn't."

He moved in for a kiss, pulling her right up against him. He captured her lips and hummed his pleasure as she opened for him. She kissed him back, moaned and pressed her body into his.

There was a difference in her. In her response to him. Still timid, maybe even a bit fearful. But tonight she was willing. Almost eager.

He kissed her long and deep, gradually increasing the pressure as the urgency of his desire grew. He reveled in the feel of her breasts pillowing into his chest. Her long legs tangled with his all the way down to his ankles. Small things in themselves, but a hundred times more meaningful for having been given so unconsciously. Last night she'd shied away from his naked body. Now she was meeting it full on.

He tightened his embrace little by little as their kiss went on and on and on. Until it became too much for her and she drew back.

"Muse," he said, panting, then lay very, very still. "Tell me what to do, *chère*."

She took his hand and placed a tremulous kiss on his palm. For a terrible second he thought she might jump from the bed and run away.

But then she looked up at him. And if he hadn't already been lying down, the need in her eyes would have brought him to his knees.

"Touch me," she whispered.

Remi groaned and told himself not to lose it.

He was so ready for this.

He wanted to rip his shirt off her. Run his fingers over her smooth skin, fill his hands with her lush curves, feel the excitement build within her body until she begged him to take her.

He wanted her so damn much.

But he would not break her fragile trust.

Slowly, gently, he reached out and touched his fingers to her cheek. "Are you sure?"

"Yes. I'm sure."

He let out a long breath, steadying the pulse that pounded like cannons through his veins.

And then he touched her trembling body.

Through her shirt he began to skim his hands lightly over her shoulders and arms and around to her back. Each time her body would stiffen a fraction, but then he'd coax her to relax, gliding his fingers and palms over her shirt, letting her know he wasn't asking for more than she was willing to give. Never once letting up on the kiss. But showing her she could trust him.

He loved feeling her heat, capturing the curves, caressing all the places he longed to taste. Taking his time, he explored every glorious inch of her. And had never been so excited in his life.

After a long while she was completely boneless in his arms, kissing him as though in a trance, unconsciously running her hands over him, digging her fingernails into his naked flesh, clutching him, holding him. Exploring his body with her fingers as naturally as he was hers.

Her sweet mouth covered his and she slid her tongue into it, imitating what he wanted more than anything else on earth.

He groaned when she found a particularly sensitive spot on the roof of his mouth, flicking the tip of her tongue over it as she pressed into his hardness.

"*Pitié d'amour!* Have mercy, *chère!*"

"Not a chance."

She ground into him. The hot crease of her cleft pushed against him, creating an inferno of heat around his arousal.

"Keep doin' that and I won't be responsible for my actions."

A sensual chuckle came from deep in her throat. She didn't believe him. He could tell from the way she just kept on doing what she was doing.

She licked at him, sucked his tongue, driving him crazy with her arousingly wanton kiss.

His whole body was poised on the brink of explosion. How could she do this to him with just a kiss?

Just a kiss. That was like saying *just* a nuclear bomb. It didn't even begin to describe the awesomeness of its power—power to wipe out all that had come before, and irrevocably change the future.

He could feel the keen, sublime tension building in his loins. If she didn't stop...

"Darlin'," he moaned. "I love what you're doing, but I jus' want you to know—"

His words cut off as she dragged her moist, skillful tongue around the depths of his mouth, igniting firestorms of sensation all the way down his body. The scorching pleasure circled his belly, homing in on his arousal.

"It wouldn' be fair, unless you let me return the favor."

"That's not necessary," she murmured, finding a remote corner of his mouth and plying it with hot velvet, pushing him closer and closer to the edge with every erotic stroke of her talented tongue. He was fast approaching the point of no return.

His desperate hands shot up and captured her face, fingers tunneling into her hair.

"Muse," he rasped out in confusion, wanting her to stop. Never wanting her to stop. "Look at me," he commanded when she continued to kiss him.

Her sultry, half-lidded eyes lifted in question, her kiss-stung lips poised just above his. And suddenly he knew what he should do. With the last fringes of conscious thought, Remi decided to give her a glimpse of the power she held over his body—over him.

"Watch," he said. "Watch what you do to me, *chère*."

Ecstasy pulsed just beyond the membrane of willpower keeping it at bay, teetering right on the brink of eruption. One heated lick or swipe of her tongue would release it.

He opened his mouth, inviting her in. With a moan of surrender, he allowed the conflagration of sensation to overtake him, gave himself over to her mastery.

As he felt the first wave of pleasure ripple through him he murmured, "And whatever you do, don' stop."

Chapter 11

Muse stared down at Remi's wrung-out but satiated face and wondered what on earth she should do next.

"Sure I should stop now?" she asked, just in case. She didn't have a lot of experience with this scenario. None, in fact. "Are you okay?"

"Oh, yeah," he said on a sigh filled with echoes of bliss. "I'm good. No, make that *you're* good."

"But I didn't do anything. I don't really understand what just happened."

Well, of course she knew *what* had happened. She just wasn't sure *how*.

His right eye cracked open and he gave a weak chuckle. "You kissed me, darlin'. That's all it took."

"But I've kissed you before."

"Not like that."

She nodded thoughtfully as he excused himself to the bathroom for a minute.

What had been so different?

Regardless of any other problems, she'd always loved kissing Remi. From the first time their lips had touched she'd been helplessly in love with his kiss.

Perhaps the difference was, now other parts of him had enjoined her devotion as well. Such as his broad shoulders and his cute butt. His nimble mind. His sensitive heart.

Had he felt all that in her kiss?

"Vien ici," he said, his arms reaching for her as he slid back into bed. She felt her eyes widen. "You didn' think we were done?" he asked in an amused tone. "Did you?"

"Um, well…actually—"

And suddenly she was terrified. Not so much by what he intended to do as by what he might feel within her as he did it.

Okay, also by what he intended to do.

"Hell, no wonder you don' like sex." He snuggled up to her, front to front. Propping up on an elbow, he rested his head on his palm, then trailed the fingers of his other hand down her arm and back up again. He gazed down into her eyes. "Wanna kiss some more?"

Terror turned to surprise. "Do you really want to?"

"I could kiss you all night, *chère,*" he murmured. "But don' think I'll be that easy every time," he added with a wink. "You jus' caught me off guard."

Lowering his head, he combed his fingers into her hair and met her lips with his, and gave her another cascade of wonderful, sensual kisses.

"This time it's your turn," he murmured, and pulled her close.

She gasped, unable to stop the terror from returning.

"Whoa, easy," he soothed, rubbing her back with a steady hand. "If you don't want to, that's all right."

"I'm sorry," she whispered, curling into his chest. "I'd rather you just hold me."

"Can we sleep like this?"

"Yes," she whispered.

She felt him smile against her forehead. "You have no idea how nice it is to finally sleep with you face-to-face."

She glanced up at him. He was right. This was the first time she could ever remember wanting to sleep in a man's arms. Up until now she'd always preferred being at his back, afraid of that uncomfortable feeling of confinement, restricted by his strong muscles and unrelenting grip on her. Along with what he might do.

But now, with Remi, she felt only cherished and protected.

She snuggled up against him, feeling his firm embrace surround her. She held her breath, waiting for the panic to come.

It didn't. All she experienced was warmth and coziness.

She sent up a silent prayer of thanks.

And fell asleep in the circle of his arms.

She was having one heck of a dream.

In her favorite position, Muse was nestled comfortably at Remi's back. Her breasts squeezed softly up against him and one arm was slung possessively around his waist.

She smiled in enjoyment. All on its own, her hand was roaming the front of him, slowly gliding over his bare skin.

Suddenly her eyes sprang open.

This was no dream!

Remi's fingers were laced through hers, and it was him moving her hand over his body. She held her breath as he sifted their joined fingers through his coarse chest hair, pausing to rub them languidly over his beaded nipples.

Farther and farther down his torso he guided her hand. Edging closer and closer to the juncture of his thighs.

Her heart pounded like thunder, her breath coming in short gulps.

"Do you have any idea what your touch does to me?"

he asked, breaking the sexually charged silence. Letting her know he was aware she'd awakened.

"I think I have some idea...."

Slowly, inexorably, he pulled her hand toward his arousal. She tried to tug it away, but he wouldn't let her escape.

"I want you to know exactly how you affect me. How easily you can control me."

She gave a gasp of shock when he closed her fingers around him, holding them in place with his hand over hers. "Are you afraid of this?" he asked.

"No," she whispered. Amazed that it was true.

"*Bon.* Then touch me."

Hard and thick, he seemed ready to explode at her very touch, at every nuance of her softly probing fingers as she slid them over his length.

He didn't suffer silently. He moaned encouragements, whispered endearments, urged her to explore to her heart's content.

"You're killin' me, *chère,*" he rasped as she gingerly took his rounded sac in her palm. Groaning long and low, he clenched his teeth.

"Am I doing it wrong?" she whispered.

"No, darlin', you've got it exactly right."

"Then why don't you...?"

Giving a strangled chuckle, he grasped her hand and moved it up and down over his shaft once. "Can you feel how hard I am?"

"Yes." She swallowed.

"Who did that to me?"

"I did."

"Do you have any idea how much power you have over me right now? How much control? How badly you could hurt me with a single movement?"

She swallowed again, tracing her fingernails over his

swollen sac and up his erection. His whole body shuddered in response.

"Or how much pleasure your touch brings me? What's in your hand—you know where I want it?"

She hesitated. "Yes."

"Where? Say it, Muse."

"Inside me."

"That's right, *chère,*" he said. "Inside you. And you know why?"

This time she stayed silent. Afraid to hear the truth.

"Not to hurt you or control you, you understand that, *non?*"

She gave a wobbly nod against his back.

"So why would I want to be inside you?"

"For pleasure?"

"But I could have that right now if I wanted it, *non, chérie?* You would willingly give me pleasure if I asked, wouldn't you?"

"Yes," she said, her fingers tightening around him. She'd give him anything he asked of her. Anything.

"But I won't ask," he murmured. "Because I don' want you to get the idea that simple pleasure is enough."

She felt the sting of tears. "It's not?"

"Not nearly enough. I want something more than my own pleasure, Muse. I'm greedy. I want yours."

In a single movement he turned to face her and grasped her gently by the arms.

"When you're ready," he whispered, and kissed her, his lips and tongue telling her she had nothing to fear. He loosened his grip and rubbed his hands slowly up and down her arms, brushing away her trembles.

"Oh, Remi."

She wound her arms around his neck, pulling him close. His body was a hot brand, burning into the front of her. Her mound pressed lightly against his hardness, creating an unimagined craving within her.

"Tonight, when you come to bed," he murmured low so she had to strain to hear, "I'm going to ask you to take off this shirt."

She swallowed heavily. "You are?"

He tugged on the hem where his hand rested on her hip. "Slowly. Button by button. I want you completely naked. So I can see your breasts."

He smoothed his hand up and over her. "I want to touch them. Skin to skin, with nothing between us."

She was too paralyzed to utter a reply.

Her nipple pebbled tightly under his palm. Her body was reacting to him more urgently, their strong attraction coaxing out a response, her trust in him overcoming her apprehension.

He tipped her chin up and locked his gaze with hers. "If you say yes to that, I'm going to ask if I can lick them." He extended his tongue and licked over her lips. "And kiss them and suck them, like I've done to your mouth. And then I'll ask to do it to the rest of you."

To her amazement, instead of raising a riot of alarm within her, his lustful declarations caused her breasts to ache and an intense hunger to stir deep in her center.

"I'm just going to ask," he quietly assured. "And I'll respect whichever way you answer."

She wanted to tell him how he made her feel, to say, *Don't wait, do it now.*

"Remi, I—" She stumbled over the words, the unfamiliar emotions making mincemeat of her attempt to verbalize them.

He laid a finger over her lips. "Don' say anything now. You have all day to think about it. I want you to be sure. Don' say yes unless you're certain it's what you want. If not, I'll understand."

With that, he slipped from the bed and dressed, leaving her to gather her scattered wits.

What kind of man gave a woman a whole day's warning of his intent, instead of just rolling on top of her and having his way, especially when she so clearly would give him anything he asked of her?

An honorable man, she realized. Beneath the roguish, rakish exterior that Remi Beaulieux showed the world beat the heart of a true gentleman.

Later that morning they made the drive to Dev's place as planned, to e-mail Morris about Grace. Afterward, over lunch, Remi listened as Dev told Muse about some nice wrought-iron fences on the estate property, at a big plantation house just up the riverbank, which just happened to be his own ancestral family home. Excited by his descriptions, she talked him into letting her include them in her book. With no references to name or location, of course. With Dev's reassurances, Remi had let her go by herself. She seemed particularly eager to be alone.

Remi waited for Morris's answering e-mail while shooting the breeze with Dev. When the computer signaled an incoming message, they both sauntered over, figuring it was for him.

It wasn't. But Dev showed it to him, anyway.

Remi read the e-mail four times and swore. *Merde.*

He glanced at his friend. "This is not good. Where did this information come from?"

"A contact at the NOPD Eighth District Station."

"The French Quarter."

Dev nodded. "Can't you get Morris to do anything?"

"I thought I had," Remi said disgustedly. "I told him specifically not to let Grace Summerville leave South Carolina."

"And now she's in New Orleans asking questions and demanding to file a missing persons report on Muse."

Remi raked his hands through his hair and swore again. "I hadn't pegged Morris as Davies's informant at the field office, but I'm beginning to think I could be wrong."

"You sure someone in the Bureau is working for Davies?"

"How else could he have known about the safe house? Not to mention my cover being blown. And now this."

"Sounds like you better not trust anyone there, Morris included."

"What the hell am I going to do?"

"More importantly, what's Muse going to do?"

He threw Dev a worried look. "Grace or no Grace, there's no way I can let her go back to New Orleans. Better lock up your guns, *mon ami,* or I could be a dead man. She's not going to like this one bit."

Dev gave him a smile of sympathy. "She a good shot?"

"Fourth place in her gun club for pistols. First for rifles," he said miserably, remembering what she'd told him that first day on her apartment stairs. *Dieu,* didn't that seem like a lifetime ago.

Dev whistled. "I think you're in trouble, buddy."

He *knew* he was in trouble. In a whole lot more ways than one. But at the moment, Grace was the trouble he was most concerned about.

Muse would be back any moment from her photo-taking jaunt. Maybe having gotten some nice pictures would temper her reaction to the situation with Grace.

Yeah, right.

When she sailed through the door all sun-pink and radiant smiles, Remi wanted to do anything but tell her the bad news. They were at an unsteady place in their relationship, and he didn't want to spoil things by having to play the big bad FBI bodyguard role again. He knew how she felt about that—he might as well be playing the Big Bad Wolf.

But he had no choice, so he took the bull by the horns.

"Your sister's turned up at the NOPD station in the Quarter, asking questions and demanding the police treat you as a missing person," he announced gravely.

"What? Oh, no!" Muse leaped off the couch where she'd just taken a seat. "I have to go to her."

Remi shook his head firmly. "Not possible. You know that."

"But I have to protect her from Davies!"

"Not your job. I've already contacted Morris again. He'll make sure she's all right."

Remi decided not to worry Muse with his suspicions about Morris. There was nothing to be gained. If Morris really was the traitor, then Davies would already know Grace was the sister and not a threat. And hopefully leave her alone. Unless it became obvious she could be used to control her twin's testimony. Which it would if Muse rushed to her.

Muse's pretty lips thinned. "But it *is* my job. It's because of me she's in danger."

"You're not responsible, Muse. It was her choice to come."

"She *is* my responsibility. She's my sister."

"I understand, but—"

"Do you?" she interrupted hotly. "What do you know about family responsibility? You don't even *have* a family."

Remi felt as though he'd been run through with a knife. All he'd done to protect the family he did love—Beau and Grandmère—flashed through his mind. If his real family gave a damn, he'd have done the same for them. Even his usurping half brother Zeph. Zeph, who'd gotten everything Remi should have.

His anger spiked. "And you're such an expert on responsibility?'' he retorted. ''Your idea of responsibility is to let your sister rescue you from trouble! Or blame everything on your father and leave town.''

Her chin went up. She opened her mouth to retort, but instead her eyes filled with tears.

Ah, hell.

''I'm sorry,'' he said and went to her, took her in his arms. ''Damn, I'm sorry.''

''No,'' she whispered in a watery voice. ''I deserved that for saying what I did. When I'm upset I say things without thinking.''

''I guess I do, too,'' he murmured into her hair. ''But you may as well go on ahead and get it all out of your system, because I'm still not letting you within a hundred miles of New Orleans.''

She stilled in his arms. ''I have to know she's safe, Remi. I have to.''

Unless he wanted a full-scale mutiny on his hands he'd better find a compromise. ''All right. We'll risk calling Morris.''

''Use my cell phone,'' Dev said, pretending he hadn't noticed their intimate embrace. ''It's not a hundred percent secure, but I've got it routed so it's pretty tough to trace.''

''Thanks,'' Remi said, and took the phone from his friend, exchanging glances. They both knew if the dirty agent learned of Remi's connection to Dev, Davies would be that much closer to finding their location. Though, Dev would never tell him a thing no matter what anyone threatened—not that they'd ever get close enough to ask.

Remi just prayed Morris wasn't the informer.

Okay, so he wasn't a complete gentleman, Muse thought, still feeling a residual sting from Remi's comment on her lack of responsibility. The fact that he was right was completely irrelevant.

They were in the Porsche cruising down the river road next to the levee, heading in the general direction of their bayou cottage hideaway. The day had turned Turkish-bath hot and humid, but the car's AC was cranked high and a crisp zydeco tune played on the radio.

Oh, what the hell. The man had only pointed out the obvious. And her comment had also been mean. Yeah, meaner.

She leaned over the gearshift and gave him a kiss on the cheek. "Thanks for calling Morris. I feel a lot better, now that I know he's taking care of her. Sorry I got cranky."

He glanced at her and smiled. "Likewise. Should we stop for ice cream?"

"That would be great."

Instead of bars, they opted to share a pint using spoons. Remi found a place to pull the car in behind a solid hedge and they climbed the levee to sit under an old live oak at a high spot overlooking a bend in the lazy river. There was a slight breeze so the heat wasn't too oppressive.

"This is nice," Muse said, dipping her spoon into the rapidly melting ice cream.

She would have said perfect, except for the confession she was about to make. She hadn't planned on telling the FBI about the videotape in her possession until the very last minute. But now Grace had arrived in the Quarter and could be in added danger because of the video.

"Remi, there's something I have to tell you."

He looked up, sucking on his spoon. "Yeah?" When he saw her serious face, a guarded expression came over his. "What is it?"

She jetted out a sigh, taking another spoonful. "Remember when we went to my apartment to pick up my things that first day?" He nodded. "And how I insisted we take the curtains to the dry cleaners?"

He snorted. "Oh, yeah. I remember."

''Yes, well, did you ever wonder why I did that?''

''No. You're a woman.''

She scowled. ''What's that supposed to mean?''

''It means… Never mind, get to the punch line. I have a feeling this isn't about dry cleaning, is it?''

''Not exactly.''

He swore softly. *''Dis moi.''*

''I have a videotape in my safety-deposit box at the bank which I stole from Gary Fox. Gary stole it from James Davies.''

Remi straightened, instantly getting that what she was saying was important. ''What kind of videotape?''

''It's a video of Davies torturing and killing a man.''

Remi froze and stared at her for several seconds. ''You're kidding me.''

''I wish I were. It's really, really awful.''

For a moment she couldn't go on; the hideously graphic images forever burned in her mind swirled through it in Technicolor black and blue and deep bloodred. And she had only watched for a few minutes before shutting it off and running to the bathroom to throw up.

There was no doubt it would be her in that dark warehouse on Louisa Street, duct-taped to a wooden chair being beaten and sliced to ribbons, if Davies caught her with the tape.

Or that her sister could wind up in the same position simply by coming to her rescue and having things go badly.

''Is that why the blond man has been following you for the past two weeks? Was he sent by Davies to get it back?''

She lifted her shoulders. ''I don't know. It's possible. At first I thought it was Gary following me. He didn't take our breakup well at all. He kept calling and— Anyway, I suppose he could just have been after the tape. After a while, though, I wasn't sure it was him.''

''Did anyone search your apartment?''

"Not that I know of. But it wouldn't have been hard to break in. The lock—"

"Is a joke," he murmured, remembering. "And if they were careful you would never have noticed. Could Fox have told Davies it was you who stole the tape?"

She thought about it for a moment. "No, I don't think so. I was never allowed access to the room where it was kept, so Davies would know Gary must have taken it himself."

"And you're absolutely sure Fox is still alive?"

She blanched. "No," she reluctantly said. "I'm not."

She'd broken up with him, but she harbored no ill feelings. Gary was definitely misguided, but he didn't deserve a gruesome death. He'd never been involved in the really bad stuff.

"He disappeared shortly after we broke up," she said. "I assumed he went underground with Davies. Besides, hopefully Davies doesn't even know someone has the tape. Gary made a duplicate and left it in place of the original."

"Clever," Remi said. "And now you have the original." She nodded. "In your bank safety-deposit box." She nodded again. "And the FBI knows about this tape, yes? It's part of your testimony. Right?" he prompted when she hesitated.

"Um…"

He groaned around his spoon. "No?"

"Not exactly."

"You didn' tell Morris? Why the hell not?"

"Because…" She finished up the last lick of ice cream and gazed out at the mud-green river slowly meandering past them. "He would have taken the tape from me. I wanted to keep it as insurance in case Davies found out I was a witness and came after me. I could pretend that without the tape my testimony was useless. Plus, as long as Morris thought he needed me alive for the trial, he'd do everything in his power to protect me."

"I see," Remi said, digesting what she'd told him. "I guess I can understand all that. But there's one thing I still don' get."

"Which is...?"

"What does all this have to do with dry cleaning?"

She smiled bleakly. Nothing like saving the worst for last. "Sure you want to know?"

"I think I'd better."

"You have to understand, if I'd told you about the video, you'd have informed Morris. We'd just met, and...well, I wasn't sure I could trust you to keep me safe, especially if the FBI took the tape."

"Muse, what did you do with it?"

"I knew Grace would come to look for me if I disappeared. That she would stay at my apartment."

His eyes widened. "Please don't tell me you left the tape for her there."

"No. But remember that key I asked you to get from the drawer?"

"Yes." Were his teeth clenching?

"That was to my safety-deposit box. I attached it to the curtains we took to the cleaners."

He regarded her warily. "I still don't get it."

An involuntary smile came over her lips. "You would if you knew Grace. She'd never stay in a bedroom with no curtains. She'd find that dry cleaning ticket in my briefcase and go fetch them within hours of arrival. She's very modest."

His brows lifted incredulously. "This is your sister?"

She thumped his knee. "Smart aleck. I told you she's the good twin."

His eyes sparkled. "Now, that's a matter of opinion."

"So you're not mad?"

"I didn' say that."

"You don't look mad."

"I'm too busy being glad I got the bad twin."

She made a face. "What are we going to do?"

He grinned. "I can think of any number of things."

She poked his knee again. "About the tape I mean, and Grace."

He gathered her to him and kissed her forehead. "Not a blessed thing."

"But—"

"You've already taken good precautions. The tape is safe where it is, and since Grace will soon be on a plane back to Charleston we don't have to worry about her finding the key. Or anyone else for that matter. Nobody in their right mind would think to look in the dry cleaning for a safety-deposit key."

She was trying to make up her mind whether to bop him a third time when he kissed her again and said, "Not bad for an amateur."

Perhaps not. "You think?"

"*Mais,* yeah. And thank you for telling me. For now we'll keep this just between us."

She was glad she'd trusted him. The tape had been weighing on her mind because of not being able to contact Grace. Now she could stop worrying.

About Grace and the tape, at least.

Remi, on the other hand, was a whole other story.

Remi was worried.

He hid it from Muse, though. He didn't want her distracted by things that might never happen.

He'd much rather have her distracted by him.

He couldn't wait until bedtime. It had been touch-and-go for a while there as to whether or not they'd be speaking tonight, let alone sharing a bed. But luckily things seem to have smoothed out between them.

They stopped in the village to pick up a few items before

going to the cottage, and to give the shopkeeper a chance to mention if he'd seen any strangers in town. Dev was right, the villagers were incredibly loyal to "Mr. Devlin," as he was known in the area. Nobody pried into their business, but everyone they met treated them like old friends needing protection.

"Haven't seen a car all day that didn't belong," the man behind the register remarked. "But I'll be sure to let Mr. Devlin know if anyone starts asking questions."

Dev had also let Remi borrow his cell phone so they could get in touch with each other easily if necessary. Though Remi didn't like the fact that it wasn't a hundred percent secure, it was nice to have the option.

He pulled into the cottage driveway and sat for a minute quietly observing their hideaway for signs of trouble.

"So, how long before Davies finds us?" Muse said into the silence, eerily echoing his own thoughts.

"Why do you ask?"

"If there is a mole at the FBI office he'll be able to connect the dots and trace the call we just made to Morris."

"It'll take an expert to wade through Dev's creative routing," Remi offered hopefully.

"Davies has experts. Trust me."

So much for not worrying her. He should have known she'd be smart enough to figure it out for herself.

He didn't answer, but reached for her hand, leaned back in the crackling leather bucket seat, and instead thought about trusting Muse Summerville.

Did he trust her?

What the hell was trust?

And why did it matter, anyway?

For some reason it did.

He trusted her with his body. Oh, yeah, no problem there.

Oddly enough, he trusted her with his life. Put a gun in

this woman's hands and he was sure she'd blast anyone trying to hurt him.

Now, that put a smile on his face. Up until a few days ago it had always been him blasting the bad guys to save his own worthless behind. It was a novelty knowing there was someone else on the planet who cared enough to cover his back.

"Remi?"

Muse cared. Of that he had no doubt. If she didn't, she wouldn't trust him to the extent she did, with her body and her life.

But what about her heart?

"Is everything all right?"

No, she hadn't trusted him with her heart, and probably never would.

And that's why he couldn't trust her with his.

"I take it this means you want to leave."

Remi drifted out of his ponderings. He'd be fine with bodies and lives. Hearts didn't fit into his plans, anyway, regardless of how his ached at the thought of their parting.

"Why would I want to leave you?"

"I actually meant both of us." She gazed at him for a long moment. "*Are* you thinking of leaving me?"

"*Non,* of course not."

"What were you thinking about, then?"

"Hmm?"

She was still staring, so he pulled himself together. And allowed more immediate and agreeable subjects to drift back into his consciousness. One in particular which had been heating his imagination all day. Anticipation was the most powerful aphrodisiac in the world.

"I was thinking how we probably have a good day or two before we have to worry about Davies finding us here, and I was wondering what we could possibly do to pass all that time together." He smiled meaningfully.

A blush crept up her neck, painting banners of pink across her cheeks. He wondered if she'd been anticipating her decision about tonight as much he had, if she'd spent the day imagining what his tongue would feel like toying with her sensitive flesh, fantasizing about the erotic suction of his mouth on the soft undersides and tight peaks of her breasts. And elsewhere.

She didn't run, didn't turn, didn't even look down.

His body quickened, knowing instinctively what that meant for the coming night.

She was going to say yes.

Tonight she would be his. Completely.

Chapter 12

"Shall we?"

Muse's pulse went into hyperspace.

Four hours later and she was still so nervous it was a miracle she could stand, for the shaking in her legs.

"You mean bed? Already?"

Only 9:30.

After Remi's suggestive remark in the car this afternoon, he hadn't once brought up the subject again of making love. He hadn't had to. It was all she could think of even without a reminder.

It was all she could think of while preparing and eating supper. And it was all she could think of talking and relaxing with a cool drink on the verandah.

Now, as he led her back into the house and gathered her into his arms for their first kiss of the evening, it was definitely all she could think of.

"Will you be joining me?" he asked, moving his lips softly over hers. "In my bed?"

She wanted to run. She wanted to stay. She wanted to melt into a puddle at his feet. He wasn't holding her tight, wasn't kissing her hard. He was making it easy for her to say no, if that's what she wanted. She knew that's what he was doing, giving her an escape.

She didn't want an escape.

She wanted him.

"Yes," she whispered, understanding all she was consenting to. Trusting him to keep her safe as he made her his. "I want to be with you."

She felt a tremor pass through his body. Could he be as nervous as she?

No, not a man like Remi, so worldly and experienced. What would he have to be nervous about?

He left the bathroom door open as he took a shower—an invitation? She didn't have the courage to go in. She left it open, too, when she took hers, jumpy as a kink-tailed cat in a roomful of mousetraps, the hot shower spray useless against her unrelenting shivers. But he didn't come in, either.

When she'd finished and dried off, she thought about going to him as she was, sliding into bed without a stitch on. But she didn't have the courage for that, either. She donned his shirt, took a deep breath and walked into the bedroom.

Remi was reclining in the bed, looking handsome as the devil and sexy as sin. He'd draped a pink scarf over the nightstand lamp, which cast a rosy glow on the walls and the bed's lace coverlet, softening the monitor's blue. The radio played in the background, but she couldn't concentrate enough to hear what kind of music. The scent of flowers filled the room, and her eyes settled on a vase overflowing with fresh-cut roses from the garden.

"Oh, Remi," she whispered, not knowing what to do with herself.

"Vien ici, mon douce ange," he said, "my sweet, sweet angel."

She took a step toward him, then another. Watching his blue eyes turn to indigo and the scar on his lip curve slowly up. No man had ever looked at her as he was looking at her now, his gaze filled with hunger and desire…and something else.

Reverence?

She reached up and with trembling fingers began to unbutton her sleep shirt.

"Non." Remi held out his hand to her. "Wait."

She hesitated, slid her knees onto the mattress and he flipped back the covers, revealing his tall, powerful body to her. As was his habit, he was already nude. And massively aroused.

Her breath backed up in her lungs.

"Do you remember what you did to me last night?" he asked, voice low and gravelly. "How easy it was to control my body, with just your kiss?"

Her eyes locked with his, soaking up the courage he was deliberately gifting her with. Slowly her breath eased out.

"I want to feel that again," he whispered, "and more. I'll do anything you want, everything you ask, to feel that again."

She licked her lips, swept her gaze over his broad shoulders, his lean hips, his muscular thighs. And stopped at the long, thick male evidence of his desire for her.

It frightened her. Terrified her.

Not because she thought it would hurt her. But because she knew it wouldn't. And that would force her to admit it wasn't sex she had been avoiding all these years but feelings.

"Straddle me," he ordered in low tones vibrating with barely restrained want.

She swallowed deeply and did as he asked.

The thin silk of her panties might as well not be there. She could feel every tense muscle, every throbbing vein, every molecule of heat generated at the top of his thighs where she gingerly perched. Her own thighs, resting astride his hips, turned to thick, molten lead.

"You're in control now," he said. "Do what you will with me."

For a moment she was astounded that a strong, powerful man like Remi would give up his dominance to her so utterly and completely.

But then, wasn't that what he'd been doing all along?

Grateful and falling more in love every minute, she looked down at his big body beneath her, and saw not an instrument of terror but one of adoration.

"I've never been on top before," she admitted.

"I figured you hadn't. Why don't you take off that shirt now? Nice and slow," he softly suggested. "Before you ravish me."

She met his gaze, the ghosts of all past uncertainties fleeing in the light of his seductive smile.

"Who says I'm going to ravish you, sugarcane?"

His smile broadened. "I do."

"You said I was in control."

"You are." He winked. "That's how I know."

She tipped her head, put her hands to his ribs, watched him suck in his breath as she slowly ran them up his chest. "Pretty sure of yourself, aren't you?"

"*Mais,* yeah. My *grandmère,* she got da voodoo. Put a spell on me to make me irresistible to women."

Muse could believe that well enough. She smiled. "Is that so."

She leaned down and kissed him. He tasted so good her throat ached.

"Yeah. Now, about that shirt…"

She was ready. More than ready. One by one she slipped

the shirt buttons from their moorings, reveling in the voracious way Remi's eyes followed her every movement. Men had looked at her before, but until now not one of them had really seen her. Strangers had seen an object, friends had seen an image. She knew Remi was seeing Muse.

It was the scariest thing she'd ever experienced.

"*Si belle,*" he murmured, and slid the shirt from her shoulders and down her arms. "So beautiful." He tossed it aside.

She had seldom been this exposed in front of a man, but instead of being frightened, she felt a heavy burden lift from her heart.

This was a man who would never hurt her or be anything but sensitive and considerate. And she was in control.

It was an amazing feeling.

"I want to touch you again," she whispered, leaning down for another kiss. Brushing her fingertips over his nipple.

He moaned softly into her mouth. "You're going to test me, aren't you, *chère?*"

"How far will you let me go?"

"As far as you take me."

She liked the sound of that. This was new for her. A completely different kind of sexual experience. One where *she* set the limits. For the first time in her life she wanted to explore the possibilities of the physical.

Starting with her lover's body.

So she put her hands on him, touched him all over, caressed his limbs and torso, watched his eyes glaze over with pleasure, heard his breath grow labored, felt his arousal thicken beneath her.

She felt powerful, in charge.

Her movements became more sure, more decisive. More demanding. She leaned down to kiss him, lacing her fingers through his and bringing his hands above his head. She held him fast, enjoying how he moved under her as he rubbed his chest up against her breasts, bucked his hardness against her belly. She kissed him hard and long, fighting him when he made to unlace his fingers and lower his hands to her. Their panting breaths mingled in his groan.

Suddenly she realized what she was doing. She jerked back, staring at him in horror and contrition.

"I'm sorry," she gasped, pulling her hands from his.

He stared in confusion, then comprehension filled his eyes. He took her hands back, wove his fingers with hers and raised them above his head. "Don' even go there, honey. There's a big difference."

"But I'm forcing you."

His lips curved. "You hear me sayin' no?"

"No," she whispered.

"Am I yellin' for help?"

She shook her head, feeling the beginnings of a smile.

"Don't think for a minute this is the same thing that happened to you. The difference is I gave you permission."

She looked down at his handsome face, his perceptive eyes, and understood for the first time it hadn't been her fault. Her soul filled with an overwhelming relief.

His sensual mouth tipped up for more kisses. She obliged with a joyful sigh. "Anything I want?" she murmured.

"*Tout quoi ti veut.* Anything."

Slowly she sat up, bringing his hands with her, placing them on her thighs.

"In that case..."

She caught his gaze and held it as she slid his hands up her legs, over her hips, up her midriff, stopping just under her breasts. She watched his eyes close, then quickly glance toward the nightstand. On it were neatly lined up his Beretta in its holster, his handcuffs and wallet, Dev's cell phone, the extra gun he'd lent her...and a short stack of small square packets.

"Take off your panties."

Her pulse stalled, then zinged.

For a moment she faltered, floundering in the unfamiliar emotions invading her, the unexpected sensations flooding her body. The fire in her breasts, the sharp need between her legs, the almost painful excitement in her belly.

Then he touched her. Slid his fingers from hers and cupped her breasts. Rubbed his thumbs over the achy, hardened tips.

She scrambled to wriggle out of the confining silk, returned to straddle him, to feel his hands on her. All over her, like hot sunshine and cold snow all at the same time.

She shivered and sweated and moaned and loved everything he did to her. Loved the sensation of him under her, moving between her thighs, blazing like an inferno against the most intimate part of her, skin to skin.

He pulled her to her hands and knees, kissing her from below, kissing down her chin and throat, licking, nipping, coming ever closer to her breasts. When his mouth finally, finally closed over one pebble-hard tip she thought she would die of pleasure.

She cried his name, wanting, wanting more.

He tongued first one, then the other, holding them, squeezing them with his fingers, suckling them so she saw stars.

"Touch yourself," he murmured, and guided her hand between her legs. "Show me how you like it."

Her eyes went wide.

"I know you've done it. Show me."

"I can't."

"I want to know how to please you. Teach me." His fingers slid over her and she gasped. To her shock, they found wetness there. "Like this?" he asked.

Blushing furiously, she managed to nod, breathless, boneless, unable to protest when his fingers nudged hers to help him discover her most sensitive, receptive, hidden spots.

He was a quick study.

Her whole body trembled, quivering with electric sensation, building fast and tumultuous as a summer storm, crashing down with a flash of blinding pleasure that stole the breath from her lungs and collapsed her limbs. She lay upon him panting.

And rose to consciousness to the feel of him grasping her hips, lifting them and slowly sliding her onto his long, thick arousal.

She'd never felt anything so good in her life.

"Okay?" he asked.

"Wonderful." She sighed with pleasure, stirring herself to move with him. To kiss him.

"C'mon now, you're in control here."

"You take over for a while."

She felt him smile against her mouth. "If you insist."

And he did.

Brilliantly.

Rousingly.

Shudderingly.

He felt so right; together they felt so right. The sensations he created within her were amazing, like nothing she'd ever dreamed were possible. She gave herself up to him completely. Surrendered to the bliss of his body and the unflinching possession he claimed of her own.

He thrust and touched and kissed and guided, and all she could do was hang on for the ride, wanting it to go on forever but craving the sweet conclusion they both were speeding toward far too quickly.

"*Vien!*" he cried, and she went with him, tumbling over the precipice, calling his name again and again in breathless disbelief that she could ever feel this much pleasure.

And as they finally crumpled to a sweat-slick heap of

tangled arms and legs, kissing each other with sated joy and winded devotion, Dev's cell phone rang.

Remi froze where he lay, instantly alert. *Bien,* as alert as a man could be under the circumstances.

Muse looked up from his chest, her blue eyes soft, face flushed and radiant and her blond hair a mess. He'd never seen anything so pretty in all his days.

The phone rang again, yanking him out of love's afterglow.

"It must be Dev," Muse murmured. "Wonder why he's calling?"

Dev would never call unless it was an emergency. Remi grabbed the phone and punched the Talk button. *"Dis moi."*

"There have been further developments with Muse's sister," Dev said without preamble.

This was not what Remi needed right now. "What kind of developments?"

"Some New Orleans cop named Creole Levalois has gone rogue, trying to hunt down James Davies in order to settle a personal score."

"What does that have to do with Grace?"

"Apparently he met up with Grace and has convinced her to pose as Muse around the Quarter, trying to lure Gary Fox out of hiding. I assume as a way to get to Davies."

Remi cursed roundly. "This from your contact at the Eighth again?"

"Yep."

"Anything new from Morris?"

"Nope."

Damn, damn, damn. "All right. Thanks, old man."

He hung up and returned the phone to the nightstand, wondering what the hell he was going to tell Muse.

She was peering up at him, alerted by the mention of her sister's name. "What's happened to Grace?"

He put his arms around her, tried to rub her back. ‘‘Nothing’s happened to her. Not exactly. But she hasn’t left New Orleans yet.’’

‘‘What? Why not?’’ Muse sat up, grabbing his hand. ‘‘Remi, what’s going on?’’

He let his gaze move over her, his beautiful lover with her wild golden halo and succulent breasts shaped like two ripe mangoes begging to be plucked. And sighed with the certain knowledge he was about to be denied his fervent desire to do just that.

‘‘She’s joined up with some rogue cop from the NOPD, and is pretending to be you all over the Quarter.’’

Horror permeated Muse’s face. ‘‘Why? Why would she do that?’’

He shook his head. ‘‘I don’t know. Dev said Morris hasn’t been in touch.’’

‘‘It’s him. Morris has to be Davies’s informer. We’ve got to go to New Orleans. Warn Grace.’’ She tugged on his hand, pulling him up.

He pulled her back on the bed. ‘‘We don’t know anything for sure. There could be lots of explanations why Morris hasn’t been in touch and why Grace is with this cop.’’

‘‘Masquerading as me?’’

‘‘Yeah.’’

‘‘Like what?’’

He cleared his throat. ‘‘I don’t know, maybe Morris got appendicitis, too. Maybe this cop is one of your old boyfriends and Grace took a shine to him. Maybe—’’ He stopped at Muse’s furious look.

‘‘I only have *one* old boyfriend, and Grace doesn’t ‘take a shine’ to men,’’ she mimicked angrily. ‘‘She’s not the type. Especially if he’s anything like—’’ This time she stopped.

He set his jaw. ‘‘Like me?’’ he asked coolly, sliding from the bed and heading for the bathroom.

"Like a rogue," she completed loudly, but he knew better than to believe that's what she'd intended to say. "Grace isn't into rogues."

"Like you are, you mean?"

"I refuse to have this inane discussion while Grace is in danger of being tortured and killed. I'm going."

She got up and had almost made it to the bedroom door when Remi caught up with her.

"You're not going anywhere," he said, grasping her arm.

"Let go of me, Beaulieux. You can't stop me."

"Oh, but I can. And I will, if I have to."

Her eyes sparked with anger. "What if Grace finds the tape and gives it to this rogue cop? What if the cop works for Davies?"

She didn't have to complete the thought. Remi got the idea. If Levalois was dirty and only using Grace to retrieve the video, he'd kill her when he got hold of it.

Still, that didn't explain the masquerade. Or why he might work for a man he had a personal vendetta against. It didn't add up.

"Morris has promised to take care of Grace and he will," Remi assured her.

"But what if he's the mole?"

"Then Davies already knows Grace isn't you and doesn't know a thing about any stolen video. Morris has no reason to let Grace get hurt. It only draws attention to himself and the case."

She jerked her arm from his grasp but didn't move. "I guess you have a point," she said grudgingly.

"Muse, I can't let you go to New Orleans. You have to see that. It's too dangerous."

"But my sister—"

"She'll be fine. I'm sure Morris and Simmons have talked to her by now and she's packing her bags for home. There's no choice here. We have to stick to my plan."

"I want to call Morris."

Remi ground his teeth. The woman was impossible. Didn't she see he was only doing this to keep her safe?

No, she only cared about her sister. Who did *that* remind him of?

"All right, fine. We'll call him."

Remi didn't know why it angered him so much that she'd choose concern for Grace over trusting his judgment. After all, Grace was blood kin and it was perfectly natural Muse should worry about her.

Nonetheless, he punched in the number with unnecessary violence and snapped at the receptionist who answered the call.

Maybe it had something to do with the fact that up until ten minutes ago he'd been experiencing the most amazing night of his life with this woman, and now she was insulting him, trying to tie knots in his plan and couldn't wait to get away from him.

All of which served to remind him once again of the perfidy of emotional relationships.

In the end the other person always chose someone else more important to them, and Remi was left holding his heart in his hand.

He wordlessly passed the phone to Muse when Morris came on the line.

Dev was right to avoid women completely. Remi'd have to seriously consider adopting the policy himself.

He looked at the naked woman standing so close to him, and had never felt so alone. The lovespell surrounding them earlier had been broken, the warm feelings between them shattered. He fought back the urge to take her in his arms, hug her tight and tell her everything would be all right.

Because she didn't want that from him.

She handed back the phone without a word, and he didn't

ask what Morris had told her. He could see she'd resigned herself to staying and that was good enough for now.

Yeah, he'd managed to sweet-talk her into his bed, and they'd had a great time. But you couldn't sweet-talk a woman into having feelings for you if she didn't. It was as simple as that.

Which was just as well. Because any kind of relationship between Remi Beaulieux and Muse Summerville beyond here and now was just plain impossible.

No matter how deeply he felt about her.

The thought was so depressing he didn't even protest when she silently turned on a heel, stalked out of his room into her own and closed the door behind her.

Chapter 13

Muse lay for a long time in her lonely bed before falling asleep, thinking about Grace and worrying herself sick.

She could kill Remi. She was devastated by this inflexible, controlling side of the man she thought was different from all the rest. In bed he was a dream come true, but with clothes on he insisted on calling all the shots regardless of her feelings, and refused to listen to her opinion or concerns.

How could he be so nurturing when it came to making love and so insensitive when it came to her worries about her sister?

It wasn't the sex, and it wasn't Remi's job keeping them apart. It was his unerring need to be in charge—a need she couldn't live with. Despite his physical warmth and wonderful sexual understanding, he was too controlling. Always, it was his way or no way.

What could it hurt to drive to New Orleans and speak to Grace for five minutes, to explain what was going on and then leave as quickly as they'd come? Davies would never be the wiser, and then she'd know her twin was safe.

But no, Mr. Macho FBI Agent couldn't deviate from his precious plan. Grace didn't figure in the plan, therefore Grace was out of luck.

Muse understood perfectly that having a well-thought-out strategy was a good thing sometimes, and certain people needed the security of always knowing where they were headed. Considering his background, it wasn't surprising Remi was one of those people. But not Muse. Okay, running for your life might be one time having a plan was smart. However, you still had to be flexible about things.

Nothing *ever* went according to plan. At least in her life it didn't. Flexibility and spontaneity were a must.

She didn't think those words were even in Remi's vocabulary.

Punching her pillow, she turned over for the hundredth time since climbing into her cold bed, trying to get comfortable. Which was tough because her pillow was soaking wet.

There wasn't a man on earth more wrong for her than the inflexible, plan-obsessed, gone-tomorrow Special Agent Remi Beaulieux.

So why did she miss him so damn much?

And why, oh, why had this happened on the most wonderful night of her entire life?

Staring at the ceiling, she let the tears trickle down her cheeks unimpeded. Best to let it all out tonight. Let the memories of their lovemaking flood her mind, recalling the joy and happiness he'd shown her she could experience with a man. Concentrate on the past night with him.

Not on the fact that she knew with sinking certainty no other man would ever be able to take his place.

Or that come morning she'd have to pretend none of it had ever happened.

Because it was that or lose her sanity completely when he moved on to his next case, leaving her behind.

* * *

Remi did his best not to think about what was happening with Muse, but didn't have a lot of success. Sleep came only in fits and starts. After Muse went to her own room, he tossed and turned, unable to get away from the scent of her and their lovemaking, or the overwhelming ache of wanting her back. He needed her sleeping next to him in his bed.

He was also unable to stop checking the security camera monitor to make sure she was safe in her room. With his protectee sleeping every night until now snug up against him, he'd forgotten what a bitch 24/7 surveillance normally was.

And he was worried about Davies.

He'd told Muse they had at least a day or two before yesterday's phone call to Morris could connect them to Dev, but one should never be complacent about such things. Especially after phoning Morris again last night.

As soon as possible Remi wanted to implement Plan B. Which meant getting out of the cottage first thing tomorrow.

And going home to Verdigris.

The next morning Remi awoke feeling like crap.

He missed Muse like hell. He wanted her back. In his bed. In his life. Speaking to him.

The silence during breakfast was deafening, broken only by the beep-beep-beep of the security monitors.

He was sorry to have to keep Muse from going to her sister, but it was the only thing he could do. His job was to protect her life until James Davies was behind bars, and no other considerations could be allowed to come into play.

He could not be swayed by the tears she was trying so hard to hide from him or the loss of the incredible closeness they had found last night.

"Come on, Muse. This is ridiculous," he finally blurted

out, as she quietly washed the breakfast dishes. "Didn't last night mean anything to you?"

She spun and gave him a recriminating look. It broke his heart to see her eyes all puffy and red, her lashes spiked with moisture.

"That's not fair. You know it did."

"Then talk to me."

"About what?"

"About whether I can have a kiss good morning."

She turned back to the dishes. "That wouldn't be a good idea."

He rose and went to her, stood close so he could smell her fruity shampoo and the unique scent of her that always made him dizzy with want. "Why not?"

Her spine straightened, and he barely resisted running his knuckles along its elegant curve. She was wearing another of those sexy summer dresses he loved so much, short and shapely in a bright shade of violet. Like the irises his *grand-mère* used to grow in her garden at Terrebeau. He wondered if they were in bloom right now. Did irises bloom in August?

"Because I might end up in bed with you again, and that would be a really bad idea."

His attention whipped back to the conversation. "Doesn't sound so bad to me." He moved in, pressing his body gently into hers. When she didn't protest he put his arms around her. "I missed you. I couldn't sleep."

A sigh shuddered through her. "I missed you, too."

"Then—"

She stepped away from him and despite the warmth of the morning a chill went down his suddenly empty arms.

"We've both agreed nothing can come of us. And even if it could, we're too different to make it work."

"This is about Grace, isn't it." It wasn't really a question; he knew it was. Muse was punishing him for doing his job.

"No. Yes. Partly. The point is, I won't start something I already know will end badly for me."

"Too late for that, *chère.* We started a long time ago, the first minute we saw each other."

She looked down at the floor, toed the rag rug with her sandal.

"And what about me?" he asked. "Won't it end badly for me, too?"

"I doubt I'm the first woman you've slept with on a case."

He wanted to deny it. Hotly. But he couldn't. Sex was sometimes an inescapable part of undercover work. But it had never been like this. Never been a woman he'd had more than a fleeting fancy for. A woman he really cared about. Deeply.

He reached out, grasped her chin and lifted her face so she was forced to look at him.

"Muse, I..." Suddenly it scared the hell out of him what might come out of his mouth. Should he tell her how he really felt? Or should he let it go, admit she was right and let *her* go? The moment stretched, along with the silence, her eyes warily watching him. His heart beat a loud tattoo, drowning out the steady beeps of the security monitors.

And suddenly he realized, there really *weren't* any beeps.

In less than a second he'd drawn his weapon, grabbed Muse and lunged for the closest solid wall.

"Get down!" he shouted over her surprised yelp, pushing her to her knees.

"What's going—"

"Somebody's breached the security system," he whispered, doing a careful visual of the kitchen, windows and doors. *Clear.* He pulled his extra weapon from his waistband and put it into her hands. "Stay down. Shoot anything that moves. I'm checking the monitors."

He sprinted low for the bedroom, scanned the split

screens and saw what he was looking for. A man crouched just inside the back perimeter. He must have somehow disabled the system. Which meant a pro.

Remi grabbed his duffel bag, which he always kept packed, rejected the idea of fetching Muse's things which he was pretty sure were spread out all over her room, and dashed back to the kitchen.

"Let's go."

Easing open the door leading to the garage, he did a quick check then hustled her into the Porsche parked inside.

"Down on the floor and stay there."

She hadn't uttered a word since that yelp, but he'd seen the look in her eyes when she'd realized what was going on. He never wanted to see that look again as long as he lived.

He started the car and hit the garage-door opener at the same time, thanking God he'd chosen the Porsche and not a tall SUV. As soon as he thought the roof would clear he gunned it, careening out the driveway like a bat out of hell.

Shots popped after them, and he heard the rip of canvas, the thud of metal being pierced, and the zing of bullets ricocheting off something solid.

For a horrifying second he thought Muse would jump up to return fire, but he sent her a warning glare and she stayed put.

It wasn't until they'd made it past the village and lost themselves in a maze of local country roads that Muse looked up and gasped, "You're bleeding!" and he realized he'd been hit.

"Pull over this instant!" Muse ordered as she vaulted up off the floor and leaned over the gearshift to check Remi's chest wound.

He batted her hands away. "I can't. We have to get away from here."

"You'll do as I say," she said steadily enough, but her heart was beating out of control. "I don't want you fainting on me from loss of blood."

He muttered something in French and pulled the car onto a dirt road and stopped behind a hedge.

She fumbled with the buttons of his shirt, finding it impossible to make her fingers work. Why couldn't the man wear T-shirts like everyone else on the planet?

"Let me," he said, taking over. The crisp white cloth had a huge pool of crimson around a long, ugly tear a few inches below his heart.

When he'd undone the last button, she anxiously yanked the shirt aside. She heard a sob and suddenly everything went blurry.

"I'm fine, Muse. Just a flesh wound," he said with a calm she couldn't understand, considering the amount of blood pumping out of his chest. "Get a clean shirt from my bag. There should be a first-aid kit in the glove compartment."

She heard the words but couldn't move. He reached past her and popped the latch, pulling out a white plastic box. "A shirt, Muse. The back seat. Sometime today."

Forcing herself to snap out of it, she floundered with his bag until she managed to unzip it far enough to drag something light tan from its depths. "This okay?"

"Perfect. Darlin', I appreciate you worryin', but remember we've got bad guys after us. Let's try to hurry, okay?"

She blinked twice and her vision cleared a little. "Okay."

She wasn't sure what he did, but within seconds it seemed, his chest was bound up in tan cloth and white gauze—apparently with her help because he kissed her and said, "Thank you," before he fired up the car again and bumped back onto the road.

She had to get hold of herself. Mental paralysis would not make matters any better.

"Where are we going?" she asked, proud of how her voice hardly shook at all.

"Home," he said, shocking her out of her daze.

"My apartment?" she asked in confusion. "Or Beau Saint-Coeur?"

"*Beau sans coeur* will never be my home," he said evenly. "We're going to Terrebeau."

"Your cousin's place? Aren't you afraid of involving them?"

"Yeah. But Beau's the only person left I can trust. Besides, I feel sorry for anyone who tries to mess with him or his people. Did I mention he's chief of police up there?"

She glanced over at the smile in his voice and felt a shade less afraid. Leaning her head back on the seat she closed her eyes. "So," she said softly, "I guess I get to meet your family."

Now that was a scary thought.

What would they be like? Would she like them? Would they like her?

And why did it matter so much?

At least thinking about meeting his favorite cousin might help distract her from worrying about Remi passing out from his wound, or about Davies's man catching up to them and then being shot down like in the last scene from that old Bonnie and Clyde movie. Neither of which she particularly wanted to dwell on.

"How far away is it?"

"Three hours normally," he answered. "But I think I'll take the scenic route."

It ended up taking more than five hours to make the drive to Verdigris, which was located a good bit up the Atchafalaya River, toward the middle of the state. They only stopped twice, which Muse insisted on to check his wound and change the bindings.

"Pretty country," she remarked as they drove down a narrow dirt road in between lush fields and groves of Spanish-moss-draped trees, with the occasional swamp thrown in just to remind you that you were in Louisiana.

"Yeah," Remi said noncommittally.

"Where are we?"

"Beau Saint-Coeur."

"Really?" she said, shocked. "But I thought—"

"I'm taking the back way into Terrebeau. You have to go over my father's land to get there."

He'd told her enough about his family situation that she wasn't quite sure what to say.

"Don' worry, I doubt we'll run into him. He's not one for working the fields. He leaves all that to Zeph."

"Your brother?"

"Half brother," he corrected, and the tone of his voice clearly said he didn't like claiming even that much.

Nonetheless she sensed he wanted to talk about it. "Who was Zeph's mother?" she asked.

After a short pause Remi said, "Sophia Lafayette. One of the housemaids."

"Ah."

"Daddy had a small house built for her on the other side of the property. She still lived there when I left."

"That must have been hard on your mother," she murmured.

He gave her an inscrutable look but didn't comment. Instead he pulled the Porsche off the road and parked on a patch of meadow overlooking the confluence of a good-size bayou and the big river.

"So Zeph works the land for your father?"

"Always did. I took off, and before that I was too busy makin' trouble. Not that he'd let me touch his beloved plantation even if I hadn't been." Remi glanced over, his expression wry. "Sorry. Didn' mean to have a pity party."

She gave him an understanding smile. ''When was the last time you were here?''

''Few years back. I was involved in a case that brought me back to Verdigris.'' He grinned. ''That's when Beau met Kit. She thought I was a jewel thief and tried to nab me. Caught the chief of police instead.''

Muse laughed. ''Your cousin Beau?''

''Get her to tell you the story. It's a doozy.''

They sat in companionable silence for several minutes, looking out at the lovely scenery.

''Don't you miss them?'' she asked, thinking of her own mother and sister, suddenly missing them with a pain that burned clear through her heart. ''Wouldn't you like to live here, close to them?''

''That'll never happen,'' he said flatly. ''Not as long as my daddy's still breathin'.''

''And when he's gone? What about Beau Saint-Coeur? Surely as the oldest you'll inherit the plantation.''

He shook his head with a humorless laugh. ''*Non,* that I doubt. I was probably disinherited a long time ago. It'll all go to Zeph, I'm sure.''

''How can you be so certain?''

''I better hope I am.'' He let out a long sigh. ''If not I guess I'm stuck with it. This place has been in the family since long before the War Between the States. God knows every one of my ancestors would roll over in his grave if I sold it or gave it away.''

Lord have mercy, that would be a difficult situation for anyone. At Dev's, she'd spoken disparagingly about his family ties. But seeing him now, here, she knew she had been dead wrong. It was obvious he took this responsibility of the land very seriously.

''You don't want it?''

He shook his head. ''Too many bad memories.'' He unbuckled gingerly and got out of the car. ‘‘Don’ think I have to worry, though. Daddy still doesn’t believe I’m his.’’

She joined him, leaning against a nearby tree. ‘‘The man needs his eyes examined. Even I can see the family resemblance. Can’t you prove it somehow?’’

He glanced at her.

‘‘You know, a DNA test or something. You could—’’

‘‘Already did that years ago. Decided not to tell him.’’

Her jaw dropped. ‘‘You had yourself tested?’’

His shoulders lifted. ‘‘Against a sample from Grandmère. I’m his, all right.’’

‘‘And you didn’t tell him? Why not?’’

‘‘Too late. The damage had been done. I didn’ care anymore.’’ His eyes narrowed and he looked out at the bayou. ‘‘Though I’ll admit I’ve dreamed of mailing the report to the old bastard when he’s on his deathbed. Just to send him to his grave feeling as guilty as possible.’’

‘‘Remi! That’s awful.’’

‘‘Yeah. But you know what they say about revenge.’’

His words were bitter, but she could tell from his face he didn’t really mean it. At least, she didn’t think he did.

Come to think of it, his expression was more than a little peculiar. She followed his gaze to where he was looking out at the water.

There was a man in a *bateau* putt-putting down the bayou. He spotted them and pulled the boat ashore.

‘‘Do you know him?’’ she asked as the tall, sandy-haired man started walking slowly up the riverbank toward them.

‘‘Oh, yeah.’’ Remi said.

She turned to him, puzzled by the intensity in his voice. ‘‘Who is he?’’

‘‘That,’’ he said, standing up straight and spreading his feet like a gunfighter, ‘‘is my half brother, Zeph.’’

Chapter 14

This was just what Remi needed to round out a really perfect day. Not.

Well, at least Muse was speaking to him again. That was worth being shot for. He'd get through this, too.

Remi did his best to appear cool and professional as his brother approached, but the effect was somewhat spoiled by the ripped, bloody shirt and bandaging around his chest.

''You run into your father?'' were Zeph's first words. He looked like he might actually believe it, too.

Remi couldn't help smiling. Zeph always did have a dry sense of humor behind the serious facade. If the man weren't a stinking, usurping bastard, he might actually like the guy.

''Nah,'' he said, and glanced down at the blood covering his chest. ''Just a little difference of opinion with some bad guys.''

Zeph's brows flicked. ''You should get some medical attention, Special Agent Beaulieux.''

Remi crossed his arms over his chest, checking the grimace of pain the movement produced. "Suddenly worried about my health, Lafayette?"

Muse cut off any interesting reply his brother might have had by interjecting, "I've been telling him that for the past five hours," She stuck out her hand. "Hi, I'm Muse Summerville. I hear you're Remi's brother. Nice to meet you."

"Zéphirain Lafayette," the other man murmured politely, shaking her hand. Zeph always was a bit shy with women. Probably something to do with being an illegitimate bastard.

"*Half* brother," Remi corrected. "Listen Zeph, we're going to be spending a few days at Beau's." He subtly adjusted his shoulder holster. "But I'd appreciate if you wouldn't mention to anyone you've seen us."

Zeph's eyes searched his. "All right."

"The bad guys were really shooting at me," Muse said into the awkward moment. "I don't relish the idea of them finding us. If you know what I mean."

"Yeah," Zeph said uncertainly, hesitated, then looked back at Remi and asked, "If I see any strangers nosing around town, you want me to phone Beau?"

Remi was momentarily taken aback, but managed to say, "That would be a big help," without sounding too astonished. Zeph was quiet and minded his own business, but he knew every living soul within a hundred miles of Beau Saint-Coeur, and therefore Terrebeau. His assistance as a lookout would be invaluable.

"Well, I'll be moving along. Pleasure to meet you, ma'am," Zeph said and took his leave, striding back down the riverbank and pushing the *bateau* onto the bayou, headed for the big river.

Remi stared after him, not knowing what to think.

"He seemed nice."

Muse's observation brought him out of his bafflement.

"Yeah."

"What?"

He shook his head. "Nothing, really." Except that Zeph seemed to be attempting to bridge the gap in their lifelong animosity. Why would he do that?

"He was right about the medical attention, you know."

He gave her a smile. "It's just a scratch. Not worth sewing up."

"You must like having scars."

He fingered the one over his lip, which he'd gotten in a bar fight down in Oaxaca. "Adds character to a man."

She rolled her eyes. "What if it gets infected?"

"I'll take a careful shower when we get to Beau's." He ran a finger down her cheek. "You can join me, smear some ointment on it." He moved closer. "Or all over me, if you like."

She demurred when he reached for a kiss.

"Aw, come on, *chère*. Just one?"

She kept her face turned downward, but she didn't step back. "Remi, don't make this harder than it already is."

"Darlin', it couldn' get much harder than it already is."

He felt the warmth of her breath on his throat as she sighed. "You're impossible," she murmured.

"*Non,* I'm pretty damn easy," he replied, tipping her chin up with a finger. "I want you, Muse. Once is not enough for me. Not by far."

"Don't do this to me, sugarcane," she whispered. "Don't make me fall in love with you. I couldn't take it when you leave me."

It had surely been a day for shocks, but this one left him reeling.

He wanted to take her in his arms, tell her, "Who says I'll ever leave you?" and end the story on that note. A lingering kiss, fade to black with the words "The End" scrolling across the screen, and they'd live happily ever after.

But the real world wasn't like the movies. So he didn't snatch her back when she walked away from him toward the car.

"Let's go," she said without a backward glance, "and meet the rest of your family."

Terrebeau had changed.

Remi could see it in the manicured oak allée, in the well-tended gardens, in the splash of whitewash on all the fences, in the very air surrounding the old plantation house.

It was bright, cheerful and welcoming. What had always been a grand old dignified antebellum mansion was now a cozy home.

Kit had worked wonders.

"It's gorgeous," Muse breathed in awe as they parked in the circular drive in front of the columned entry.

Before they could open the doors, a small black-haired toddler burst onto the front verandah and yelled, "Who dere? Who dere?" then squealed, "Unca Remi! Unca Remi!"

The child plunged down the front steps like a Tasmanian devil and launched himself into Remi's arms with no regard to blood or bandages or gunshot wounds.

"T-Bone!"

Remi throttled the pain of being mauled by his three-year-old cousin-once-removed and lifted him into a big hug. He needed a hug bad, and this was just the guy to give him a real good one.

"*Ça va, mon 'tit garçon?* How's it goin'?"

"We *va!*" T-Bone wriggled in his arms and looked at Muse. "She you sis'er?" he asked loudly. "I'ma havea sis'er!"

"*C'est vrai?* That's great!"

"I'ma be da big sponsapildy." His eyes glowed with pride.

Remi chuckled and looked up in time to see Kit coming out of the front door, belly first. "Remi!" she called in joyful surprise.

Damn, it was nice when people were glad to see you.

She rushed down the steps and added her rounded figure to T-Bone's exuberant hug. "We didn't expect you! What brings you to— Oh! You're hurt!" she exclaimed, and peeled her baby off him as she looked in horror at his mess of a chest. "My God, what's happened?"

That's when she noticed Muse standing uncharacteristically quietly by the side of the Porsche. Muse smiled at Kit's frozen confusion. "Hi, I'm Muse," she said, but didn't budge an inch. "I tried to get him to the emergency room, but he wouldn't listen."

Kit swung her gaze to Remi and back to Muse. "Oh, what a surprise," she said just as Beau's head poked over the side of the second-floor gallery.

"Hey! Remi! What the—" Beau's smile vanished along with the rest of him. The sound of French doors slamming heralded his cousin's quick assessment of the situation and momentary arrival.

"We, uh, ran into a little trouble," Remi told Kit and allowed himself to be ushered along with Muse into the foyer of the big house, where Beau was already sprinting down the elaborate, curved staircase.

"They ran into trouble," Kit repeated to her husband and set T-Bone onto the floor, where he promptly scurried away.

"Well," Beau said, halting at the foot of the stairs. He planted his hands on his hips, looking every inch the aristocratic Southern gentleman. "I can see that. Delia," he addressed their matronly housekeeper who had appeared from the kitchen, wiping her hands on a towel. Delia had been with the Terrebeau Beaulieux family since forever—as long as Remi could remember, anyway. "Set two more places for supper, if you will, and call Jamie to fetch our guests' luggage from the car. Tell him to put it in the Oriental room. Or...?"

"That would be fine," Remi gratefully agreed.

At precisely the same time Muse said with a blush, "I'd prefer two rooms, if it's not too much bother."

Unless you knew Beau extremely well you'd have missed the amused quirk that flashed past the very corner of his mouth. *Saloperie!* There was such a thing as knowing a person too well. Beau certainly hadn't missed the implications of that unfortunate little exchange.

"The Oriental room and Lady Jane, then, Delia. Please." Beau instructed, his eyes sparkling annoyingly.

Remi groaned inwardly. Lady Jane was the name given to the virginal Victorian bedroom that connected to the opulently sensual Oriental den of sin, both decorated long ago by some long-dead Terrebeau patriarch, as obnoxiously witty as the present one. No doubt Remi'd be stuck sleeping on the narrow, rock-hard, unadorned virgin's bed staring at a dour portrait of God knew which ancient relative.

He looked to Kit for support, but she just stifled a grin.

"Old man, I think you'd better introduce us to your lady, and tell us about the trouble you're in."

Beau put his arm around his wife, who gave Remi a wink and added, "Oh, and about the shooting, too, of course."

Kit insisted Remi clean up and change his bandages before doing anything else. When he reluctantly went with Delia and Beau to be seen to, Kit turned to Muse.

"Would you like to freshen up, too, Miss Summerville?"

"Please, call me Muse. And yes, I'd love to."

Kit gave her the cook's tour of the house as they went up to the third floor. It was huge and beautiful and amazing. Muse had seen grand homes like this in Charleston, of course, but only after paying an admittance fee.

"It's mostly Beau's doing," Kit said, looking somewhat

awed herself. "It's been sort of a life-long mission for him to return it to what it was years ago." She leaned in conspiratorially. "Honestly, I don't dare touch a thing. I'm still getting used to it all."

"Not from around here?" Muse asked.

"A farm in Iowa," Kit said with a self-deprecating smile.

Muse had liked Kit immediately, and the woman's natural modesty and pride in her husband's heritage only reinforced her feelings. She could imagine Kit felt as much a fish out of water as Muse would under the circumstances. Thank goodness Remi had no plans to take on his own family estate, if it was anything like this.

She halted that thought in its tracks. Even if he did, it would be no concern of hers. It's not as if he would ask her to live there with him. Or that she would say yes if he did.

Would she?

"Looks like you could use a sympathetic ear," Kit said with an understanding smile.

Muse sighed, and then did something totally out of character. She walked into her assigned bedroom, sat down on the bed and spilled the whole tangled tale, Remi included.

"You're really worried about your sister, aren't you?" Kit said when she'd finished.

"Incredibly worried. And that's what Remi doesn't get. I just don't understand why he's so inflexible about this."

Kit leaned back against the scarlet silk-upholstered headboard and regarded her. "How much do you know about Remi's childhood?"

"Enough to know it wasn't very happy, except for the times here with Beau and his family."

"Remi's a very strong man. A lot of people would have gone under with an upbringing like that. But once he was old enough, he managed to pull himself out of it by concentrating on what he wanted. He set goals and, one by one, accomplished them all. For a long time his plans were his only anchor in life."

"He claims they still are," Muse said wearily. "Because of his undercover work."

Kit nodded sagely. "He would. He's still caught up in that mentality. I think it's time he realized his life is now his own, and he doesn't need to compensate for the past anymore."

Muse stared at Kit, the words resonating. "You think that's what he's doing? Compensating for the past?"

"Isn't it obvious?"

The exact diagnosis Grace would give, no doubt. Except Grace would go one step further. She would say Muse was doing precisely the same thing with her own lifestyle, chasing after the approval of an absent father who didn't deserve the agony of heartache she'd spent on him—avoiding life's real responsibilities. Hadn't Grace been saying that for years?

Muse had always told her she was the crazy one, and laughed it off. After all, Muse had a college diploma and a good job as a paralegal.

But could it really be true? Did responsibility go beyond those superficial material things, down into the realm of the emotional? She'd never thought so before, but now she wasn't so sure.

And if it did, what did that mean to her relationship with Remi?

It bore thinking about.

Kit stood, glancing at the clock. "Well, we'd better see what our boys are up to. Delia probably has T-Bone down for his nap by now so we can all talk in peace." She gave Muse the grin of a mother who loves her baby but knows very well he's a handful and is grateful for the break.

"This'll just take me a minute," Muse said, going into

the adjoining bath to freshen up. "T-Bone is an interesting name," she called, not wanting to stop their chat.

Kit laughed. "It started out as T-Beau, which stands for *petit*—little—Beau in Cajun. Then a friend of ours got to calling him T-Bon when he was being good, but of course to him that meant his favorite meal—steak—and he decided he liked that one best of all, so he's been T-Bone ever since." She made a face as Muse returned to the bedroom. "The joys of a bilingual family."

Muse grinned. "And you've got another on the way?"

Kit groaned. "Six months and the baked-potato jokes are already old. I feel sorry for the poor baby girl."

They laughed together and went down to join the men.

"Good news," Remi said as soon as they walked into the living room. It was formally decorated, brimming with antiques and expensive-looking artwork, but somehow it still managed to look cozy. "I checked in with Dev, and he says Morris sent another e-mail. He and Simmons met with Grace and that cop Levalois this morning. They've assigned two men to guard her until she leaves town."

"She's going right away, right?"

"He didn't say. But I assume so."

"Thank God."

Muse heaved a sigh of relief, feeling less stressed-out than she had in weeks. Ever since she'd broken up with Gary Fox, her life had been filled with tension and chaos. First the blond man following her every move, then running for her life with Remi, now Grace being in danger because of her. This was the very first time she could actually relax and feel relatively safe; for the moment all factors seemed under control.

Taking a seat on the luxurious sofa next to Remi, she curled up and sat back to listen to him and Beau tell stories of growing up on Terrebeau, and the one about how Beau and Kit met.

A while later, when a sleepy T-Bone toddled in from his nap and crawled onto his mama's lap to listen, too, Muse's heart melted in her chest. He was so cute and looked so much like his daddy, and the family was so obviously blissfully happy together. It brought the sting of tears to her eyes.

How perfect their life seemed! How she longed to share a similar happiness with a man and a couple kids of her own.

Remi had shown her last night that against all odds it might be possible. After so many years of not believing it could ever happen to her, to suddenly think it could… The thought filled her with hope.

Which was immediately crushed.

The only man on earth she could imagine such a life with was Remi. But he didn't want a life like this. Not with her, not with anyone.

Even if she could talk him into staying with her for a while, he was bound to get restless and leave her in the end. He was like her father. Not willing to make the sacrifices necessary to keep a family together.

And like her. She'd inherited those same traits from her father. Hadn't she always been a gypsy, moving on at the first sign of anyone wanting to tie her down?

She took another long look at Beau, Kit and T-Bone, sitting close and laughing, exchanging kisses and looks of loving affection.

And wondered if she wasn't wrong about that, too.

The afternoon went by quickly. Remi showed Muse the cemetery fence he'd told her about, and she took some photos while listening to Beau tell the old family legend associated with it.

As it got closer to suppertime, they were joined by the rest of the Terrebeau clan—Beau's parents, Dori and Gunny, and his sister, Jolene. The only one missing was Remi and

Beau's grandmother, Madame Beaulieux. But just as they moved into the dining room to eat, Delia walked in with her on her arm.

Remi's whole face lit up when he spotted the old woman. "Grandmère! You look wonderful!" he said, embracing the frail figure. "It's so good to see you up and about again."

"*C'est le contentement, ça.* The happiness of seeing my family together again and thriving, it does my heart good."

"Mine, too, Grandmère. I'm glad I don't have to sneak in to see you anymore."

Remi had told Muse how he'd had to slip in secretly to see his grandmother during the long years of his supposed estrangement as the family's black sheep. She was the only one he'd entrusted with the secret of his FBI undercover work—because she was ill he didn't want her to pass on thinking he was a notorious criminal. But thanks to that case involving Beau and Kit, everyone knew and he was able to visit more frequently, without having to sneak around Beau to see her.

As Muse watched them hug, Madame Beaulieux's gaze lit upon her. "Ah!" the old woman exclaimed, and an odd light of recognition passed through her eyes. She turned to Remi expectantly.

Remi paused for a millisecond as he searched her face. "Grandmère, may I present Muse Summerville. She is—"

"I know who she is," Madame Beaulieux interrupted with a look of satisfaction as she grasped both of Muse's hands in hers. "I am so happy to meet you. This explains everything."

"*Comment?* What everything?" Remi asked.

"Didi La Roi telephoned earlier and said I would need a reading. She's coming over this evening."

Beau's eyes rolled eloquently. Kit and Jolene exchanged a wide-eyed glance. Remi actually scowled at his grandmother.

"Now, Grandmère, you know all that stuff is just nonsense."

"What stuff?" Muse asked, totally lost.

"Didi is a voodoo priestess," Madame Beaulieux announced crisply. "She reads my tarot and does spells, too. Only good ones, of course."

Muse gave a cry of delight. "Voodoo? Oh, I love voodoo! I mean, I've done some research, for my book, and I think it's fascinating. I've never participated in any—" She stopped because everyone was staring at her, expressions ranging from horror to glee. Remi was shooting her dagger looks of warning. "Um..."

"You come to me tonight, *ma chérie,*" Madame Beaulieux said, ignoring them to give her a hug. "My rooms at eight o'clock. Together we do our reading with Didi."

"I'll be there," Muse murmured and kissed the lovely old lady on the cheek, flouting Remi's glare. "I can't wait to have my fortune told."

At this point she'd take any advice she could get about her messed up life.

Besides, Madame Beaulieux seemed nice, and it would give her a breather from Remi's disquieting presence. A respite she badly needed.

"You don' really believe in all that stuff?"

Muse stopped to sniff an old garden rose that smelled of sweet cloves before answering Remi's question. They were walking along the moss-covered path behind the house, touring the extensive flower and herb gardens.

"Of course not. Nobody can predict the future," she answered.

"What about influence it?"

"Everything you do influences your future."

"Including voodoo?"

She smiled and looked at him when he halted. "Grace would say voodoo is just projected wish fulfillment."

One brow lifted. "What's that supposed to mean?"

"You want something bad enough to do a voodoo spell for it, you're probably going to work hard enough to get it, anyway. The spell's just window-dressing."

He reached over and plucked a gardenia from a nearby bush. "Your sister sounds like a pretty smart lady," he said, and slid it into her hair, over her ear.

Before she knew what was happening, his lips were on hers.

She tried to resist, but he pulled her into his embrace with a velvet iron grip. Gentle but unrelenting. The taste of him caught her by surprise, so good, so right. So just what she needed. A little moan slipped from her throat, and he changed angles, deepening the kiss. The warm breeze and scent of gardenia, the taste of him, the feeling of safety in his arms, all conspired against her. She relented, melting into his kiss, surrendering to his will.

"Who needs voodoo?" he whispered. "I've already got everything I want right here."

"Separate bedrooms," she murmured, "remember?"

"*Adjoining* bedrooms," he reminded her.

"I locked the door," she countered.

"I was a thief for years."

"You'd break into my room?"

"I'd rather have an invitation."

Just then T-Bone came tumbling around the corner of a hedge, calling, "Moose, Moose, it amos' eight! Grandmère *te cherche*!"

She pulled from Remi's embrace and caught the little guy up in her arms. She smiled. "I assume that means Madame Beaulieux is looking for me?" She was rewarded with an enthusiastic nod. Giving the boy a kiss on the cheek, she said, "You go tell her I'm on my way, okay?"

Another big nod, a wriggle, and he was gone.

She looked up. Remi was standing there, hands in pockets, watching her with a funny smile on his face. He'd changed into a suit for dinner, black with a white shirt and silk tie, which showed off his broad shoulders and tall frame to perfection.

Mercy, he was handsome.

And tonight he could be all hers.

"Leave the door unlocked, Muse. Better yet, come tuck me in when you're done".

She made herself shake her head. "Nothing's changed since this morning, Remi," she said softly. "Getting in deeper would just hurt both of us." He regarded her searchingly and she added, "Me, anyway."

He let out a sigh and looked toward the house. "You better go on. Grandmère will be waiting."

Remi watched Muse walk away and barely suppressed the urge to yell after her, "I'll be hurt, too, you know!"

The truth of the statement nearly blinded him with its sharp clarity. He would hurt when they parted. More than he cared to contemplate.

How could he let her go?

Yet, how could he ask her to stay?

Stay where? His present apartment wasn't fit for a nice woman to live in or even visit. Sure, occasionally he'd rented higher-class digs to impress his targets, but only for a few months at a time as necessary. Never with the thought to stay permanently. His life had been exciting, every day an adventure, not geared to one special place. He did, however, have a healthy bank account and brimming investment portfolio. Maybe he owned a property somewhere they could move into?

But he liked the whirlwind of activity he called his life.

Didn't he?

Or was all that adventure simply designed to conceal an almost visceral loneliness he'd felt every single day of his life—every day except those he'd spent with Muse Summerville?

A sinking, leaden feeling crept through his stomach.

Did he really want to resume that homeless, fast-paced life? Spend the remainder of his days without this woman at his side?

With a mounting sense of dread, he realized the truth.

No, he did not.

Hands in pockets, Remi watched the door close behind Muse as she disappeared into Beau's beautiful home.

And he made a monumental decision.

He loved her.

He didn't want to be that lonely, rootless man anymore. He wanted a home and he wanted her in it, in his life, filling them with love and meaning.

He'd do whatever it took to get her there. And keep her there forever.

Chapter 15

Muse took a seat at the small round table, joining Didi La Roi and Madame Beaulieux. They'd already spent quite a while drinking tea and chatting out on the gallery, and now they'd moved inside and it was time for the real fun to begin.

She watched with interest as Priestess Didi did a tarot spread for Grandmère, one that boded continued good health and more great-grandchildren. That last one was a no-brainer, but left Madame Beaulieux with a broad smile nevertheless.

Then it was Muse's turn.

"I see much change in your life," Didi said solemnly, turning over the first two cards—a tower and something else. She looked up. "It is in complete chaos now, *n'est-ce pas?*"

"You could say that." Not too hard to guess, either, based on their earlier conversation.

Didi turned over two more cards. A moon and a hideous

devil. ''There is much secrecy. Something in the past you've been hiding. You have been alone because of it, and afraid and confused. Limiting yourself.''

That could describe any number of things about her life. Or anyone else's. ''I suppose that's true.''

Two more cards. ''I see much strength within you and around you. It is your loved ones who help give you this strength.'' Muse nodded. ''There is a man,'' Didi continued. ''This man is also strong. Very strong.''

Madame Beaulieux gave her a little wink. ''He is handsome, this strong man? Tall and black-haired?''

Didi looked imperiously at Grandmère and said something to her in French that Muse didn't catch. Madame Beaulieux just grinned.

''This man is your passion, your protector, and he is your future,'' the priestess said, and turned two more cards, to the right of the others. ''But he could overwhelm you. You must not let that happen.'' Didi considered. ''There is something you want very badly, but you are afraid for some reason.'' She looked into Muse's eyes. ''Why are you afraid?''

But Muse hardly heard her. She was stuck way back at the words *he is your future.* Remi? Her protector, yes. Her passion, certainly. But…

''He's not my future,'' she said.

''The cards say otherwise,'' the priestess replied.

''Maybe it means my future depends on him. That would make more sense.''

The priestess regarded her carefully. ''It is possible. But that is not what I am sensing. Is it him you fear?''

Just nonsense, Muse reminded herself. There was no way cards could tell the past or the future or who she was afraid of.

''No. It's my sister I'm afraid for,'' she evaded. ''She could be in danger.''

Didi nodded sagely and turned over another card. The Lovers! Muse held her breath.

"You feel responsible," Didi said.

Her breath whooshed out. What did that have to do with lovers? "Yes."

"And there is some kind of choice involved?"

"Yes," she admitted.

"Well, let's see the outcome of this choice."

Didi carefully turned over the last card in the spread, hesitated and placed it on the table.

Muse gasped.

Death!

Both old women took Muse's shaking hands and patted them, making assuring noises.

"Who is it?" Muse cried. "Who will die? My sister?"

"The card doesn't mean someone will die," the priestess said more than once, trying to calm her down. "Almost never. It means a new beginning. Transformation. Severance with the past."

"Are you sure?"

Nonsense or no, Muse was just superstitious enough to be more than upset by the card's prediction.

Didi stood, walking purposefully to a roomy carpetbag that Muse hadn't noticed before. She opened it onto Grand-mère's coffee table, revealing a jumble of tied herbs and jars of mysterious substances.

"I will prepare for you two gris-gris bags. A powerful one to ward off death. And another to make sure this strong man stays in your future."

"How?" she asked, thinking of the first.

"By making him fall in love with you," Didi answered.

Muse looked up in alarm. "No! I didn't mean— That's not necessary."

"You'll need one of his hairs," the priestess explained, not paying any attention to Muse's protests as she chose and added ingredients. "Plucked. Put it inside the gris-gris bag, then place the bag under your pillow when you sleep to-night."

Muse made a mental note not to let it get anywhere near the bed without careful consideration.

"Every day you must hold it in your hand and think of him. Think of your future together, how you would like it to be."

"We have no future together," Muse said softly, more to herself than the priestess.

"Then that is how it will be. As for the other," Didi said firmly, "have it with you always. *Always.* If you do not," she warned, "it cannot keep you safe."

"What about my sister?"

"Hold it and visualize her. It will work for her, too."

Muse gratefully accepted the second gris-gris bag, and reluctantly took the first, as well, a small red satin pouch, emanating the scents of sweet spices and pungent herbs. Then she took her leave of the two old ladies, pleading fatigue from the long day.

But instead of going to her room, she made a detour out through the gardens.

She wouldn't be able to sleep, anyway. No time like the present to do her thinking.

Muse wandered the beautiful moonlit paths not seeing anything but the darkness ahead nor feeling anything but the fear of making the wrong decision.

This time it wasn't about her sister. By now Grace was surely back in Carolina.

No, this decision was about Remi.

Did she dare do the spell, resolve in her mind and her heart to try to win him for always? Get him to change his stance on commitment, persuade him to quit his wild and woolly life undercover to settle down with a woman who was, ultimately, unsure she could do the same?

Seemed like a long shot.

The whole idea of them being together was crazy insane.

And yet, her heart told her she'd regret it till the day she died if she didn't try.

She wanted him so much, with a need that took her breath away.

But how could she prove to him—and, more importantly, to herself—that she was ready to take on the responsibilities of a real relationship?

In front of her a twig snapped.

"How'd it go?" Remi asked from the darkness.

Her heart stopped. He was sitting on a black wrought-iron bench, blending in perfectly with the shadowed green skeletons of the night garden.

She kept her voice steady, despite the pounding of her heart. "Interesting."

She stood there squeezing the two gris-gris bags, torn by uncertainty.

He spotted them and leaned back on the bench in a relaxed sprawl. "Didi fix you up with some good spells to ward off the evil eye?"

"I thought you didn't believe in voodoo?"

"Hell, I'm *Créole pur,* born an' bred, and have seen Didi's work all my life. I'd be the last one to scoff."

"Really."

He shrugged, crossing his ankles. "Strange things happen in the bayous of Louisiana. Call it what you will."

She held out the gray bag in her hand. "So you think I should keep this with me as protection?"

His grin glowed white in the darkness. "Surely can't hurt." He nodded toward the other bag she clutched. "What's that one for?"

She shifted on her feet. She knew damn well he knew

what it was for. The red satin was unmistakable and, as he said, he'd grown up with this stuff.

"Just some silly love thing," she mumbled.

He hummed a few notes, caught the tune and sang, "'Just an old silly love song...'"

He got to his feet, all six-foot-plus of him, and strolled over to her. Casually. As though he weren't about to blast her universe out of the water.

"Here." He reached up and plucked a single black hair from his head. "This is what you need, *non?*"

He pried the red bag from her fingers and with deliberate cool deposited the hair inside it, then handed it back to her.

She was speechless.

Luckily he didn't wait for an answer but leaned down and kissed her. Short. Unadorned. Straight to the point, then over.

But she'd never experienced a more intense kiss.

"Dream of me," he whispered, and then he was gone, too.

He was following her. Again.

The fine hairs on the back of Muse's neck stood on end. For a split second she slowed her pace, confused. She was back in the French Quarter.

She glanced behind her along the midnight street, feeling evil lurking in the shadows. Davies? Had he finally caught up with her?

Where was Remi?

Above, the clouded moon from the tarot card glowed down menacingly. Suddenly something leaped out of nowhere and grabbed her. She screamed. "No!"

"Your future! Your future!" Didi cried shrilly. Her bony fingers dug painfully into Muse's arms.

"No!"

Ahead of her, Grace appeared, caught by the hideous

tarot devil, who laughed hysterically as Grace screamed for help. Muse tried to run to her but was held by a grip of iron.

"Your future! Your future!"

"Remi!" she screamed. Where was he? He'd promised to protect her. He'd promised.

The devil danced with Grace up to the top of the tarot tower, ready to push her from the parapet.

"No-o-o-o!"

Then he looked straight at Muse. "It's you I want!" And just that fast he was on her, grabbing her, holding down her leaden limbs with hands of fire. "You, Muse!"

Memories of that horrible night so long ago flooded through her like a tidal wave. She fought for her life, for her sanity, kicking, clawing, screaming.

"Muse!"

She forced her eyes open. A dark shape loomed over her, holding her down. Shaking her. Just as he had that night.

"Muse!"

No. Not like that night. This man held her in a totally different way. Gently, soothingly.

This man's body didn't threaten. It offered safe harbor.

"Remi?"

"It's me, *chère*. You're having a bad dream."

She threw her arms around him. "Oh, Remi."

"I'm here now, darlin'."

"I was so frightened."

He kissed her, took her deeper into his calming embrace, weaving his own special, magical spell around her. "I'll always be here for you," he promised.

Deep in her soul she felt something shift within her. A hard, dark kernel thawed, softened and soaked up his nurturing like a thirsty seed.

"Will you?" she asked, wanting, needing to hear the words she so longed for.

"As long as you want me."

"I want you now," she whispered. "Please, Remi. Make love to me."

He didn't hesitate but slid in next to her, filling the bed with his body, his scent, his calming presence. She sat up, tossed off the nightshirt Kit had loaned her and waited impatiently the the two seconds it took for him to shed whatever he was wearing.

And then she was in his arms again. Held close as skin to his powerful, muscular body.

She felt no fear. Nothing but sweet desire.

He moaned and canted over her, whispering her name, murmuring endearments in a sultry patois of French and English as he lowered himself between her legs and slid home.

"Muse," he said again and again, kissing her lips, her cheeks, her eyelids. *"Mon doux amour."*

He moved over her, firmly, steadily, not holding back. She was amazed, stunned by the pleasure she felt. No panic, no fear, nothing to mar the incredible bliss of being completely his.

She wanted to whoop and ring bells and shout to the world how wonderful he made her feel!

"Wrap your legs around me," he ordered softly.

She did. He rolled, and suddenly she was on top of him. She laughed, covering his face with kisses, and rolled them back so she was on the bottom again. Over and over, back and forth they rolled on the bed, laughing and kissing and moaning with pleasure, until she didn't know where she was or who she was. All she knew was she was with him, part of him, and she never, ever, ever wanted it to end.

"Mine," he whispered, "You're mine. Just mine."

"Yes," she answered. "I'm yours."

Her body tightened around him possessively, making him tip back his head and groan. "Ah, *chère.*"

She felt his hands glide over her, touching, sending ribbons of desire spiraling through her body.

He drew out, plunged home. She cried out, drowning in the sensation of him. "Yes," she moaned. "Yes."

His fingers found her breast, squeezed, rolled the yearning tip between them, shattering her with sharp, splintering pleasure.

Her breath caught, the world froze, he moved, hard and thick, filling every inch of her. She sobbed once. And surrendered to the sweet power of his love.

It came like waves, the pleasure sweeping over her, robbing the air from her lungs, making her cling to his arms, his back, his heart and soul. When she heard his answering roar, she knew she'd never be the same again.

It was midmorning and they'd made love for ages. Now Remi lay there in bed, Muse sleeping contentedly in his arms. He wasn't sure what magic had happened between them during those incredible hours. But whatever it was, it had been monumental.

He'd made love before, many times. But it had never been like that.

He felt the hands of fate, sealing his. To her.

There was no way he would let her go, *could* let her go. Not now. Not after this.

She stirred, and he held her tighter, awed and humbled by the change in her. By the courage and ability she'd found to let the past go, to allow herself to trust again to this degree.

Could he muster that same courage?

Somehow he had to find it. For her. So they could be together. Always.

Today he'd tell her. He would quit his undercover work. Move to Carolina with her if that's what she wanted. Buy her a big house on the beach, with a darkroom, pamper her for the rest of her life. And let her pamper him.

But first a nap. Neither of them had gotten much sleep last night, and none since dawn.

With a happy smile he cuddled closer to his woman and let his eyelids shut out the bright light of morning.

And told himself Davies would never find her. Between Beau and himself, they'd keep her safe. Nothing would stand in the way of his future with Muse.

Nothing.

When he woke she was gone.

Gone from the bed, gone from the house, gone from Terrebeau.

And so was his extra gun.

"How?" he demanded of Beau when he found his cousin helping Kit prepare Sunday dinner in the kitchen.

"The Porsche," Beau replied, pointing out the window at the empty spot where the car had been parked. "I saw it pull out about half an hour ago."

"And you didn't think to tell me?"

"I assumed you were with her. How was I to know you'd turned into such a slug?" He glanced pointedly at the clock. It was well after noon.

Remi ignored the gibe and narrowed his eyes at Kit. "Do you know anything about this?" He waved the note he'd found on Muse's pillow, reciting, "'Forgive me, Remi. You were right about responsibility. I'm sorry. I have to go. Love, Muse.'"

Kit shook her head as she washed carrots from the garden. "No, but I'm not surprised."

"That she left me? Why? Am I that terrible?"

Kit's mouth dropped open. "Remi, no! She didn't leave you. She went to Grace."

"Same thing," he muttered, crumpling the note in his fist.

His heart felt like a knife had been thrust into it. Once again a woman had put her feelings for another above him, betraying his love and the trust he'd begun to have in her. He should have known it would happen.

"It's not the same thing at all," Kit said patiently, drying her hands. "Though I can see how it might feel that way right now." She came over and gave him a hug.

"You were perhaps a bit…rigid…about her sister," Beau offered. "Now, I'm not saying you were wrong. But maybe it wouldn't have been such a bad idea to take a quick trip to N'Orleans to see Grace. Before Muse set off by herself."

Remi clenched his teeth. *His own cousin…* He jetted out a breath, taming the urge to smash plates.

"Go to her," Kit said. "She's crazy in love with you, Remi. Any fool can see that."

He snorted. "She has a strange way of showing it."

Beau looked over at him and smiled.

Remi slammed his eyes shut. He knew just what the annoying bastard was thinking. Beau had said those exact same words four years ago when Remi'd given him the exact same advice about Kit.

Saloperie! Damn it, didn't he see the circumstances were completely different?

"Admit it," Beau quoted further, irritating him even more, "You're miserable without her. Tell her so. Get down on your knees and beg if you have to."

"Very funny." Remi set his jaw, but turned and stalked upstairs to get his things.

He'd go after her, all right. And he'd find her, too. Aside from anything else, this was his job she was messing with by defying his orders to stay put. No way was he losing an FBI witness. If Davies hadn't already killed her by now, Remi might just do the deed himself. *After* she'd testified.

* * *

When he got the phone call from Dev twenty minutes out of New Orleans, Remi thought he'd been prepared for anything. But he wasn't.

"Davies has her," Dev announced grimly. "Morris just called."

Remi almost drove Beau's Mercedes off the road. "*What?* How? Where?" he demanded, grabbing hold of the wheel to keep from pulling his hair out.

"Snatched from Muse's apartment just a few minutes ago."

He forced himself to calm down. "How the hell did that happen?"

"Davies's goon, Gary Fox, showed up this morning and took back that videotape Muse stole."

"Grace removed it from the safety-deposit box at the bank?"

"Apparently so. Anyway, since Fox didn't kill her then, Morris didn't think she was in any danger so he pulled off the two men guarding her."

Remi's mind whirled in confusion, then realized with a snap that Dev wasn't talking about Muse. "You mean Grace? Davies kidnapped Grace?"

"Who did you think I meant? Yeah, that cop, Levalois, called Morris just as he was charging to the rescue."

"Was Muse there?"

"Muse? No. Why? *Hell,* Remi. Are you telling me you *lost Muse?*"

"I didn't lose her. She bolted."

There was a short pause. "Jeezus. How long?"

"Thank God not long enough. Where did they take Grace?"

"Unknown. Hang on. It's Morris on the other line. I'll patch us."

Remi waited anxiously until he heard Morris say, "Beaulieux? Ask Muse where Davies could have taken her."

He swore under his breath. "Muse is not available at the moment. You're sure it's Davies?"

"Positive ID from Levalois. Davies took him, too. Signs of a struggle in the apartment."

"Anyone injured?"

"No traces of blood. Ideas on destination, people?"

Dev recited a list of property owned by Davies or his front companies, which he'd already pulled up on the computer.

Morris cursed. "Could be any one of them, depending on what Davies is planning to do."

Morris's grave mistake was assuming Davies was remotely rational. But talking with Muse had convinced Remi he wasn't.

"Guaranteed he's planning to kill them," Remi said, feeling sick to the stomach. "As payback for Muse daring to steal his favorite home movie. She told me what was on it. My guess is he'll have his fun first, then dump the bodies."

"According to Levalois the video was a recording of Davies torturing and killing his foster brother. That correct?"

"His brother? Brutal. Muse didn't know who it was, but, yeah, that's what she said."

Guess that answered the question as to whether the cop worked for Davies or not.

Remi thought for a second. "She also said it was filmed at some kind of abandoned warehouse. They might go to the same place now. Dev, what fits?"

He could hear computer keys clicking in the background, then Dev said, "He owns three warehouses." And gave their addresses. One was on the river close to the Quarter, one in a run-down area on the outskirts of New Orleans well-known for drug activity, one in a town about an hour's distance from the city.

"My money's on the second," Morris said.

"You take that one," Remi said. "I'll check the one near

the Quarter since I'm almost there. It'll take me fifteen minutes, tops.''

''Call in,'' Morris ordered, and then there was a click.

''I'll alert NOPD for backup,'' Dev said.

''Give them all three addresses. Just in case.'' In case Morris was trying to lead him astray on purpose.

''I'm on it. Where do you think Muse is?''

''She's been to the apartment by now,'' Remi said, putting the gas pedal to the floor.

''There'll still be agents there processing evidence, so she should be safe.''

''She'll also know what's happened to Grace.'' Remi's mind went very, very still. ''She knows Davies better than any of us, and where he's likely to take her sister.''

He just prayed it was one of the addresses he and Morris were headed to.

''You believe she's gone after them?''

He thought of the gun she'd taken with her. Cold panic slithered up his spine, along with dead certainty.

''I'd bet my life on it.''

Chapter 16

Luckily it was Sunday, so traffic didn't slow him down. Remi made it to the dilapidated warehouse on the banks of the Mississippi in record time. Nerves screaming, he parked a block away and ran the rest, keeping to the lengthening shadows, sprinting along the edges of the tumbledown structures, closing his senses to the fetid squish and decay of the wharfside refuse underfoot—and the cloying smell of his own fear.

Far in the distance, he heard the wail of a police car.

There! To one side of the partially boarded-up front entrance was a long, black limo. On its fender sat a bald guy who looked like a gorilla, talking to a woman who looked suspiciously like…

Muse!

Remi halted in his tracks, panting with relief at seeing her safe—and fury at the fact that she was standing in a flirtatious pose in that sexy sundress, chatting with a man who must be Davies's goon and flipping her hair as if she didn't have a care in the world.

Remi counted to twenty, then did it again, battling the urge to run screaming to her like some kind of barbarian idiot, throw her over his shoulder and carry her off to the safety of some nearby cave. *Le Bon Dieu.*

The sirens grew louder. *Switch the damn things off!* he thought angrily.

She was all right, he told himself. Obviously Muse knew the bald guy from her days with Fox. But what the hell did she think she was doing? She couldn't possibly be planning to rescue her sister single-handedly? Surely she wouldn't—

He watched in horror as she turned with a little wave of her fingers at the man and sashayed toward the entrance of the warehouse, then disappeared into it.

Merde!

It took Remi three seconds flat to reach the limo. "I'm with her," he called, and rushed after her, to the surprised shouts of the goon.

Drawing his weapon, Remi ducked through the door. Right into the bowels of hell.

In the middle of the room was a circle of bright yellow klieg lights, illuminating a macabre vignette. In the spotlight a man and a woman sat duct-taped to wooden chairs. Remi knew they must be Levalois and Grace, but she looked so much like Muse his knees almost buckled from shock.

A second man stood over Grace with a lighted cigarette, ready to brand her exposed breast with it.

Davies!

Remi raised his weapon and— The room erupted in chaos.

Levalois roared in anger. *Crack! Crash!* He was on his feet, the heavy chair fractured to kindling.

Bang! A gunshot cracked through the room.

Everything froze, and for a second it was deathly quiet.

A delicate spray of scarlet sprinkled over Grace as a coin-size hole appeared in the middle of Davies's forehead. Then the creep collapsed to the floor in a heap.

Sacré...

Suddenly the warehouse was full of uniforms and suits running and shouting. Morris was in the center of it all, barking orders.

Desperately Remi scanned the swarming room. *Where was Muse?*

She stood stock-still amid the bedlam, not ten feet away, holding the Beretta between her hands with perfect pistol form, the end of the barrel still pointed at Davies.

Ah, non.

In two steps he was by her side. "Muse, darlin', let me have the gun."

The only thing she shifted was her gaze, which flicked from Davies's fallen body to her sister and back. Then Levalois moved in to block Grace from view.

"*Chère*, honey—" Remi ran his hand gently along Muse's stiff arm "—lower your weapon, baby."

It began to tremble. He carefully cupped his hand under the Beretta and continued to rub her arms, coaxing them down. "You've gotta give me the gun, Muse."

From the corner of his eye, he saw Levalois pull Grace to her feet and into his arms, giving her a very uncoplike kiss. *What the...?*

"Beaulieux, do you have Miss Summerville under control?" Morris's anxious voice asked from behind.

"Under control, sir."

"She shot Davies?"

"Looks that way, sir."

Finally Remi was able to ease the Beretta from her fingers—along with a little gray gris-gris bag. He slid the weapon into an evidence bag Morris held up for him, then put his arms around her, sliding the bag into his pocket. She seemed numb with shock.

''How'd you get here so fast?'' he asked his boss suspiciously, as he held her tight.

''A local patrol car happened to be out by the other address, so we had them check it. Needless to say the warehouse was empty. We came here instead.''

''Lucky.'' Or had he known all along?

''Right,'' Morris said, then turned his attention elsewhere.

That's when Remi saw Grace look their way, over Levalois's shoulder, and heard her cry out.

''Muse! Oh, my God, it's Muse!''

Remi watched as the sisters hugged and cried, hugged and cried some more. That story, at least, had a happy ending.

Unlike some he might name.

He sighed and forbade himself to think about how Muse had chosen her sister over him, and left him without even looking back. There would be time enough to lick his wounds later. After he'd made certain she was safe.

Because he still had a job to do, and he was a hundred percent certain there was a traitor in the FBI who'd worked for Davies and fed him information. Now that Davies was dead and several of his henchmen under arrest, that traitor was a loose cannon.

Chances were the informant would panic. Try to cover his tracks. Silence anyone who could finger him. Eliminate loose ends.

Loose ends like Muse.

Even though she had no idea who he was, the informant couldn't know that. And with Davies gone and his henchmen arrested, she would be free to come forward, openly, with all her information. And possibly land the guy in a heap of hurt.

Remi shoved his hands in his pockets, fingering the small bag there.

Morris hadn't done anything suspicious that Remi had noticed since his timely arrival. He and Simmons were processing bad guys and evidence, presiding with cool efficiency over the whole messy crime scene.

Could he be wrong about Morris? Or was he just playing the part, and looking for his opportunity…

Damn. He had to get Muse out of there as fast as he could. Out of New Orleans. To safety. Until he could figure out who the mole was and put him behind bars, where he belonged.

She wasn't going to like it.

She was *definitely* not going to like it.

She'd made her choice, Grace over him. She would see it as her duty to stay with her sister, especially after what had happened…and nearly happened…to her because of Muse. Not that her appearance at the warehouse had made any difference to the eventual outcome. Remi'd arrived in plenty of time to save Grace, as had both the FBI and the NOPD.

But imminent danger or no, there was no way he'd ever pry Muse from Grace's side as long as she felt her twin needed her.

Not unless…

His gaze fastened on Levalois.

Hmm.

The man stood in the middle of the room, watching Grace and Muse, brewing like a dark storm cloud, ready to burst thunder and lightning. The harsh angles of his cheekbones were covered in a wash of black stubble, his wide stance spoiling for a fight; the feral look of possessiveness in his black eyes spoke volumes about his feelings for Muse's sister.

Dieu. If Grace wasn't into rogues, she was in big trouble.

But Remi'd found his salvation.

He sauntered over, positioning himself between the big

man and the door. What was the guy's first name again? Creole, that was it. Remi estimated thirty seconds before ol' Creole decided either to go over there and bodily rip Grace away from Muse or storm himself right out the front door.

Three, two, one... Levalois spun on a toe and ran smack into him.

He almost smiled.

"Sorry, didn't see you."

"No problem," Remi said, instantly recognizing the desperation in the man's eyes. A kindred soul on many levels.

The poor devil. He hated to do it, he really did, but he had no choice. After a minute of strained chitchat he broached the favor he wanted to discuss.

"Muse will never leave Grace as long as she thinks her sister needs her," Remi said to the stone-faced Levalois.

"So?"

"So I want you to make it clear she doesn't. Need her." Remi paused meaningfully, enduring a scathing, narrowed look. "Don' even try to deny you're in love with Grace," he went on. "I've seen the way you look at her."

Takes one to know one.

"You're imagin—"

Remi raised a hand, cutting off the man's brittle denial. "Don' worry, it's not obvious to anyone who isn't in the middle of it himself."

Creole stared at him, then let out a particularly potent Cajun oath. Remi gave him a smile of wry understanding, and in that moment a tentative friendship was born of mutual misery.

"Thanks, *mon ami.* I owe you big-time."

Merci, Dieu. Now Muse wouldn't worry about her sister while Remi carried her off...somewhere far away. Exactly where, he'd figure out later.

But before the night ended, he vowed they'd be on their own again, just the two of them. Safe and sound.

Whether she liked it or not.

And whether or not his heart was breaking in two.

It was strange how one's body could recover so quickly from killing a man. Fooling one's mind into thinking everything was okay. That you could talk and laugh and hug and pretend it didn't bother you. Because you really thought it didn't. The man was scum, after all.

Muse knew better. She'd been through denial before. No doubt she'd be in therapy for years after her true feelings surfaced. But for now she was all about Grace.

And trying to ignore Remi's Benedict Arnold gaze.

She hugged her sister like there was no tomorrow, grateful she'd gotten there in time to make sure there would be. If she'd listened to Remi— Well, there was no imagining what might have happened.

Muse sent a sidelong glance to Grace's erstwhile savior, Creole Levalois, shocked as was humanly possible at the obvious romantic connection between the two unlikely lovers. But lately, impossible things had been happening at an alarming rate, so Muse decided to take her sister's falling for a bad-boy cop as just another.

The four of them, including Remi, were taken to the district station and thoroughly grilled and debriefed by both the FBI and NOPD. Afterward, they went to grab a late supper at a nearby restaurant.

That's when Remi hit her with the news.

"It's not over, you realize that, right, Muse?"

She blinked. "What?"

"I have to get you out of New Orleans tonight."

She gazed at him in disbelief. "Davies is dead, Remi. In case you didn't notice, I shot him." She gave a little chuckle but nobody laughed with her.

"We still don' know who the informer is. You're in danger until he's exposed."

"How so?"

He gave her some convoluted explanation about loose ends. She dug in her heels. "No. Grace needs me."

Creole's arm rested casually along the back of her sister's chair, making a powerful statement by its mere presence there. "Grace will be all right," he said.

"I'm fine, Muse," she agreed quietly. Grace had been unusually quiet all evening.

Muse glanced between Creole and her sister, and it dawned on her maybe she was intruding where she wasn't wanted.

All right, fine. Family loyalty and responsibility weren't just about riding to the rescue—though it might have been nice to receive a thank-you. Had she ever thanked Grace when she'd pulled Muse out of scrapes? She'd have to remember to do so again, just in case. Anyway, no, family loyalty and responsibility weren't just about helping but also about butting out when you're not wanted.

"Okay, so Grace doesn't need me."

And being happy for your sister when she'd finally found someone who so obviously loved her.

And Muse *was* happy.

She gifted them with a smile, then turned to Remi, whose expression had gone, if possible, even more sullen. "What?"

"We'll talk about it after we get out of here." He finished the last bite of his meal and reached for his glass, draining that, too.

"I don't want to leave town."

"You'll go where I tell you to go."

Her jaw dropped. "Excuse me?"

His lips thinned. "You're suddenly so big on responsibility. Well, you're *my* responsibility. Morris hasn't taken me off the case, or relieved me of my baby-sitting duty. I'm in charge of you, and until that changes, you'll do as I say."

"Baby-sitting?"

She regarded him, speechless. Was this the same man who'd shared her bed last night, who'd surrendered to her every whim, who'd made her feel if she'd asked for the moon and the stars he'd somehow get them for her?

With whom she'd fallen so much in love that it hurt?

Was it all a lie? Just to get her where he wanted her?

She shoved her plate away. "Right. Let's go."

Grace peered at her as though she hadn't heard a word. Creole just squirmed in his chair, then rose along with Remi.

Out front he hailed a taxi. Muse managed to hold it together long enough to say a warm goodbye to Grace and give Creole a hug.

"Don't worry, I'll see she gets back home safely," he assured her.

"Then I'll see you soon," she said, throwing a glare toward Remi. "Just as soon as my bossy, overbearing, so-called bodyguard stops jumping at shadows."

"Agent Beaulieux has your best interests at heart," Creole replied softly. "You do what he says."

Obviously, a conspiracy between overbearing men. Poor Grace.

Still, she couldn't help but like her sister's new admirer. He exuded empathy and solid goodwill, and Muse knew he really was only thinking of her. Unlike a certain other man.

She slid into the taxi, careful not to bump up against Remi as they drove to the warehouse to retrieve their cars.

How had it all come to this?

Suddenly the weight of the day was too much to bear. Her heart was stone heavy, her shoulders seemed to carry a ton of burdens. All she wanted was to find a corner somewhere, crawl into a ball and sleep. Or cry. She'd been doing that a lot lately.

Why did everything always go so terribly wrong in her life?

All she'd wanted was…was to show Grace and Remi, and herself, that she was capable of being like her sister. Loyal, reliable, responsible. Muse had done everything she could to prove she was worthy of their trust.

Yet Grace hadn't seemed particularly surprised or overjoyed at her actions. And all Remi saw was that she'd disobeyed his orders, taking it as a personal betrayal that she'd chosen to defy him and his blessed plan for the sake of her sister's safety.

Didn't they realize she'd do anything, anything at all, to win their respect? Even kill the man who'd threatened them both?

She scrunched back in the uncomfortable taxi seat and felt the stinging in her eyes begin.

She'd killed a man.

Actually *killed* a man.

Oh, God help her.

The floodgates opened, and every emotion she'd felt over the past week descended on her like a tidal wave. Crushing her.

"Muse?"

"Go away," she gasped. What was the use? He'd never understand what she'd done or why.

She hadn't even understood it herself, until just now. And the most terrible part was, it had all been an exercise in futility.

"Chère?"

She felt herself being lifted from the seat, but was oddly powerless to resist. Her arms wouldn't function, she couldn't even find her hands, and she couldn't see, either.

A warm cocoon enveloped her and she slowly sank into beckoning layers of numbness.

She didn't sleep, not really. Didn't pass out. She understood what was happening when Remi called one of the remaining agents at the warehouse—Simmons?—to drive the Porsche back to the Bureau for him, and carried her to Beau's Mercedes. Driving to a small hotel in the nearby Quarter, he checked them in, asking the desk clerk to call a doctor. She managed to put up enough of a fuss that he and the clerk relented and didn't, deciding together to call one if she wasn't better by morning, just a few hours away.

All this she understood, but she felt nothing.

Or maybe she felt too much.

Either way, it was strange allowing Remi to undress her, tuck her into bed and join her, his big body wrapping around her protectively, all this without feeling a trace of fear. A trace of anything, really. It was also a little weird that he took the pillow from beneath her head and put it under her feet, and that she couldn't stop shaking.

Eventually she must have slept, in fits. Every so often she'd look up at Remi and he'd smile down at her, tightening his arms around her, asking if she needed anything, until one time his eyes were closed and he'd fallen asleep, too.

He looked so worried, skin pale, his broad forehead marred with creases, his long eyelashes resting upon dark smudges. Was that a hint of gray at his temple?

The diamond in his ear winked at her, and she felt a lone tear trickle down her cheek. How she loved this man! It would be hell to leave him. But she must.

She'd never change him or his controlling ways. And she couldn't live like that.

What irony! Searching all these years to replace a father who didn't want to claim any part of her life, only to fall in love with a man who wanted to dominate every last detail of it.

She had to get away from him. Had to think.

And there was something else she must do, as well.

With a sigh, she slid from the bed, eased on her clothes, and at the last minute patted the pockets of his jacket. She smiled tenderly when she found the gris-gris bag deep in one of them. So that's where it had gone. Carefully, she slipped it back in and said a little prayer that it would protect him from harm for all the days to come. Then she found what she was searching for. With one last longing look at Remi's sleeping form, she slipped quietly from the room.

''Muse!''

Muse whirled guiltily from the Mercedes's door, expecting to see Remi's angry face. Instead she saw the last man on earth she ever wanted to see again.

''Gary! What are you doing here?''

''Where have you been?''

''I—'' She took in her former boyfriend's furious expression, his agitated posture, the fire in his eyes, and suddenly she was frightened. ''Gary, what do you want?''

''You know what I want, Muse. What I've always wanted. You.''

She'd never thought of Gary as a violent person, but now she prayed she hadn't been deluding herself.

''I'm sorry, Gary. We didn't work. I've moved on. You should, too.''

''We worked fine. Your problem, and mine—when we were together nobody ever knew. It was perfect.'' He grabbed her arm and indicated the Mercedes. ''Whose car?''

She curled her fingers around the keys, which she'd taken from Remi's pocket. ''A friend's.''

He put his face close to hers and sneered. ''That man you've been with? The one upstairs you were in bed with?''

Now she was really scared. ''What do you know about him?''

''I've been following you for weeks. And I know all

about your FBI lover boy. You lost me for a few days, but I have my sources.''

Relief at finally knowing who her stalker was hardly put a dent in her growing anxiety. Had his stalking escalated?

He was talking crazy. His eyes were bloodshot and glazed. There was also a videotape tucked into the waistband of his pants. The one she'd stolen from him, which Morris said he'd taken back from Grace yesterday morning.

''Gary, have you been walking around since yesterday? Have you slept?''

''I knew she wasn't you. I could tell. She'd had sex with that cop. You never had sex. Not until—''

She yelped as he suddenly jerked her arm and grabbed the keys from her hand.

Opening the car door, he shoved her in. ''Drive! Your place.''

It was only a few blocks to her apartment, and she used every minute to try to talk him down, reason with him.

''Whatever it is you're planning, Gary, don't do it. It's not worth it. Davies is dead, and the rest of the gang arrested.''

''I know. It doesn't matter.''

''You can make a new start. You were always better than them, Gary.''

He made her park illegally in front of her building, and dragged her up the stairs to her apartment. There was a new dead bolt lock installed, but the key had been left under the mat. Grace always was far too trusting.

Thank goodness Creole had already put her sister on a plane back home. Grace had been through enough and didn't need to witness whatever Gary had in mind for Muse.

He slammed the door behind them and stalked across the kitchen toward her.

''You had sex with him, didn't you?''

''Who?''

"That man in the hotel. You let him touch you."

"Calm down, Gary."

"You never let *me* touch you. All that time and I never touched you!"

"You didn't want to. Neither of us wanted to."

"I want to now!"

"Gary, you can't."

"If I can't, I'll find something that can." He looked around frantically, his gaze landing on an antique candlestick on her table. He grabbed it.

"No!"

He reached for her, brandishing the candlestick. He grasped her hair and backed her toward the bedroom. "I can be like him. I can satisfy you as well as he can! Come back to me, Muse!"

"Gary, please. This isn't—"

His voice rose hysterically. "I want you back!"

She tried to appear calm, though her whole body trembled. "It's not possible."

"Do you love him? You love him, don't you!" he screamed, eyes wild. "How can you love him after just a few days?"

He shoved her onto the bed.

It was happening again. Oh, God, it was happening again!

"Please don't do this," she pleaded. She wanted to kick and scratch and fight him with all her might, but tried reason one last time. "I'll never come back if you do this to me."

"You won't, anyway." He raised the heavy candlestick high above his head, his face contorted with rage. "But if I can't have you, no one will!"

"Gary, *no!*" She threw her arms over her face.

"No one!" he yelled. "No one!" But he didn't move.

She peeked out from behind the protection of her arms

and saw the despair and indecision in his eyes as he gripped his makeshift weapon.

"I'm not her, Gary. Someday you'll find the right girl, I promise. But I'm not her."

The candlestick wavered. "I don't want anyone else. No other woman will ever treat me like you did."

The plaintive note in his voice made her ask, "How, Gary? How did I treat you?"

A muscle in his cheek quivered. "With respect."

"Oh, Gary."

All her fear evaporated when his eyes filled. She sat up and took him in her arms as he broke down and cried. She lifted the candlestick from his hand and let him hug her, rocking back and forth, back and forth.

"What am I going to do without you?" he murmured over and over.

"You'll find someone, I swear," she whispered. "And with her your problems will all disappear."

"How can you know that?" He pulled back and peered at her.

"It happened to me, didn't it?"

He didn't see the lie behind her words because just then the door flew open with a crash.

Remi burst in, swooping down on them. Her heart leaped at the sight of him, her avenging angel, gun drawn and eyes blazing.

Chapter 17

"Freeze! FBI!"

Muse held her breath as Remi's eyes raked over her and Gary sitting on the bed. He halted in his tracks. "What the *hell* is going on here?"

Another man appeared in the bedroom doorway, whom she remembered from somewhere. Simmons? From last night?

Gary jumped to his feet. In about ten seconds he was on his face on the mattress, arms handcuffed behind his back, Remi's knee at his spine.

Muse didn't object but pressed her palms to her eyes and tried to gather her wits.

"The hotel clerk reported you were kidnapped. Wanna tell me what this is all about?" Remi's voice was even, but far from cool.

"Meet Gary Fox," she said, letting her breath out. "And yes, he forced me here. Then he tried to rape me. Or maybe kill me. I'm not sure, exactly. I talked him out of it."

For a second she thought Remi might murder Gary on the spot. But he just growled to Simmons, "Get him out of here."

Simmons quickly grabbed Gary off the bed and propelled him toward the front door, amid loud protests. Something nagged at her memory about Simmons, but she couldn't put her finger on it.

"Wait!" she said, and got up to follow them into the living room. "Where are you taking Gary?" He looked terrified.

"Jail. For attempted rape and murder," Simmons said, ducking down to check Gary's handcuffs.

"That's not necessary."

"What?" Remi gaped at her.

God knows why, but she felt sorry for Gary. "Don't arrest him. I don't want to press charges."

"Are you nuts? He just tried to kill you!"

"Well, not really."

She glanced at Simmons, wishing she could get a better look at his face. But he kept turning away from her, finding things to fiddle with.

"He won't bother me again." She turned to Gary. "Will you?"

He shook his head vigorously. "No. I swear."

"Give them the tape, Gary. Davies is dead, but it could help convict the others. If they name you, it'll help your case."

"The tape's here?" Remi asked, surprised.

She scanned Gary's waistband. Empty. He blanched, his eyes grew wide, as though trying to convey something to her. What? They jerked to Simmons. And suddenly she remembered where she'd seen him before.

The tape!

Omigod-omigod-omigod. Simmons had been one of three

men watching Davies torture and kill that poor guy on the video!

He had a gun. She couldn't let on that she knew.

With as much indifference as she could muster, she gave Gary a slight nod and said to Remi, "He must have dropped it when you handcuffed him. I'll check the bedroom."

She spotted it immediately, a corner peeking out from under the bed. With a toe she pushed it all the way under. And walked to the TV stand opposite, where she kept her own video collection. She chose a similar case and prayed Simmons wouldn't notice the deception.

"Here it is." She went back and handed it to Simmons, putting on her most sincere face. "Make sure Morris gets it."

"Sure." He slid the tape into his jacket pocket and pushed Gary out the door. "Let's go."

As soon as the door was closed, she whirled to Remi. "It's him! Remi, it's Simmons!"

"What?"

"The informer. It's Simmons! It has to be! I recognized him."

"Of course you did. He was at the warehouse yesterday, and last night he helped with the Porsche."

"No." She shook her head impatiently. "The tape. I remember him from Davies's tape. He was there at the warehouse. *On the video.*"

Remi swore. And ran for the phone.

She went back to the bedroom and fetched the real video from under the bed. "I still have it," she said, interrupting Remi's phone call to Morris. "I gave him *Bringing Up Baby.*"

Remi swore again, then said, "She switched the tape. I've got it here. But you'd better pick him up quick or Fox is a goner," and hung up.

"He'll call NOPD?"

Remi nodded. "You're sure it's Simmons?"

"I'm sure." She shivered at the memory of his cold observation of the torture.

Remi slid the video from her fingers. "We better take this in before anything else happens."

She hung back. She shouldn't. There was something else she had to do. And she still needed to think. "Do you need me to go?"

Remi halted abruptly on his way to the door and stood with his back to her.

And just like that the atmosphere changed. From helpful and professional to thickly tense and very, very personal.

Fisting his hands on his hips he asked, "So this is it, then? Goodbye?"

Maybe thinking wouldn't be necessary, after all. She didn't think a heart could hurt this much. "Is that what you want?"

"Seems to me I'm not the one who left you. Twice. Glad you recovered from the shock you went into last night, by the way."

"Thank you for taking care of me."

His shoulders shifted. "All part of the service, ma'am."

His words cut like a knife. "Remi, look at me."

He shook his head. "I don' think so."

"Afraid you'll see how I really feel about you?"

"Exactly," he said.

And walked out the door.

It was a full five minutes before she could feel her body again. She just stood there, paralyzed, her heart shattered in a billion pieces on the floor.

She wanted to run after him. Scream and cry and hold him and beg him to stay. Tell him she'd changed. Beg him to change, too. Beg him to love her.

Beg him to love her enough to change, as she had. Because of him.

But she had no right.

He was who he was. Who was she to ask him to be someone different? She had to accept the reality that they could never be together.

And that's why she didn't run after him and beg him to stay.

Of course, she changed her mind almost immediately.

With the return of feeling in her body, came the feelings in her heart. She sprinted down the stairs and dashed out onto Burgundy Street hoping to catch him. But it had been almost ten minutes, and he was long gone.

Should she take the Mercedes and go after him to the FBI building? No. A public scene was the last thing he'd want.

A group of tourists gawked as she leaned against the warm red brick of the courtyard wall and fought the emotions tearing her apart. She didn't care that she must look like a well-used voodoo doll. All she cared about was that she'd lost Remi.

Forever.

She shuddered out a sigh.

Maybe not forever.

Maybe he'd come back for her. On his own. Without her having to beg.

Maybe he'd deliver the tape to Morris and decide he couldn't live without her. And come back to her.

As she slowly returned to her apartment, she thought about it.

What would she do if he came back?

With another sigh she changed her mind again.

How could it possibly work? Just because you loved a person more than life itself didn't mean you could live with them. It didn't solve the differences and the problems between you. Insurmountable problems. Like his love for his rootless job. And his obsessive need to micromanage all things.

Well. Not all things.

Not sex. The sex was good.

Really good.

Again she changed her mind.

Maybe there was hope. Making love, he had no need to plan every little detail. Or direct her. And when he had taken control—after she started trusting him and lost her fear—he'd involved her in a way that touched her heart. She'd loved it then.

Maybe that was the key.

Trust.

She did trust him. But maybe not enough? Maybe she should simply trust, trust him enough not to be afraid of the rest. Afraid he couldn't always be the way he was when they made love.

Was that possible?

Maybe.

Maybe not.

How could she know?

If he delivered the tape to Morris and decided he couldn't live without her. And came back.

That's how she'd know.

Of course, he didn't come back.

Noon came, then afternoon, and as night fell the certainty that he wasn't coming slowly enveloped Muse in a blanket of sorrow.

She called Kit to let her know she had the Mercedes and that she'd return it in a day or two.

Meanwhile she busied herself cleaning the apartment, then tackled the job of clearing out her closet. Out with the old and in with the new. No time like the present to start her new lifestyle. Later, she'd buy some less…revealing clothes. Longer hems, higher necklines, lower heels. What she needed now was a pair of jeans and a baggy T-shirt.

By the time she'd stuffed her old wardrobe into big plastic bags and loaded them onto the back seat of the car, the sun was just peeking over the horizon.

She made herself a cup of coffee and perched on the sofa, drinking it with unsteady fingers.

She hadn't wanted to leave her apartment, just in case… But by now the truth was painfully obvious.

He didn't love her.

He didn't want her.

He wasn't coming.

With one last sigh she gathered her purse and keys and walked to the car.

And wondered where she'd find the strength to go on.

Remi stared at the ceiling from his bed, watching the dingy paint brighten and the resulting shadows creep inch by slow-moving inch across the rectangle of cracked plaster.

The dark, cylindrical silhouette of the still-rolled-up shade had reached about a quarter of the way across the expanse when he managed to tear his attention from it and gaze blankly out the window instead.

Blue sky. White puffy clouds. The occasional bird winging past. All reminders of the world that continued to live and thrive beyond this room.

Beyond the aching. Beyond the heartbreak. Beyond the misery.

Face it, mon ami. *You're miserable without her.*

Yeah, yeah, yeah. Damn, he hated it when Beau was right.

Which he usually was. The man had an infuriating way of seeing right through the turmoil, straight into the eye of the hurricane.

Never mind they were Remi's own words. That only made it worse.

With a curse he jumped out of bed and stalked to the shower, hoping a good dousing of cold water would drive the heat from his blood.

No such luck.

The only thing that would cool this passion he had for Muse Summerville was about a hundred years of living and sleeping by her side.

Probably not even that.

He hadn't ever had a chance to tell her he loved her. Tell her he wanted to share her life. Her smile. Her luscious body. The way she laughed. Her quirky, infuriating habit of going off and doing whatever the hell she felt like doing, regardless of his opinion.

Bien. Maybe not so much that last one.

He yanked on some pants and a shirt, reaching for his holster. And his handcuffs.

There was more than one way to make a woman do what you wanted.

Oh, hell.

He plunked down on the bed and raked his hands through his hair, disgusted. As if he would ever actually handcuff the woman he loved. Get real.

No, the way to win Muse was with flowers and consideration and being nice. Not brute force or ordering her around.

That ordering-around thing was probably the kicker. She hadn't liked it when he'd done that. And he'd done it plenty over the past week.

But how else could he get the stubborn woman to fall in with his plan for the future?

She'd told him repeatedly she wasn't the type to settle down.

Of course, she'd also said she didn't like sex. And they both knew how wrong she'd been about that.

Get down on your knees and beg.

He could do that.

And he would if he had to.

Or…he could make her think marrying him was *her* idea.

Muse drove slowly through the sleepy village where she and Remi had hidden out for two idyllic days and nights. How long ago it seemed now, after all that had happened since.

Pulling over, she went into the small grocery store where they'd talked to the owner, hoping to find out who might keep an extra key to Dev's cottage. He did.

"My wife locked up after you and your husband left," he said after a warm greeting. "Mr. Devlin told us you were both all right, but it's nice to see for myself. Your hasty departure caused quite a stir."

She smiled at his obvious concern and made the appropriate responses, all the while thinking she just wanted to get out to the cottage and retrieve her things, and then get out of there. She knew Davies and his gang, including the FBI informant, were all behind bars, but frankly the whole place gave her the willies.

After promising to return the key she borrowed, and asking him to thank his wife—who had apparently gathered all Muse's belongings and stowed them carefully away for her—Muse drove to the cottage.

She parked the car in the driveway and sat for several minutes, gathering courage. It was ridiculous to think anyone lurked inside ready to attack her. Still, her heart pounded when she inserted the key in the front door and opened it wide.

She gasped.

A man sat on the sofa, watching her with hooded gaze.

"Damn it, Remi! You scared the spit out of me!"

Muse dropped her purse on the floor and shut the door behind her.

Remi! He was here!

Had he come for her?

"Sorry."

"I thought you were a hit man."

The corner of his mouth twitched. "No such luck." His eyes traveled over her, taking in her jeans and T-shirt, ending with her face, nearly devoid of makeup. "You look beautiful."

She smiled nervously, hoping he didn't hate her new image. "You do, too, sugarcane."

And he did. Oh, how he did! His gorgeous body, his disreputably long black hair, his bone-melting smile—conspicuously absent at the moment—oh, just the sight of him twisted her insides into a tangled knot of yearning and sweet desire.

"You forgot this," he said, pulling a small scarlet bag from his breast pocket.

It had nearly torn her heart in two to leave Didi's love spell tucked under the pillow at Beau's. Seemed best at the time. She bit her lip. "So I did." Did she dare take it back?

"Anyway, I figured you'd come back here. For these." He indicated the photos and papers that made up her book, neatly stacked on the coffee table.

"Yes, I was worried they'd be ruined or lost."

"I told Dev to make sure they were safe when I called him from Beau's."

"Thank you." She couldn't believe he'd remembered, when she herself hadn't, not until much later.

He shrugged. Their eyes met. There were a million things she wanted to say, but not one of them would squeeze past the melon in her throat.

The silence lengthened until she thought there was no way he had come for her. She had to stop hoping.

"So," he said. "What are your plans now that you're a free woman again?"

Her turn to shrug. She folded her arms across her abdomen. Looked at the hardwood floor. Anywhere but that tiny satin bag in his hand. "I was thinking about moving back to South Carolina. To be close to my family. Make a new start."

"Sounds good." He slowly nodded. "What's it like in Charleston? Nice? I've heard the sea islands up there are really something."

"Gorgeous. Charleston's the prettiest city in the whole country."

He got to his feet, just as slowly. "Yeah? I was thinking of buyin' a place up that way."

What?

Her heartbeat kicked up. "What about your job?"

"Oh, didn' I tell you? I gave Morris my resignation yesterday."

"You...you did?"

"Mmm-hmm." He tossed the bag in his palm. "Time for a change."

She couldn't believe what she was hearing. "What will you do instead?"

"Not sure." He tipped his head. "Something that doesn' involve planning. Someone recently pointed out I'm a bit rigid about my plans. I'd like to give spontaneity a try."

Her pulse went into overdrive. "Really?"

"You're about the most spontaneous person I know, *chère*. Think there's any hope for me?"

She took a few steps toward him. "Oh, I don't know about that." And another few. "You're a tough case. I think you'll need careful guidance." They were almost touching now. "By an expert."

"Got anyone in mind?"

The musky heat of his closeness nearly undid her. "Maybe. Depends."

"On…?"

"On whether your heart is really in it."

He lifted her hand and put the scarlet bag in it, closing her fingers around it. Then he leaned across the chasm of the universe and put his lips to hers. "Heart and soul," he whispered, and kissed her. Wrapped his arms around her, pulled her close and kissed her like she'd never been kissed before.

"Oh, Remi, I'm so sorry I left Beau's without telling you."

"I should have listened to you a lot sooner. I swear I'll listen to you from now on. If only you'll give me a second chance."

"I'm the one who needs a second chance."

He kissed her again and his lips told her everything she wanted to hear without uttering a word.

"What will you do without your undercover work?" she murmured.

"Whatever you want me to do."

"Where will you live?"

"You decide. Here." He fished his handcuffs from his pocket and placed them in her hand. "I'm yours. Do with me what you will."

She looked down at them, more than tempted to slip them on his wrist and hers, so he could never, ever leave her. "Be serious."

"I am serious. I trust you, Muse. With my life. With my love."

She looked up, her heart bursting with joy. "Your love?"

"Ah, *chère.* You must know I love you madly."

She threw her arms around him. "Oh, Remi, I love you,

too.'' She didn't think it was possible to feel so happy. ''Will you come with me to South Carolina?''

''You want me to?''

''More than anything.''

''Then I'll come.'' He kissed her deeply, holding her tight to his chest. ''Anything else you'd like me to do?''

She smiled. ''Meet my mother.''

He chuckled. ''Can't wait. What else?''

''Live with me.''

''She won't mind?''

''Not when she meets you and sees how wonderful you are.''

''You think?''

''I know.''

''Anything else?''

''Make hot, passionate love to me.''

''Count on it.'' He glanced toward the bedroom. ''How 'bout now?''

''Now and every night for the rest of our lives.''

He stopped, about to lift her from her feet into his arms. He gazed down into her eyes and asked, ''The rest of our lives?''

''Yes! Marry me,'' she blurted out, then slapped her hand over her mouth. ''I mean—''

He grinned. ''Did you just ask me to marry you?''

''Who me?''

''Yeah, you.''

''Um. Maybe.''

''You better make up your mind, because I won't decide for you.''

''No?''

He shook his head, still grinning. *''Non.''*

''Ah.'' She swallowed. ''I'd like to ask you. I really would. But...I don't have a ring or anything, and—''

''You mean—'' he produced a small velvet box from his pocket and held it out to her ''—like this one?''

Her heart went still. He pried open the box. It was—

''Oh, Remi! It's beautiful!'' Reverently she reached for the box, touched the gorgeous diamond ring inside. ''But I don't think it'll fit you.''

''Guess you'll just have to wear it, then. That is, if you decide to propose to me.''

She glanced from the ring to Remi's endearing, sexy, mischievous smile. ''You planned this, didn't you?''

''I'll try to be better. I really will.''

''Not possible,'' she whispered as he slipped the ring on her finger. ''You're already perfect.''

Absolutely perfect.

Epilogue

Three Years Later

Muse grinned at her sister as they lay on a blanket in the backyard, watching their husbands with amused interest. Remi and Creole were standing hands on hips, staring at a pile of lumber, metal poles and bolts that had just been dumped in the grass at the edge of the driveway.

The project for the day was to build a swing set.

Remi and Creole were experts at many things, but Muse wasn't altogether sure swing-set construction was one of them.

Grace chuckled. "Think we should give them a hand?"

"What, and spoil their fun?" Muse replied with a wink. "Besides, you can't. You just had a baby."

"True," Grace said, and tenderly kissed the four-week-old in her arms. "Guess we'll just have to relax and watch."

Muse let out a mock sigh. "Mmm. What a shame." After a pause she added, "Think they'll take off their shirts?"

"I'd say that's a given, show-offs that they are."

"How lucky can a woman get."

Muse reached over to stroke the cheek of her own precious baby, sleeping contentedly next to her in a shady spot on the blanket. She truly was the luckiest woman in the universe.

Thanks to the amazing man who had shown her that love was possible, even for her, all the dreams she'd been so afraid to hope for had come true. Every one. A husband, children of her own, her family close enough to hug whenever she felt the urge…all hers.

Luke, Grace and Creole's toddler, ran up and announced, "Unca Remi say bad word!"

Smothering a smile, Muse did her best to look serious. "He is very naughty, isn't he?"

Luke giggled. "Unca Remi naughty! Unca Remi naughty!" he called, and ran back to the men, who turned in unison, looking guilty.

"Hey, you tattled!" Remi said, grabbing the toddler as he zoomed by and giving him a good tickle. "When did you learn to speak French?"

Luke squealed with delight, playing keep-away around Creole's legs. "Dada save me!" Then he took off across the grass.

The pile of lumber forgotten, the two men chased after Luke, playing an impromptu game of tag.

Muse followed their antics, joy and contentment filling her to the brim. "Good thing baby Julia is only ten months old. This could take a while."

Grace laughed. "As long as they're having fun."

She gazed fondly at her sister. "Oh, Grace, how did we manage to snag the two most incredible men on the planet?"

Grace's eyes softened. "They are pretty wonderful, aren't they?"

"Doesn't come close."

The men in question came trotting up, Creole toting a panting, grinning Luke on his shoulders, and Remi carrying several sheets of paper. He flopped down next to Muse and gave her a big kiss. Swiping her iced tea, he took a big gulp.

"Listen, you! Yours is on the tray!"

In two swallows her tea was history. "Excellent," he said, switching glasses, "this construction thing is thirsty work."

He polished that one off, too, and gave her an unrepentant grin.

She grinned back. "I can see that."

He put his arms around her and nuzzled up her throat, ending with another loving kiss. "We've run into a little hitch."

"Oh, yeah? What's that?"

"We have no idea what we're doing."

All four laughed, making baby Julia gurgle in her sleep.

"That could be a problem," Grace agreed.

Remi thrust the papers into Muse's hands. "Here. You ladies read the directions. Tell us what to do."

She met Grace's mirthful eyes over Creole's shoulder. "What do you think? Shall we bail them out?"

"I suppose we'd better, if we want this swing set finished before Beau and Kit come to visit next week. T-Bone would be so disappointed."

"True." Muse sat up, shoulder to shoulder with her sister, holding the papers so both could see. "All right, let's see…" They read the first paragraph, something about checking shipment contents and sorting carriage bolts.

"Doesn't look too difficult," Grace murmured.

"Nope."

Muse looked up at Remi, who had gotten to his feet and was watching her expectantly. Eyes full of love. And trust.

How incredible was that? Day to day, in every way, she

trusted and relied on Remi, and every day that trust and reliance was returned. She didn't think it was possible for two people's lives and wills to be so intricately intertwined. Like the rose and the briar—putting down roots together, supporting each other as they climbed and grew closer every year, changing and blooming as one single, strong vine.

"Ready?" Grace asked the men, a definite twinkle in her eyes.

"Ready as ever," Remi said.

So handsome. So good. So sexy.

So easy.

"All right," Muse said, keeping a grin at bay, "here goes."

No, she wouldn't change him for the world. Not for the sun, the moon and the stars. He was everything she wanted forever and ever. Just as he was.

Well. Except for one teensy weensy detail…

"Step one," she and Grace said together. "Take off your shirts."

* * * * *

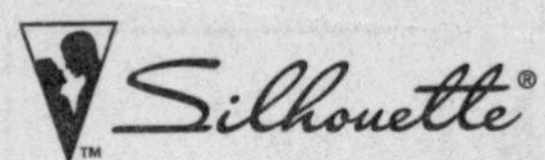

COMING NEXT MONTH

INTIMATE MOMENTS®

#1279 THE RIGHT STUFF—Merline Lovelace

To Protect and Defend

Major Russ McIver had strict rules against dating other military personnel—that was, until a mercy mission stranded him in the jungle with independent Lieutenant Caroline Dunn. Would their heated encounters and the threat of death from rebel forces make him reevaluate his ironclad position on love?

#1280 ONE TRUE THING—Marilyn Pappano

Heartbreak Canyon

Retired police officer Jace Barnett's instincts told him that Cassidy Rae was hiding something. Jace felt compelled to protect his attractive new neighbor, liar or not, from the man she claimed had murdered her husband. But with no way of knowing the truth, was he conspiring in a crime…of the heart?

#1281 DOWN TO THE WIRE—Lyn Stone

Special Ops

DEA agent Joe Corda took the missions that scared everyone else away. That was what led him to rescue emissary Martine Duquesne from a brutal Colombian drug lord. They'd sent Joe to get her out alive—but the problem was, saving her life was only the beginning….

#1282 EXTREME MEASURES—Brenda Harlen

With a potential murderer on his trail, Colin McIver took refuge in the hometown he'd never forgotten—even though that meant facing the woman he'd never stopped loving: his ex-wife, Nikki. Stunned when she revealed she'd given birth to his child, he was suddenly ready to risk everything to keep danger from his family's doorstep.

#1283 DARKNESS CALLS—Caridad Piñeiro

Powerful, dangerous and the key to catching a psychotic killer, Ryder Latimer was everything FBI agent Diana Reyes couldn't have—and everything she wanted. But once she learned his secret, would his sensual promises of eternal love be enough to garner her forgiveness? For Ryder was more than a lover of the night…he was a vampire.

#1284 BULLETPROOF BRIDE—Diana Duncan

Gabe Colton had been on the verge of telling Tessa Beaumont who he really was—until his accidental hostage distracted him with her intense response to his bad-boy bank robber image. Now, on the run from the authorities, and with the *real* criminals chasing them, he must use all his skills to protect her…and his true identity.

SIMCNM0204